Warmth and pass...
Coolness and fear.

Laurel's response to his kiss was a study in ambivalence.

Her lips parted for his, and she allowed him access to her mouth, but she took no liberties with his. Her body was pliant, but there was no shivering response, no arching to get closer. Her hands resting lightly on his biceps weren't pushing him away, but neither were they clinging.

And she was whimpering—tiny sounds of pleasure and agony that tore at his gut.

Still, her lips remained hesitant beneath his, her body accommodating rather than passionate, and he knew her trembling had little to do with arousal.

Once, he would have taken whatever she had been able to give. But not anymore.

He wanted it all.

Dear Reader,

If you're looking for an extra-special reading experience—something rich and memorable, something deeply emotional, something totally romantic—your search is over! For in your hands you hold one of Silhouette's extremely **Special Editions**.

Dedicated to the proposition that *not* all romances are created equal, Silhouette **Special Edition** aims to deliver the best and the brightest in women's fiction—six books each month by such stellar authors as Nora Roberts, Lynda Trent, Tracy Sinclair and Ginna Gray, along with some dazzling new writers destined to become tomorrow's romance stars.

Pick and choose among titles if you must—we hope you'll soon equate all Silhouette **Special Editions** with consistently gratifying romance reading.

And don't forget the two Silhouette *Classics* at your bookseller's each month—reissues of the most beloved Silhouette **Special Editions** and Silhouette *Intimate Moments* of yesteryear.

Today's bestsellers, tomorrow's *Classics*—that's Silhouette **Special Edition**. We hope you'll stay with us in the months to come, because month after month, we intend to become more special than ever.

From all the authors and editors of Silhouette **Special Edition**,
Warmest wishes,

Leslie Kazanjian
Senior Editor

MARY ALICE KIRK
Promises

Silhouette Special Edition

Published by Silhouette Books New York

America's Publisher of Contemporary Romance

For those with the courage
to struggle for love.

SILHOUETTE BOOKS
300 East 42nd St., New York, N.Y. 10017

ISBN: 0-373-09462-0

First Silhouette Books printing June 1988

All the characters in this book are fictitious. Any
resemblance to actual persons, living or dead, is
purely coincidental.

® are Trademarks used under license and are
registered in the United States Patent and
Trademark Office and in other countries.

Printed in the U.S.A.

Books by Mary Alice Kirk

Silhouette Desire
In Your Wildest Dreams #387

Silhouette Special Edition
Promises #462

MARY ALICE KIRK

is a full-time writer who holds degrees in American Studies and International Relations. Throughout her life she has been driven by creative energies, but she refused a scholarship in the performing arts to pursue an academic career. Although she enjoys many hobbies, the need to write stories about people's lives is the most compelling force for her, she says. Aside from her family, it's the one thing from which she derives her deepest satisfaction.

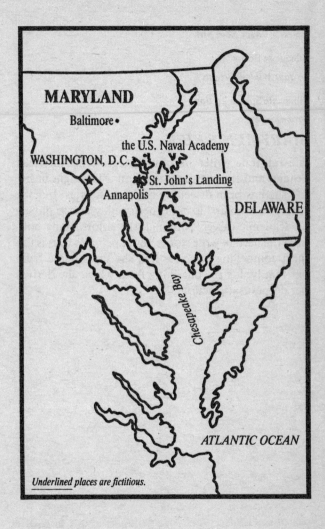

MARYLAND

Baltimore •

the U.S. Naval Academy

WASHINGTON, D.C. •

St. John's Landing

Annapolis

DELAWARE

Chesapeake Bay

ATLANTIC OCEAN

Underlined places are fictitious.

Chapter One

She was making a mistake. Laurel knew it, even as she knew there was nothing she could do about it. She had made the commitment to attend the conference months ago; it was too late now to change her mind. It was not too late, however, to wish she could change it or, for that matter, to brood over the possible consequences of her rash decision. Such fruitless activity had occupied her thoughts for the past twelve hours, from London to Boston. No doubt it would keep her busy for the next leg of her journey, as well.

The automatic door connecting Logan Airport's international and main terminals opened with a subdued whoosh of air. Laurel passed through it quickly, pausing only long enough to scan the overhead screens for information about her next flight. Then she hurried down the corridor, heading directly for her gate with an air of assurance that spoke volumes about how often she traveled. Airports, no matter how complex, had ceased to confuse her years ago.

Her gray eyes held a determined look. Her short, businesslike haircut, her stylish spring clothing, everything about her five-foot-ten-inch slender frame bespoke purposefulness and sophistication. Nothing hinted at the uncertainty she felt. Nothing but the dark circles under her eyes and the condition of her delicately shaped lips—devoid of lipstick and slightly swollen from having been worried between two rows of straight white teeth.

It would be smart, Laurel knew, to ignore the negative aspects of the upcoming week in Annapolis and to focus instead on the conference itself. After all, it was an honor to be asked to participate in the annual Foreign Affairs Conference sponsored by the United States Naval Academy.

The prestigious event brought together several hundred of the country's brightest students of foreign policy and a select group of government professionals who worked day in and day out on the issues about which the students were reading. As one of the employees of the Arms Control and Disarmament Agency who represented the U.S. in negotiations with the Soviet Union, she had been asked to coordinate the mock negotiations program for this year's conference. The program's purpose was to teach the students what was really involved when world powers met to discuss arms control. And of all the people the conference committee could have chosen to demonstrate this complex, critical process, they'd chosen her. Yes, Laurel concluded, she should forget everything else and appreciate how good it felt to be so highly regarded.

At the moment, however, she would have sacrificed the ego boost the invitation had given her for the chance to reconsider.

By the time she reached the security checkpoint, Laurel had her ticket ready. The plane was due to take off in ten minutes, and she was quite certain her flight had been called. Only when she reached the boarding area did she slow her pace, and her tense expression softened a little as she spotted the person waiting for her.

Her father, Vice Admiral James Randall, was standing apart from the last-minute stragglers in line to board the plane, looking tall and imposing in his black uniform with its three gold stars and anchor prominently displayed on the shoulder boards of the jacket. A concerned frown appeared on his brow as he glanced at his watch. Laurel's heart beat faster in a rush of anticipation, and she started toward him. When he raised his head to scan the corridor, she caught his eye, smiled and waved. He waved back and came to meet her.

"Laurel! I was afraid you weren't going to make it. It's so good to see you, honey!"

"Dad." For a moment Laurel enjoyed the luxury of being close to her father as he caught her in a quick hug. "It's good to see you, too."

"Two years!" he exclaimed. "Has it really been that long?"

"Almost," she confirmed.

"Well, we've got from here to Annapolis to catch up." He held her at arm's length for a brief, assessing look. "Ready?"

Laurel nodded, draping her garment bag over her arm as her father collected her small case.

Walking toward the ramp, he said, "When I heard your flight out of Heathrow had been delayed, I started dreading having to tell Captain Anderson that his mock-negotiations coordinator had missed her plane."

"Oh, I'm sure the conference would have survived until I got there," she replied. "But for your sake, I'm glad it didn't come to that."

They filed down the center aisle of the plane, and as Laurel slid into her seat, she felt her stomach take a nervous flip. She wasn't afraid of flying; she was afraid of being in Annapolis, Maryland. And she was counting on idle conversation with her father to keep her from dwelling on where this particular flight would end.

"So, are you going to tell me why you cut your hair?" Her father was regarding her shorn locks with a mixture of horror and curiosity.

"It had to happen sooner or later, Dad," she teased gently. "I've been too busy to fuss with a waist-length mop. Besides, I want to be taken seriously at the negotiations table by my Soviet counterparts—which means not looking like their idea of an American teenybopper."

He shook his head and sighed. "But all your beautiful hair! Maybe by the end of the week I'll be used to it." With a knowing grin, he added, "It's certainly obvious you're being taken seriously. It's still hard for me to believe my little girl's on a U.S. arms control negotiating team with all that military and academic firepower. Besides being the only woman on the team, I suspect you're also the only negotiator under fifty!"

"Believe me," Laurel returned, "I was as surprised as anyone when I got the appointment. I guess I was in the right place at the right time. They were looking for a woman to balance the team, they wanted someone from inside the agency—ergo, they picked me."

"You shouldn't be so modest," he chided her. "You were the best person for the job. I know you'll never admit it, but I hope you don't mind if *I* gloat a bit this week."

"Please, feel free. The job has few enough rewards. Some strokes from my Dad would be most appreciated."

"I'll be glad to oblige." He gave her arm a squeeze, but then his tone became somber. "Before we get too involved, though, talking about other things, I wanted to tell you how sorry I was to hear about Jonathan Coltrane's death. It was sad news."

Laurel hesitated, wary of this new topic. "Yes, it was," she agreed quietly.

"I imagine Nathan was pretty broken up," he went on. "His uncle was the last of his family. Besides which, this leaves him holding the reins on the estate. I wonder what he's going to do with all of it. Do you know?"

Shifting to find a more comfortable position in her seat bought Laurel a little time to plan a response. Unwittingly, in the space of a few perfectly normal remarks, her father had hit upon the one topic she wanted to avoid. She couldn't talk about Nathan. Not now. Not when she was about to spend a week in Annapolis, where the memories would surround her.

Her voice was casual, but her hand trembled as she lifted it to inspect a fingernail. "Frankly, Dad, I don't even know where Nathan is. I was in Geneva last fall and didn't get to the funeral."

She frowned at the nail she had nibbled ragged somewhere over the Atlantic, then abruptly hid it in her fist, dropped the hand into her lap and shot her father a quick smile. When he spoke, she knew she'd have to do a better job of dissembling.

"It's going to be a hard week for you, isn't it, honey?"

Laurel's gaze slid away from his as she hedged, "Maybe. I don't know, really." And she wondered why her father had suddenly become concerned about her personal life. They had always cared for each other in a reserved, polite way; in the past, though, his attention had been divided between his Naval career, his alcoholic wife and his two daughters—in that order. With his position secure on the permanent faculty at the College of Naval Warfare in Newport, Rhode Island, and his wife having died two years ago this coming August, Laurel guessed he finally had time to think about his daughters.

"You've never told me what happened between you and Nathan," he noted, surprising her even further. "I realize, when you two were having trouble, I was tied up with your mother's illness and didn't have time for anything else. But I'm not tied up anymore, and if you want to tell me, I'd like to know."

Her reply was calculated and brief. "Nathan and I made a mistake, Dad. We shouldn't have tried to turn our friendship into any more than it was. Instead of making it better, we ruined what we had."

Praying her tone had warned him that she didn't want to pursue the issue, she willed the knot in her stomach to go away. His next question, however, only made it tighten.

"Are you all right, honey? You look—" he hesitated over the word "—upset."

"I'm fine," she insisted, forcing a smile. "A little tired, that's all. The last couple of weeks in Geneva were pretty grueling. And you know I've never been good about transatlantic flights. I can't get used to being cooped up that long. But don't worry. By tomorrow I'll be as good as new. Now, why don't you tell me about Lilly? How was she when you saw her last month?''

Her father's eyes searched her carefully disciplined features once more, then he went on to talk about Laurel's younger sister, who was due to have her third baby soon. With some encouragement, he also filled her in on his own life, an account that consisted mostly of Navy talk.

Feeling bad about deceiving him, Laurel realized that at least part of what she had said was true. Though she'd mastered the mechanics of maneuvering through airports, she would never get used to flying. She would never find it easy to say goodbye to one place and hello to another.

The memory of one particular parting flashed through her mind, and as the big jet approached its destination, she thought again and again about that first, horrible time she'd had to say goodbye...

"You'll write to me, won't you?" The little girl with the long dark braid gave her young friend a sad, half-hopeful look.

"I already promised I would." The boy leaning against the big oak tree tried to pick a blade of grass between two bare toes.

"How much longer is your family going to be here in Spain?" she asked.

The boy pushed off from the tree to grab the swing that hung from a low branch. "I think maybe another six months, but I'm not sure."

"Don't you hate not knowing where you're going to live?"

"Naw, it's sort of neat. I remember being in Charleston and San Francisco before that, and I liked those places fine."

"I don't want to move." The girl frowned, a stormy expression darkening her wide gray eyes. *"I hate moving. I hate having my room packed in boxes. And I know Mommy hates it, too. I saw her crying twice yesterday."*

With a sensitivity rarely found in such youthful form, the boy sought to comfort his friend. *"You'll be okay, Lauri. It'll be hard for a while, maybe, getting used to a different school and all, but I'll bet you end up liking Charleston."*

The girl's eyes filled quickly, unabashedly, with tears. *"But I'm going to miss you, Nathan. I might never ever see you again!"*

There was no denying it, and the boy didn't try. The sadness in his brown eyes said that he didn't like the idea any better than she, but, being the more optimistic of the two, he tried to look on the bright side. *"I'll write. And I'll never stop being your friend, no matter where we are. I promise. My Dad says, when you're in the Navy, you're all part of the same family. It's sort of like we're related, and you don't ever stop being related once it happens. Now, come on. Don't you want one last swing ride before you go? Get on, and I'll push you…"*

Laurel looked out over the jet's wing and watched it slice through a bank of clouds as the pilot announced their descent into Baltimore/Washington International. She recognized her present feelings as the same ones she'd had on that sunny morning in Spain—fear, loneliness and a longing for someone she never expected to see again. The difference was, this time it was true: she would not be seeing Nathan again. He would not be at the airport to greet her as he had been all those times she had come to visit him in Annapolis. Nor would he be there to say goodbye. They had said their final goodbye.

But that had been more than three years ago.

Why then, Laurel wondered, did the knowledge that she had lost her dearest friend still have the power to fill her with such deep despair?

The passengers disembarking from Flight 566 out of Jacksonville, Florida, into BWI airport were a typical mix of students returning to college after spring vacation and weekend travelers who wanted to be home in time to watch the Sunday-afternoon Orioles game. Nathan Coltrane, Captain, U.S. Navy Medical Corps, was neither. But he had long since grown accustomed to standing out in a crowd, if for no other reason than his size. At six-foot-six and two hundred and thirty pounds, he was built like a linebacker, and without a lot of conscious effort, he made sure he stayed in peak condition. Physically, at least. Emotionally, well, the haggard look on his strong-featured face told another story. He looked like hell, and he knew it.

As an excuse to those who'd expressed concern, Nathan had confessed he'd been working too hard. After all, wasn't a doctor supposed to take exhaustion for granted? The truth, though, was that his burned-out look came not from his work but from having spent the past three years trying to glue together the shattered pieces that used to be his life. His appearance was merely an indication that, thus far, he had not succeeded.

Nevertheless, the lines that shot downward from the corners of his mouth spoke of determination, and the long strides that carried him toward the main terminal were unhesitating. He was through pouring his energy into work in a futile effort to forget. He was through trying to become involved with women he did not want and to whom he had nothing to offer but an already occupied space in his heart. He was allowing himself thirty days in which to let go of the memories and the hopes. When he left Annapolis at the end of May, his heart was going to be his own, for he would have rid himself of everything that reminded him of Laurel.

Nathan hitched his garment bag over his shoulder, his attention focused on the escalator that led to the baggage claim area. The sound of a familiar voice calling his name was only a little surprising, and he cast his gaze over the heads of the crowd until he saw Louise Halliday. Dressed in her Sunday church clothes, the tiny black woman who had been the Coltrane family housekeeper for the forty years prior to Jonathan Coltrane's death was standing—or, more precisely, jumping up and down—at the foot of the escalator, waving a white-gloved hand in a furious effort to get his attention.

In a flash, Nathan's grim expression disappeared and was replaced by a delighted grin, and he began walking down the moving stairs toward her. When his parents had died in a car accident in Naples and Uncle Jack had brought him to Annapolis to live, he'd been ten years old; from then on, "Aunt" Louise had been the closest thing to a mother he had known. Nathan adored her, and the tears he saw on the old woman's weathered cheeks made it obvious the feeling was mutual.

Having dropped his bags in the rush to get to her, Nathan literally scooped Louise off the floor into his arms, laughing at her shriek of protest as he scolded, "I thought I told you not to meet me!"

"Oh, pooh!" she shot back, returning his hug as far as her arms could reach around his shoulders. "You knew when you said it you were wasting your breath. Now, put me down so I can look at you."

With a final squeeze, Nathan complied, bending to retrieve the hat that had fallen off her head, handing it to her, and then straightening to endure the thorough once-over she gave him.

"Hmph," was the quick verdict. "What's the matter with the United States Navy? Can't they tell when a man needs a good night's sleep?"

Nathan neither apologized for his sorry appearance nor tried to explain it. "That's what I'm here for, Aunt Louise. A vacation. I've got a whole month with nothing to do but fish and sail and sleep."

"Looks like you ought to start with a nap and leave the fishing and sailing for later. What is it about you doctors, anyway? Always busy telling other people what to do, never finding time to take care of yourselves." Louise shot another sharp look at his face and nodded. "Let's get you home."

Home. Yes, Nathan thought, that was part of the problem. St. John's landing had remained home no matter where the Navy had sent him. But it was time to make a new home—one that did not rely upon memory.

"Your rental car's parked in the garage," Louise informed him on their way to the luggage carousel. "Keys are in it. And I got the cottage ready for you. Food's in the refrigerator, bed's made, clean towels are in the linen cupboard. But I don't know why you won't tell those Historical Society ladies to take their brochures and leave the Landing so you can sleep up at the big house. Perfectly good house sitting there getting dusty while a bunch of tourists traipse through it, looking at things they've got no business seeing. Mr. Jack would be furious if he knew about it.''

One corner of Nathan's mouth turned downward. She was right. Uncle Jack would have been furious if he'd known the Annapolis Historical Society was running tours through the ancestral halls of St. John's Landing. God knows what he'd have said if he had known what else his nephew and heir was planning to do with his legacy. Fortunately, Uncle Jack would never know.

Unfortunately, Aunt Louise would. And Nathan was not eager to hear what she would have to say on the matter.

When they reached the baggage area, he checked the flight roster, noting, ''There's a flight from Boston unloading ahead of mine.''

''Boston?'' Louise piped up, craning her neck in an effort to see through the mob around the conveyor belt. Since her head barely cleared the shoulders of the people around her, the effort was almost comical.

Nathan smiled down at her affectionately. ''It'll be a while before my stuff comes through. Let's go get you a cup of tea and me some coffee.''

''I don't mind waiting here,'' Louise assured him. Then, without pausing for breath, she asked, ''Haven't heard from Laurel since the funeral, have you?''

Nathan flinched inwardly but answered steadily enough, ''No, I haven't. Why?''

''Hmm. Just wondered. Seems strange she hasn't written you, doesn't it? I'll have to ask her in my next letter if she's forgotten her manners.''

''She sent flowers,'' he reminded her.

"True," the old woman agreed. "And wouldn't have known to do that if I hadn't called her."

"I appreciate it that you did."

"You could've done it yourself."

"I would have found a way to get in touch with her if I hadn't known you'd already talked to her."

"Would you?"

"Yes."

"Hmph. I wonder."

Nathan sighed and ran a hand across his face in a gesture of frustration. "I haven't heard from Laurel in three years, Aunt Louise. I've got no idea where she lives or what she's doing."

"Well, you know I'm not one to pass gossip," Louise supplied with a careless flutter of her hand, "but I understand she's working for the government again, something about controlling arms. Talks with the Russians about bombs and treaties or some such nonsense."

Nathan's gaze zoomed downward, expecting to meet Louise's upward glance. Instead, he focused on the pink silk carnations edging her straw hat as she went on checking out the crowd. "The Arms Control and Disarmament Agency. She got appointed to one of the negotiating teams?"

"Whatever it is, she had to find a place to live in Geneva, Switzerland, besides the place she's got—" Louise stressed the words "—in Washington. Are all these people off that flight from Boston?"

"Hmm? Oh, no. My flight was pretty full. Most of them are off that one, I guess." Preoccupied, Nathan was barely aware of the people shuffling around them.

He wasn't surprised to hear that Laurel was with the Arms Control and Disarmament Agency again; the U.S.

government liked to hang on to people in whom they
had an investment. Laurel had started as a Congress-
ional liaison for ACDA during graduate school and
had continued doing research, writing position papers
and going on speaking tours for them up until the time
he had gotten his first overseas assignment. Her degrees in foreign relations and her amazing analytical
skills had quickly made her a valuable asset to the
Agency. Even when she had been in San Diego and Japan with him, no longer officially working for ACDA,
they had called upon her to speak at chambers of com-
merce and college consortia, explaining U.S. positions
on particular issues of military diplomacy. No, it wasn't
surprising to discover that they had taken her back into
their fold. And, really, her appointment to the negotiating team was probably the next logical step.

Logical or not, Nathan couldn't stop the surge of
undiluted pride that shot through him. Neither could he
prevent the taste of bitterness that followed it. He knew
how hard members of the negotiating teams worked. He
knew what their lives were like, always between resi-
dences, never knowing when they might be called back
to the city they had left two months before. Compared
to that life-style, the Navy represented the height of
stability. And it struck him as cruelly ironic that this was
what Laurel had chosen over being with him.

Yet he knew it was not that simple. When Laurel had
left him, it had not been because she was seeking to
satisfy her career ambitions. And if there was anything
ironic, it was that neither of them had ever been com-
pulsively ambitious in that regard. Yet here he was, a
Captain in the Navy, when by normal standards it
should have taken him another seven or eight years to
receive the commission. And there was Laurel, holding

a position usually reserved for career diplomats, Henry Kissinger and four-star generals. And the truth was, the only thing either of them had ever really wanted was to be happy. Together.

At that moment, Nathan's attention was caught by a sight that brought home exactly how far short of success he and Laurel had fallen: a boy and a girl, close to college age, hurrying toward the terminal exit. The boy had one arm wrapped around the girl's shoulders as he carried a suitcase in the other hand. The girl was talking excitedly, and the boy's gaze was directed more toward her than where he was going. They were obviously delighted to see each other. As they approached the doors, the boy gave in to his excitement, sliding his arm up to hook the girl's neck and pull her toward him for a kiss that was somewhat less than discreet. Neither of them seemed to care in the least that they had an audience, as they slowed their pace and enjoyed the moment for all it was worth before breaking apart, exchanging knowing looks and continuing on their way.

How many times had that been he and Laurel? Nathan wondered. How many times had he come to BWI to meet her at the beginning of summer vacation, at Christmas—whenever she could get away and her parents would let her come to visit? How many times had he stood at the arrival gate, waiting for her to get off the plane, his heart pounding, his stomach a knot of nerves, his mind racing with all the things he wanted to tell her? It had been that way when they were children. It had been that way when their friendship had shifted to accommodate a growing sexual awareness of each other and the beginnings of romantic love. And at that moment, if he saw her standing across the concourse, it would still be the same.

Which was why, since he was not likely to see her ever again, he was going to have to stop remembering their hellos and remember, instead, that they had said their last goodbye.

Laurel's view out the window of the rental car her father was driving was both familiar and somewhat bleak. The road from BWI to Annapolis passed through some of Maryland's finest farmland. In April, though, the open fields on either side of the rural highway were newly tilled, leaving only dark soil churned into long, straight rows between fieldstone walls. There were few houses to be seen, only an occasional weathered gray barn with two or three horses grazing in an adjacent paddock.

They had been driving for some time in silence when James spoke. "You've been awfully quiet."

"I'm tired, Dad," Laurel replied, wondering how many times she could excuse her silence as exhaustion before he called her bluff.

"I don't imagine you'll get much rest this week," he remarked. "The conference agenda is heavy, and they like to keep their round table moderators busy. Are you going to see Louise Halliday while you're here?"

Relieved that she could finally give him a definite answer and that there was at least one thing to look forward to about being in Annapolis, Laurel smiled. "I wrote to Aunt Louise months ago to tell her I was coming. She'd never speak to me again if I didn't see her."

"Perhaps we could take her to dinner one evening. You should call George and ask him to drive over from D.C. to join us. He must be very proud of you. With his transfer to the Soviet desk at the State Department, you two make quite a team. By the way, have you set a date yet, or are you determined to make this the longest engagement on record?''

Laurel hesitated for an instant before announcing, ''I'm not seeing George anymore, Dad.''

James's thick brows, which were graying like the hair at his temples, rose in mild surprise, but his gaze remained steady on the road ahead. ''Oh? What happened? I thought you said your goals were so compatible.''

Laurel's tone was controlled as she answered, ''It wasn't a matter of goals so much as likes and dislikes—that sort of thing, you know.'' Her gaze flickered to his long enough to see that, no, he didn't know. Then again, he didn't seem very concerned about George's fate. The sad part was, neither was she.

Ironically, she realized it was George Ackerly—or, rather, her engagement to him—that had lulled her into believing she could waltz into Annapolis as if the past had never happened. Of course, the conference invitation had arrived *before* George broke their engagement. With an engagement ring on her finger, she had felt immune to any power Annapolis might still have to prompt memories of Nathan; thus she had accepted the invitation without a qualm. Then George had made his announcement, which at the time had made pitifully little difference to her, and since then her work had kept her too busy to anticipate how her broken engagement would color her perception of this trip. At least it had until last night when she had tried to sleep. Then it had hit her. With her engagement ring missing, she was returning to Annapolis not from a position of power but in a weakened state, vulnerable and totally unprepared to face her past failures.

Yet the past loomed before her as the car turned off North Street and into State Circle, and Laurel felt her entire body tense as though preparing for impact. Suddenly her heart was pounding and her hands were clammy. Seeing the steeple of St. Anne's soar above the old building in the middle of the circle was like looking through her own photo album. She closed her eyes, but it did no good. Against the backdrop of her memory, the scenes sprang up one after the other and, along with them, a frighteningly vivid image of Nathan.

In a flustered effort to wipe out the image, Laurel ordered her brain to logical thought. Obviously, there were still some remnants of emotion that needed to be put in their proper place. That was normal. Annapolis had been Nathan's home; for a while, when her father had been stationed at the Naval Academy, it had been her home, as well. Probably she was suffering from a delayed case of melancholy. This desire she felt to see and talk to Nathan must be only a sentimental yearning for the good old days. She would remember soon enough that the good old days were gone and that many of them had not been very good in the first place.

The need to prove that this hastily constructed theory was true was fast becoming necessity. When her father pulled their car to a halt in front of the bed-and-breakfast run by Mrs. Honey Clarkson, Laurel took one look at the restored eighteenth-century town house—where she had never stayed and which, therefore, might have provided some refuge from other, too familiar places—and made an impulsive decision.

"We made good time," James remarked. "After we register, I think I'll take a walk and stretch my legs. Would you like to join me?"

"I don't think so," Laurel replied, her gaze wandering toward the city dock and the street that led to the bridge across Spa Creek. "In fact—" she turned to him "—would you mind registering for me? There's something I want to do. And I'd like to use the car, if you won't be needing it."

"No, I don't need it," he replied. After pausing a moment, he added, "If you're going to the cemetery, I'd be glad to come with you."

Laurel shook her head, not bothering to correct her father's misconception that she wanted to pay her last respects to Jonathan Coltrane. "I appreciate the offer, Dad, but I want to do this by myself. I'll be fine."

With a sigh that sounded disappointed, her father reached across the seat and patted her arm. "All right, then. I'll meet you in the parlor at seven-fifteen. You're not going to refuse me the pleasure of walking into that reception tonight with my accomplished daughter on my arm, are you?"

She smiled warmly. "Only if you refuse me the pleasure of walking in on the arm of my distinguished father. I'll be ready at seven-fifteen."

A few minutes later, Laurel was headed out of downtown Annapolis, certain that what she needed to do in order to regain her composure was face the worst and get it over with. And that meant facing St. John's Landing.

Traveling along the familiar road, she held on to the thought that memories weren't real. They could not hurt her. Nor could they force her to think or to feel any certain way. Nathan—who *could* hurt her and who could, she feared, still make her think or feel almost any way he chose—was somewhere on the other side of the world. There was no danger of actually having to face him in her current unnerved state. Or ever, for that matter.

Yet her hands trembled on the steering wheel, and the knot in her stomach had become genuinely painful. The truth was, she was scared and thoroughly bewildered by the violence of her reaction. And when she reached the initial stretch of low fieldstone wall that bordered the Coltrane property, she knew the word *memory* did not begin to describe the almost desperate longing for Nathan that was, by this time, throbbing inside of her.

This wasn't a memory. It was a vision, crystal-clear and powerful. It was as if he were there, beside her. The air was heavy with the scent of him—not of the cologne he wore, but of that elusive fragrance that was dark and male and entirely his. She could see his intense brown eyes and the broad planes of his face. As though she could reach out and touch it, she recalled the way his sensual mouth looked when he smiled. The way it felt as it rocked across her own in a seeking caress. The way it moved, open and wet and hungry, across her breasts. Her breasts that were, at that very moment, aching for the touch of the first—and only—man whose impassioned loving had ever aroused them.

Laurel shuddered helplessly. It *must* be only nostalgia, her mind clamored, groping for a hold on rationality. Surely she was merely feeling lonely and sorry for herself. The last three years of forgetting couldn't possibly have been a complete waste of time. But with growing dread she heard the voice of her heart answer insistently that they had been.

Chapter Two

Sitting on the end of the Coltrane dock, with his back against a piling and his gaze fixed on the waters of the South River, Nathan rested one arm on his suitcase and wondered how long he could pretend he was relaxing rather than admit he was avoiding the cottage.

Aunt Louise had wanted to help him get settled in, but he had sent her on her way with a promise to be at her house at noon the following day for lunch. He had checked on his rental car in the garage, then walked through the main house—ostensibly to make sure the Historical Society was doing its job and that things weren't getting dusty, as Aunt Louise had claimed. Then he had started down the path to the cottage with every intention of unpacking and taking a nap. Faced, however, with the imminent threat of seeing the old place—and worse, lying in the bed that awaited him— he had not been able to follow through. And he was beginning to wonder if this whole plan didn't have some serious masochistic overtones.

Maybe he should take a real vacation. Go lie on a beach in Bermuda. Spend a couple of weeks in New York, seeing shows. Was it really necessary to put himself through this agony?

Unfortunately, he thought it probably was. The five days he had been here when Uncle Jack died had taught him that. At first, his attention had been focused on his dying uncle. Later, however, through the funeral arrangements and meetings with his lawyer, he had been stunned by how powerfully—and how painfully—the Landing made him think of Laurel. There was nowhere to go, no place to rest his eye that did not hold some memory of her. Long before his leave was over, he had been frantic to get away. It had taken a long time to come to grips with the experience and to realize what it meant in terms of his future.

He had come to the Landing a scared, heartbroken little boy, and Uncle Jack and Aunt Louise had tried in their separate ways to make him feel welcome. Uncle Jack had taken him sailing and told him about his ancestors, how the Coltranes had always drawn strength from their land and how it could give him solace for his grief. He belonged here, Uncle Jack had said; St. John's Landing was his destiny. Aunt Louise's tactics had been slightly more effective; she had baked him cookies and told him stories about his father as a child. But he was living with strangers, and the things they said had made little sense at the time.

Only recently had he realized in a conscious way that, finally, it had been his friend Lauri and the continual assurance she offered him that he was loved for himself alone that had eased his sorrow and turned St.

John's Landing from a formidable, foreign environment into a place where he could feel at home. He had always known her love was important to him, but he'd never known *how* important. Until last fall, when he had been at the Landing without her, he had never fully realized how closely entwined were his sense of the Landing as home and Laurel's presence in his life.

When Laurel had left him, she might as well have taken the Landing with her. Uncle Jack's will said it was his, but it had ceased to be a place he thought of when he wanted comfort. It would never again bring him that feeling of well-being he used to get when he thought of his ancestors who had settled the tract of land and turned it into a profitable plantation—the bounty from which Coltranes had benefited for more than three hundred years. Yes, it was his, but without Laurel it was an empty shell, a body without spirit. And he could barely stand the sight of it.

The past winter in Jacksonville had been long and painful as he wrestled with his conscience. But he was sure, now, of what he had to do. He would not be able to live at the Landing alone, and the notion of ever bringing another woman there was unthinkable. Nor would he ever be able to pass the legacy on to any child he might produce; no matter how unfair it was, he would always be plagued by the thought that a child of his that was not also Laurel's was not the child that should have St. John's Landing. Thus, the Landing was useless to him—except as a source of constant pain. And so, as sad as it made him, he was going to sell it.

His lawyer, Ted Gilliam, could have handled everything. Technically, it wasn't necessary for him, personally, to negotiate with the Historical Society, which had expressed interest in purchasing the property. Emo-

tionally, however, it was important that he be the one to
sign his name on the dotted line and hand over the keys.
Before he could get on with his life, he had to accept the
fact that Laurel was truly and irrevocably gone, and
part of that acceptance was saying goodbye to his
memories of her. He knew that if he cheated himself of
that opportunity, he would always regret it. And there
were enough regrets in his life already.

Nathan glanced down at the sailboat floating beside
the dock. *The Scallop* had been his since his graduation from high school. How many hours had he and
Laurel spent on it? More, he knew, than he could begin to count. As he stretched one long leg out to rest his
foot on the prow, he rubbed his eyes with a weary hand
and sighed. He was tired. So very tired. Too tired to face
any more great emotional battles. All he wanted was
some peace. He only wished the price he had to pay for
it were not so high.

The white stones crunched beneath the car's tires as
Laurel turned into the winding road that led to St.
John's Landing. The driveway was canopied by old
oaks and maples, their limbs newly budded. Beneath
the shelter of the trees, white dogwood bloomed, and
clusters of crimson and pink azaleas bordered the gravel
drive. Situated on the banks of the South River, a narrow waterway that emptied into the Chesapeake Bay
several miles south of Annapolis, what remained of the
Coltrane property comprised thirty acres of heavily
wooded land, a quarter mile of which wound along the
shoreline of inlets and sloughs. Originally, the tract had
covered the entire peninsula along the South River, east
to the modern town of Edgewater and north to Annapolis on the Severn. It had been a thumb grant given in

1661 to St. John and Elizabeth Coltrane. Jealous
neighbors had claimed that Lord Baltimore must have
used an exceedingly small map when he set the tip of his
thumb to it and parceled out the grant; however, over
the years, as the Coltrane heirs had turned their attention from planting tobacco to other interests, St. John's
Landing had been reduced to a mere fraction of its
original size.

As Laurel turned the last bend in the drive, the main
house came into sight. Big and white and meticulously
kept, the early Georgian mansion sat on a bluff over-
looking the river. The drive circled past the carved oak
front door, and Laurel slowed her car to gaze at the
beautiful fanlight, remembering the first time she had
seen the Landing, the summer her father had been
transferred to Annapolis.

She had been nine, and the place had greatly intimi-
dated her. It had seemed so big, so perfectly groomed.
And so rich. Walking up to the front door with her
hand tucked in her father's, she'd found it unbeliev-
able that her friend Nathan, whom she had left behind
so long ago in Spain, lived in such a house. The Nathan *she* remembered always looked a little scruffy, and
he collected rocks and thought nothing of picking up
dead birds and worms.

Just when she'd been ready to tell her father he must
have driven to the wrong place, Nathan had come
bursting through the front door, dressed only in ragged
cutoffs and hollering, "Hey, Lauri! I caught two catfish this morning, and Aunt Louise's gonna fry 'em for
dinner! She said we could watch her skin 'em! Come
on!"

Though a bit abrupt after such a long separation,
Nathan's greeting had served a purpose. Laurel's ini-

tial fears about St. John's Landing were instantly over-shadowed by the gruesome possibility of having to eat something called a catfish that had to be skinned.

At thirty-four, she no longer found catfish—or much else, actually—intimidating. And as she parked her car, thinking about how much of her life she'd spent at the Landing, Laurel concluded that this place was the closest thing to a home she had ever known. Yet this was not a homecoming. The house was empty. There was no one to greet her. Uncle Jack had been buried last September. Aunt Louise lived in her own place now.

And Nathan? If he had been there, would he have welcomed her? Would she have wanted him to? The latter was a question she had to answer.

Feeling as though she were about to dip her heart in acid like so much litmus paper, Laurel turned away from the house and let herself be drawn across the lawn toward the spot where a path led into the woods. When she reached it, she faltered for an instant, wanting to turn back but compelled to go on by the almost perverse need to see, to touch, to remember. It was absurd. Nothing had changed. The earth had not moved, yet it felt as though it had, for certainly her entire vision of reality was shifting.

Against all common sense, she moved forward, her low heels causing her to stumble a little over the uneven terrain, until she came to the edge of an embankment. There, she grabbed hold of the slender trunk of an oak sapling and paused to look down. She could see patches of water glittering in the afternoon sunshine through the trees and low-blooming azaleas and rhododendrons. The view tempted her to go down to the dock.

She had learned to fish on that dock. Nathan had taught her. She had learned to kiss there, too. They had taught each other. The memory of their first, innocent and breathless kiss washed through her, raising goose bumps on her skin and bringing a flush to her pale cheeks. Her lips parted, trembling, as her mind conjured up an image of two young people standing on the pier, both of them tall and slender and glistening with water from a recent swim.

Laurel was shaking as she hurried on, certain she was questing after something she would regret having found.

The house St. John had built for Elizabeth when they first settled the land was nestled in a small clearing deep in the woods, some distance along the path. A simple white structure with a gambrel roof and two windows flanked by dark green shutters on either side of a heavy front door, it was every bit as enchanting as Laurel remembered it. As she slowly approached the cottage she felt the veil of unreality wrap her more closely in its folds.

She tried to believe it was only time and distance and loneliness that made this place seem so perfect in her memories. Memories were like that, weren't they? Improving or worsening with age until the past appeared either black or white, good or bad, with no gray areas of ambiguity. It was only a trick of her imagination that she remembered the days she and Nathan had spent in this cottage as being everything romance and love could ever hope to achieve. Surely, with all the heartache that had come afterward, the memories this place evoked would be tarnished.

Maybe, a voice whispered as she reached out a trembling hand to take hold of the iron door latch.

It was locked. Not surprisingly, Laurel supposed with a sigh. Moving to the window on the right side of the door, she gazed for a moment at the lower right pane where the first inhabitants of the cottage had etched their names and the date, according to traditional practice of the time. Her finger reached out to trace the faint milky lines. Then, refocusing her gaze past the wavy, leaded glass, she looked inside.

The great room, as the central living area of early colonial houses was called, was as it had always been. The paneled walls were painted a delicate shade of spring green. Paisley chintz cushions rested on benches in recessed windows, and Persian carpets were scattered over the glossy wood floor. A single sofa dominated the room, set at an angle to the fireplace. There was a mahogany desk against the wall, an old sextant on its left-hand corner. And on the far side of the room sat a spinning wheel, the one Elizabeth had brought from England.

Drawing back a little, Laurel spread her hand wide on the cottage wall. As though she could somehow absorb the richness, the wholeness, of the cottage itself and all it contained of her own life, her fingers moved over the weathered wood, touching it lovingly, as her eyes tried to take it all in at once. Slowly, she walked toward the window at the far end of the small dwelling.

Nathan's presence was so strong now. So alive. She could hear his voice, gentle and deep as he spoke love words to her in the dark. Apprehensive, she leaned forward and peered inside.

It was still there. And the force of its presence took Laurel's breath away. She sagged against the window, her forehead resting on the glass, her gaze transfixed by the large canopied bed that dominated the bedroom. As she had known it would, the image of a young man and woman floated before her eyes, and down to its smallest detail the picture mirrored the one that was engraved in the pages of her memory: the candles on the bedside tables; the bouquet of red roses, gardenias and baby's breath on the window seat, streamers of white satin ribbon trailing to the floor; moonlight streaking into the room, bathing it in silver. The woman was dressed in a satiny white negligee that clung to the soft curves of her slender body. The man wore the black trousers of a tuxedo and a white shirt that hung open, baring a darkly matted, powerful chest. Standing at the crossroads of youth and adulthood, they looked very happy and very much in love.

Unable to prevent it, she allowed the scene to play itself out in her mind, and she knew that therein lay the truth inside her heart . . .

"You are incredibly beautiful," the man said, his large hands cupping the woman's face.

"So are you," she replied, turning her head to brush his palm with her lips.

He brought his mouth down to hers and kissed her long and tenderly. Her fingers—a band of diamonds on one of them glittering in the candlelight—clung to his shoulders. When their lips parted, both of them were breathless.

"You're trembling all over," he whispered, his hands running down her arms. "Are you scared, Lauri?"

"A little," she whispered back, dropping her gaze. "Oh, Nathan, I know it's silly. We've known each other forever. We've kissed thousands of times before. It seems as if I've always known what you taste like, how it feels to have you hold me." She ran an adoring hand across his chest, under the shirt that was so invitingly

open. "I've touched you before, and you've touched me, but..."

"But we've never made love," he finished for her when the words wouldn't come. And, lifting his bride's face to his own with a finger under her chin, he made it clearer still. "We've never been in bed together, with nothing on and all the time in the world to do exactly what we've been wanting to do for a long, long while."

Her eyes locked to his, she said solemnly, "I guess I'm worried you'll be disappointed."

"Not a chance."

"I'm not, well—" Her lashes lowered. "You know this is my first time."

"Hmm. Mine, too."

Startled gray eyes clashed with gently amused brown ones.

"You thought I was sowing wild oats when I claimed to be studying or out with the guys, didn't you?"

She blushed and nodded. "I'm sorry, Nathan. I should have known better."

"So, now you know," he told her. "I've never wanted anyone but you. And I'm probably as nervous as you are. But I love you, Lauri, more than I'll ever be able to tell you. I want to show you how much I love you. I've wanted to show you for so long."

"Oh, Nathan!" she cried softly, throwing her arms around him. "I love you, too. Let's not wait any longer. Please, love me, and let me love you!"

And then she was trembling with something beyond fear as he began scattering kisses with eager abandon over her eyes and cheeks and lips. Inexperience was forgotten as, for the first time between them, passion was entirely unleashed. Neither was afraid. The end was *a goal they both sought, and they had their love to guide them to it.*

White satin slithered to the floor, and ivory skin was revealed bathed in amber candlelight. A ragged breath was drawn. And then there was the moist sound of feminine flesh being tasted, suckled, until it flushed and swelled with pleasure. A zipper rasped, followed by a low growl as gentle hands discovered and measured the full extent of masculine arousal.

The diaphanous white drapes of the canopy enveloped the lovers as they sank down upon the bed, oblivious to the visual harmony their bodies, together, created. He was so very large, she so very slender. His skin was dark. Hers was ivory. His hair, lustrous and thick, was almost identical in color to the mantle of luxurious, nearly black silk that spread across the pillow beneath her shoulders. Never had two lovers so clearly belonged to each other. They were matched. Perfectly. As though fate had made them for precisely this moment.

And if that were true, then fate had planned well. For when the moment came, they fit together with a flawlessness that was breathtaking. For a time they lay still, their gazes locked, their limbs entwined, their lips barely touching—both captivated by the realization that they were, indeed, joined. But their destiny lay yet ahead of them, and they began moving toward it together.

They knew the way. They had known it forever. Perhaps even when they'd been too young to understand, they had known intuitively that someday their love would lead them to this: this incredible feeling of being lost in the other. Of giving up separate thoughts, separate wishes, so that they might live and breathe as one. There was no question of mistrust or of holding back.

*They gave everything freely, joyfully. And when their
knowledge of the other became complete, it was with an
innocent and boundless faith in the future. They took
what love gave them and returned it in full measure,
certain that in doing so, they had become a part of each
other for all time....*

No! Not for all time! It wasn't true that a man and a
woman could be fated for each other! It wasn't true that
people had no control over whom they loved! And it
could not possibly, in a million years, be true that her
wedding night with Nathan had been as glorious as she
remembered it.

More than fourteen years had passed since they first
came together on that bed as husband and wife. No
memory of passion could survive that long unchanged.
And Laurel was convinced it was the ensuing years of
struggling to salvage their marriage that had painted the
memory of their wedding night in such rose-colored
hues. They had had two short weeks of the sort of happiness that could have been lifted from the pages of a
storybook. Then Nathan had announced that, if he
were going to finish medical school, he had no choice
but to apply to the Navy scholarship fund. And nothing had ever been the same again.

He didn't like it any better than she, he had said. But
Uncle Jack had refused to keep paying the tuition, so it
was the only way. He knew it would be hard for her, but
they could make it work. She would see. Everything
would be all right. How could it not be, when they loved
each other so much?

It hadn't been all right, though, and none of the
hundreds of things Nathan had done for her had made
it so. She had tried so hard to give up her intense longing for a home and a way of life she had never had the

chance to enjoy. Again and again she had let Nathan talk her into believing that, if only she tried harder, everything would be okay. She had loved him so much and so blindly that it terrified her even now to think about it. And in her bedazzled state, she had not been able to see that she was destroying everything that had been good between them in her vain effort to fit into a life she would never be able to accept.

Then, one morning, in the space of a few dreadful and unforgettable minutes, her world had exploded in front of her. The fierce, unwavering love she had come to expect from Nathan, the love that she had cherished all her life, was gone—vanished—as though it had never been. In its place was resentment and unbridled fury. Leaving him had been an act of sheer desperation. If she had stayed, she would have had to live with the knowledge that he didn't love her anymore, that he was only determined she honor her vows to him, no matter what. And so, in order to do what she knew had to be done, she had convinced herself that she must not love him, either, and that the power he held over her emotions stemmed only from dependency.

But it wasn't so. As she stood there on that warm afternoon in April, leaning against the cottage with her eyes closed and her arms wrapped around her, Laurel could only wonder at the thoroughness—and the foolishness—with which she had gone about believing her own lie. The truth lived in the longing of her heart and in the aching, sensual awareness the memory of her wedding night had aroused in her body. She could no longer deny it. She was as much in love with Nathan at that moment as she had been on the day she married him.

Suddenly, the cottage no longer seemed a place of beauty and enchantment; it had taken on the qualities of a prison. It frightened her to think her heart might be trapped inside the modest dwelling and that she might be doomed to live without it—and, therefore, alone—forever. She needed to get away, to go someplace where she was reminded that she was whole and thoroughly in control of her destiny. With a purposeful shove, she pushed herself away from the cottage and turned to go.

And then she screamed, a choked sound, totally disbelieving.

"My God, Laurel, it *is* you," Nathan whispered.

With one hand splayed on the wall behind her and the other clenched at her waist, Laurel stared at the real, flesh-and-blood man who had been the object of her love for as long as she could remember. The feeling that she had bidden him to appear—snatched him, by sheer longing, off the deck of some aircraft carrier—was overwhelming, and she wondered dazedly if she might simply faint.

"Are you all right?" he asked, taking a couple of steps toward her. "I'm sorry. I didn't mean to scare you."

Laurel straightened, the thought that he might touch her sending a bolt of panic through her. Breathlessly, she spoke. "I'm fine. I didn't hear you coming."

"I was down on the dock and didn't hear a car, so I— You cut your hair."

"Yes. It seemed—" Her hands fluttered. "Well, I thought it was time."

"I didn't recognize you at first."

"I'm sorry, I—"

"It's a little shocking. That's all."

"Of course," she agreed stupidly, forcing down a bubble of hysterical laughter.

They stared at each other. Then Nathan's gaze made several rapid trips over her, returning always to her face. Laurel couldn't prevent her own eyes from performing the same almost guilty appraisal of him, though it was torture to be confronted with the broad shoulders and narrow hips and long, muscular legs that, only moments before, she had been imagining magnificently nude. Acute embarrassment infused her face with color as she wondered how on earth to explain her presence there and what she could possibly say that wouldn't come out sounding like *I love you*.

"You look well." Nathan's rasped comment broke the silence.

"So do you," Laurel countered, willing her eyes not to wander downward and thinking that, in fact, his face looked fairly wretched. As her head cleared somewhat, she realized that, unfortunately, she did have something else to say to him. "Nathan, I'm sorry about Uncle Jack."

He nodded once and uttered a stilted "Thank you."

"He loved you very much, you know," she added, not knowing what had made her say it.

A brief, almost confused frown appeared on his face. "Yes. I loved him, too."

"Were you able to get home before he died?"

"We had a few hours together."

"I'm glad."

She bit her lip. If she didn't get out of here soon, she was going to make a complete fool of herself.

Before she could think of any way to escape, Nathan asked, "Did you want to go inside?"

"No. That is, I— I had some time this afternoon. I'm staying in town and wanted to... well, to see..." She floundered in a well of emotion. Not for anything in the world would she have walked through that cottage door with him. But then, he didn't look too happy about the idea, either. They had not parted friends. The realization that he might still be furious with her was unspeakably painful.

"I've been in Geneva most of the past year," she went on, trying to justify her presence. "That's where I was when Aunt Louise called to tell me about Uncle Jack. I couldn't leave to come to the funeral. I got here this afternoon and wanted to—"

"You don't have to explain."

"Well, it's been so long since I've been at the Landing, I thought I'd—"

"Why *are* you here? In Annapolis, that is."

It was clear to Laurel that the question was torn from him. He had waited as long as he could to ask it and did so now reluctantly.

"I'm attending the Foreign Affairs Conference at the Academy," she informed him, sounding nearly apologetic.

His frown cleared as comprehension dawned. Haltingly, he said, "Aunt Louise told me about your appointment to the negotiating team. That's quite an accomplishment, Laurel."

They both knew what the admission had cost him, and Laurel had no desire to make him pay more. "Thank you," she replied simply. "She's told me something about your work, too. She said you've had special duty on the design of the new hospital ship. I've heard wonderful things about the project."

Nathan shrugged. They both also knew what that bit of praise had cost her. That was the trouble. They knew too much about what the other thought and felt. Trying to pretend they didn't was insane. What was even more insane was that they were standing ten feet apart, behaving like virtual strangers, when Laurel found the urge to throw herself into his arms, to greet him fully, overpowering. But she couldn't follow her heart's lead, for in spite of what Nathan had tried so hard to make her believe, love did not conquer all.

Suddenly, it became impossible to remain standing there. "I have to be going," she said, taking a single step toward the path. "My father's expecting to meet me at seven-fifteen. There's a reception this evening at the officers' club."

Nathan's expression stopped her. His narrowed eyes and the tautness of his features registered renewed shock. "I'll see you both later, then. When the Commandant heard I'd be home this month on leave, he invited me to the reception."

Laurel's complexion lost some of its heightened color at this news. "Oh," she replied weakly. "Well, Dad will be delighted to see you. He's going to be a moderator this week, too."

Laurel wondered if Nathan had even heard her. His eyes were roaming again, lingering on the curves of her body, shooting upward to skim over her hair with unmistakable displeasure.

She was about to say a quick goodbye when her gaze fell upon his luggage, dumped in a heap several yards back along the path. "Are you, uh, going to be staying up at the house?" she asked.

"No." His eyes locked with hers. "I'll be here. At the cottage."

Her mouth formed a silent O. And then neither of them could look at the other.

"I really should be going."

"I'll walk you back to your car."

"Oh, no! I mean, there's no need—"

But he was motioning her to lead the way, and she could not very well refuse. She moved quickly, keenly aware of how much distance Nathan was leaving between them as he followed.

When they reached the lawn, Laurel frowned, noticing that in addition to her car, there were five or six others parked in the drive. They hadn't been there when she arrived.

"It looks as though you've got trespassers," she commented in an almost normal tone.

"The Historical Society is running tours through the house," Nathan explained, coming up beside her. "They've been taking care of the place for me. It must be time for the Sunday afternoon showing."

Laurel winced at the thought of what Jonathan Coltrane would have said about strangers wandering through his home, peering curiously and dispassionately at the things that had meant so much to him. Opinionated, overbearing and honorable in the manner of the Old South, Uncle Jack had been snobbish to a fault about his time-honored position in Annapolis society. He had possessed a good head for business and an almost unbearable pride in having saved the Coltrane yacht brokerage from bankruptcy after his father died.

Laurel had always found his condescending attitude irksome, but it was balanced by his generosity and unfailing hospitality. She hadn't loved him, and there had been times when the things he said to Nathan had made her genuinely dislike him. But she had always respected Uncle Jack, and she knew he would have been furious to know Nathan had turned his precious home into a public spectacle, no matter how tastefully the deed was being accomplished.

"I imagine the Society is grateful you've given them permission to show the house," she said as they reached her car.

"Hmm," Nathan replied absently. "Laurel, I—"

When he didn't continue, she looked at him. "Yes?"

He shook his head.

"You wanted to say something?"

"It was nothing. Forget it."

It wasn't nothing. She knew he had started to say something important but had thought better of it. And she didn't dare press him further. She had lost her right to question him about either his thoughts or his actions. She wasn't his wife anymore—and he had made it clear the last time she saw him that he did not think of her as his friend. Pain shot through her, and she turned away.

"I have to go," she mumbled, her fingers tangling in the car keys she had dropped into her blazer pocket. She slid behind the wheel, quickly turning the key in the ignition.

Nathan's hands gripped the door as he closed it for her; his fingers, wrapped over the edge of the open window, brushed her shoulder as he leaned down to look at her. It took every ounce of restraint Laurel possessed not to move the inch that would keep them from touching.

"Well, until later, then," she tossed out with a pasted-on smile, her voice cracking with false brightness. Though she avoided looking at him directly, she could feel Nathan watching her. She could also feel, in his hesitation, all the things he wasn't saying. When he did speak, it was as though, in sifting through his choice of words, he found the only ones left to him entirely unsatisfactory.

"Goodbye, Laurel."

She couldn't look at him as she delivered a nearly inaudible "'Bye." With the car in gear, she waited until his hands dropped away from the door. Then she managed, somehow, to drive away.

This had to be the epitome of self-inflicted torture. Nathan lay sprawled on the bed in the cottage, staring up through the canopy and thinking that, if he had a grain of sense, he'd be heading back to the airport—right after he let Aunt Louise know how little he appreciated not being warned that Laurel would be in Annapolis. He was quite certain the wily old woman had known.

But *was* he driving back to the airport or giving Aunt Louise a piece of his mind? Of course not. He was lying here on this frilly old relic of a bed—not that he had any expectation of resting. Oh, no. He was lying here because, in some mixed-up way, the damned bed made him feel closer to Laurel. And for some peculiar reason, he wanted to remember that, once, they had been very, very close. He wasn't saying goodbye to his memories of her, as he had vowed he would do. He was reliving every last one of them and drowning in regret that they would be all he ever had.

She was so beautiful. If he lived to be a hundred, he would never forget how elegant her slender body was, how startlingly clear her gray eyes could be, how white and smooth her skin always looked next to her dark

hair.... *Her hair.* God Almighty! How could she have
cut it like that? She would never have done it if they had
still been married; she knew how he liked to wrap his
own body and hers together in those long, thick strands
of silk....

Blood pooled insistently in his loins in response to the
erotic images his mind was conjuring, and he groaned,
rolling to his stomach to bury his face in a pillow. His
fist came down hard on the bed in a gesture of supreme
frustration. He wanted her. He wanted her so badly it
hurt. Three years of trying to forget wiped out in a single, ill-fated moment.

Dammit! He didn't *want* to want her! What was she,
after all, but a woman? There wasn't anything magic
about that. There had been plenty of other women who
could have helped him forget Laurel. If he had let them.
None of them had *been* Laurel, though. None of them
had known him as well as she did. And there *was*
something magic about being with a woman, of making love with a woman, who knew as much about you
as you did yourself. There was something magic about
falling in love with your closest friend and having it
work out that she fell in love with you, too. They'd been
so happy. They'd had such plans.

And it had not been entirely Laurel's fault that the
plans had gone awry. Nathan's conscience reminded
him of that, even as another part of him persisted in
believing it should have worked, and that it wasn't entirely *his* fault that it had not.

Turning his head to stare at the empty pillow beside
him, Nathan allowed another memory to carry him
back in time, this one not as wonderful as those that
had haunted him earlier....

"*What do you mean, no?*"

"Just what I said. No, I do not want a baby. Not as long as we don't have a home."

The man frowned, his fingers stopping in the act of buttoning the shirt of his summer white uniform. He watched his wife as she pulled her bathrobe from the closet and put it on. "You mean," he began slowly, "all this time you've been putting off starting a family because of school and this and that and the other thing, you knew you weren't ever going to do it?"

"I've been trying to reconcile myself to the idea," she told him as she began making their rumpled bed. "But I don't think I ever will. I just can't bring myself to subject a child to the kind of childhood I had. Nathan, for heaven's sake!" She spread her arms wide. "Look around you! We've been in the Philippines two months, and only half our things have gotten here from Japan. We probably won't see the other half ever again. We've got a stack of claims forms—and every other form the government ever invented—to fill out for the stuff, and we'll be lucky if the money comes any time in the next year! You're about to go off for twelve weeks on a cruiser, and I've been told it's best not to leave the base—or even the house, if I can help it—because I might get attacked by a mugger or shot by a political terrorist! And you want to have a baby?"

She shook her head. "I want a home, Nathan. I want our children to grow up with the same friends and the same schools. I don't want them scared of investing themselves in something because it might get snatched away from them. And I don't want their lives to be at risk because they happened to be born in a country where the crime rate's sky-high and a lot of people don't even like Americans!"

"They wouldn't be any more in jeopardy here than in a lot of cities stateside." The man left his shirt half unbuttoned to pick up a white belt, which he threaded through the loops in his white slacks. "You're blowing things all out of proportion because you're mad you had to leave Japan in the middle of that research grant, and you've decided this is the way you're going to make me pay for getting transferred."

"That's absurd," she shot back. "I know you don't have control over your assignments."

"That's right! But you blame me for them, anyway!"

"I don't!"

"You do!" Taking a stance at the foot of the bed, he gave up the notion of dressing and, instead, exploded. "I've had it, Laurel! I'm sick of waiting for you to decide that you're in this with me! I've spent ten years feeling like I'm the one who's married here and you're only along for the ride, and I'm through with it! I'm through watching you wait for the ax to fall! I'm through racking my brain, trying to second-guess what it'll take to satisfy you! You've never even tried to get over all the crap you believe about the Navy. You made up your mind in the beginning we weren't going to make it, and you're itching to be able to say 'I told you so.' Well, let me tell you something. I didn't want to be in the Navy, but I've made the best of it. I'm a physician with highly specialized training in trauma medicine, and I'd never have been any kind of physician with any kind of training if it hadn't been for the Navy! I'm not going to be made to feel sorry I dragged you into this, when the truth is, it's gotten so I'm damned glad to be here! You've got no right to try to make me feel like I ought to be ashamed of what I've done or what I am. I'm not *ashamed! But I'm sick and tired of having a wife who's ashamed of me, and I want it to stop! Now.''*

The woman, who stood clutching a pillow to her waist, stared in astonishment at her raging husband. *"If you aren't ashamed of anything,"* she began in a shaky whisper, *"then why wouldn't you tell me the reason Uncle Jack cut off your tuition—"*

"Ah, dammit, Laurel!"

"—so that you'd have to accept a Navy scholarship, when we both know, from the way he talked about your father, how he felt about the Navy?"

The man flung one arm wide and heaved an exasperated sigh. *"Are we going to go through that again?"*

"We've never been through it once," she insisted, her lower lip trembling. *"You've never answered the question."*

"I told you why Uncle Jack cut off the tuition."

"You told me you had a fight with him, but you've never said what the fight was about."

"What difference does it make? It's been ten years!''

"I don't know what difference it would have made! You won't tell me!" Her voice rose suddenly to a fever pitch, and she dumped the pillow on the bed. *"You and Uncle Jack always had fights, and it was never the end of the world! You'd say one thing, he'd contradict you and the bell would ring to start another round. You always ended up doing exactly what he didn't want you to do. Then he'd make you sit through one of his lectures on what it means to be a Coltrane. Then you'd apologize, and he'd get a little sentimental, and the two of you'd go off sailing together, the best of friends. Now, you tell me why you refused to apologize that time, when the consequences meant more than all the other times put together? Why was that fight so awful*

*that you hardly even speak to each other now? Why
wouldn't you let me even talk to him about it? What on
earth did you say to make him so angry?"*

In the silence that ensued, the humid air in the room
hung like a sultry mantle, the only breeze coming from
an old wooden ceiling fan that made a swishing sound
as it sliced through the heat. The two recipients of the
fan's dubious benefits stared at each other. The man's
jaw was set in a hard line, and when he finally spoke, his
voice was flat.

"It's too late, Laurel. I'm not going to rehash it.
You'll just have to believe me. Uncle Jack wouldn't have
changed his mind, no matter what I said. I didn't have
a choice about applying for the Navy scholarship, if I
wanted to finish school. You agreed to the decision.
And dammit—" his control broke once more "—it's
time you learned to live with it! You're going to stop
acting like a scared rabbit who's waiting for the big bad
wolf to eat her up! And you're going to stop cringing
whenever you see me in this uniform! It's gotten so you
cringe even when I'm not in uniform! It's gotten so I
feel like I go to bed every night with a scared virgin!
Every time we make love, I've got to convince you it's
okay and that I'm not going to eat you alive!"

"I do feel like you're going to eat me alive," she
cried, her voice quavering. "You don't make love anymore! You make war!"

"Well, if that's the way you see it, then you've only
got yourself to blame!" he roared. "It wasn't that way
in the beginning. And the only reason it's that way now
is because you can't separate me from the big bad Navy!
I'm fed up with it! You say you want a home and a
family. So, prove it! Prove you're committed to me and
to our marriage!"

Pacing to her dresser, he snatched up a small, flat package and turned to shake it in her direction. "While I'm away on this tour, you're going to stop taking these damned birth control pills. And when I get back, we're going to get you pregnant!"

"How dare you," she breathed, crossing the room to tear the pills out of his hand. Slamming them onto her dresser, she met his look defiantly. "How dare you stand there and tell me what you're *going to do to* my *body!"*

His eyes narrowed. "It may be your body, but you promised to have my children. And speaking of promises, what about 'to love, honor and cherish?' Haven't seen much of that going on around here, either. But I'm going to see all of it real soon. And if I don't, I'll know one thing for sure. You don't love me. You never loved me. You loved St. John's Landing. And you thought you'd get it by marrying me. Well, I've got news for you, lady. Right now, I'd burn the Landing to the ground before I'd ever see you living in it...."

How could he have said such things? What cruel streak could have made him accuse Laurel of coveting St. John's Landing when, even as he said it, he had known it was a lie? The idea must have been buried in his subconscious, though, and a part of him must have been afraid it was true; for in the heat of their fight, the words had come tumbling out without premeditation and without his being able to stop them.

Two days later, Laurel had left Subic Bay and gone back to the States. He had tried to change her mind, but he had been angry, and all the apologies he'd started had come out sounding as if he was blaming her for the fight. She'd been so cold, so completely shut off from him. And finally he had given up, devastated by the realization that, in one vicious outburst, he had lost the thing he most valued in the world: Laurel's love. The love that had always been there to make the world seem right. The love that, when taken away, had left him feeling scared and alone and bereaved, as though she had not simply left him but had actually died.

Three years had not been long enough to recover from the loss. It had, however, been long enough to compile quite a list of regrets: he never should have allowed his anger to get away from him; he never should have let his patience wear so thin; he never should have taken her strength for granted or expected her to get over the scars of her childhood by simple virtue of the fact that he loved her. There had even been times when he wondered if, in spite of all his best instincts, he should have told her the truth about that final blowup with Uncle Jack, and why, indeed, he had turned to the Navy.

Hindsight was always twenty-twenty, Aunt Louise would say. And "should have's" and "if only's" were a deadly way to view life. He wasn't even certain to this day that, given the choices Uncle Jack had left him, things could have gone any differently. In any case, it was too late. Too late to take back the fight with Uncle Jack that had started the whole thing. Too late to give up a career he had worked so hard to establish. Too late to retract the words that had turned Laurel's love for him into the tortured look he had seen on her face that afternoon.

Nathan rolled onto his back once more and began thinking hard. This afternoon by her car, he had started to tell Laurel he was sorry for ever suggesting she had married him for the Landing. But he had been so shocked at seeing her that he hadn't been able to make the words come. He would have to find the words, though, for if she found out he was selling the place, as she surely would, and he hadn't apologized, she could be hurt badly, thinking he was getting rid of it to spite her. And nothing could have been further from the truth. More than that, the thought of her going through life thinking he believed such hateful things about her made him feel sick through to his soul. He had to find a way to tell her he was sorry before fate turned his failure to apologize into one more "if only" he would have to live with forever.

Rising from the bed, Nathan went to the carved antique wardrobe where he had hung his garment bag. A glance at his watch told him he would have to hurry if he wanted to shower and shave before the reception. He removed his uniform from the bag and hung it on the open wardrobe door, then quickly pulled his sweater over his head and tossed it onto a chair. He stopped abruptly, though, in the act of unbuckling his belt to stare at the familiar white shirt and slacks hanging before him.

His eyes came to rest on the shoulder boards, and he thought about the hours of hard work that had gone into putting the four gold stripes there. Laurel probably didn't know he had made Captain. Would she be impressed or disdainful? He guessed he knew the answer to that question. What he didn't know was why he should still care.

There was no choice, though. He would have to wear the uniform. He couldn't attend a reception at the Naval Academy in civilian clothes. Problem was, if he wanted Laurel to listen to anything he had to say, this was not the way to go about it. One should not approach the peace table wearing the very thing that had caused the war in the first place.

Chapter Three

He was late. Which was nothing new. Laurel glanced at her watch, then the door—not for the first time in the past half hour—thinking it was oddly comforting that Nathan still hadn't learned how to be on time. There was little enough about him she had ever been able to regard as less than perfect, and his habitual tardiness had always been reassuring rather than annoying. On this particular occasion, however, reassurance felt more like a bad case of nerves as she waited for him to appear.

Diligently, she tried to pay attention when one of the bright-eyed coeds among the small group with which she was standing asked her a question.

"Do you feel the manipulation of military values for a domestic constituency corrupts our foreign policy?" was the zealously intellectual query that came from a girl whose name tag announced, "Hi! I'm Jenny from Swarthmore."

Laurel clenched her teeth against a giggle that rose in response to the self-consciously erudite question. "Well, Jenny," she began carefully, "to tell you the truth, that's not something I've really thought much about." Then, offering the girl a benign smile, she tossed back, "I understand Ambassador Hillyer is lecturing at Swarthmore this year. Did you attend any of his lectures?"

Jenny started to answer, but the young man to her left—Mark from Antioch—was too shrewd to let Laurel get away with such a ploy. "Excuse me, Ms. Coltrane, but I don't believe you answered the question."

"I never discuss domestic politics, Mark," Laurel said in her clearest and most ladylike tone. To her distress, it looked as if Mark was going to persist. Fortunately, at that moment, her father arrived to rescue her.

"Pardon me," said James, smiling at the group of young people, "I'd like to borrow Ms. Coltrane for a moment, if you don't mind."

Laurel wished the students a pleasant evening and allowed her father to guide her toward the bar. "I always forget how incredibly pedantic students can be," she whispered discreetly. "I know these kids represent the best and the brightest. But I think by the end of the week, I'm going to believe that talking with an idealistic undergrad is more trying than hammering out a verification agreement with a hard-nosed Soviet."

"You looked as though you were about to go down for the third count," James noted. "What on earth's wrong with you, Laurel? And don't tell me again that you're tired. I may not have been around much when you were growing up, but I paid attention when I was there. I've never seen you so distracted!"

Embarrassed at having been caught in the act, so to speak, Laurel gave him a faintly sheepish look. "It shows, does it?"

He smiled. "Probably not to most people."

They had reached the bar, and Laurel had turned to face him when her eyes were caught by the sight of a set of massive shoulders filling the doorway.

Her heart skipped a beat, and her hands grew instantly cold. "The answer to your question is walking in the door," she said.

Laurel heard her father's breath catch at the same moment she noticed—with a jolt—that those familiar, brawny shoulders on which her gaze was fixed now boasted a set of Captain's stripes. He'd gone from Commander to Captain in a little over three years? Lord!

Nathan shook hands with the Commandant, but as he spoke to the older man, his eyes scanned the crowd and came quickly to rest upon hers. The message he silently relayed to her was clear: don't move. Then he had to tear his gaze away and turn to greet the Commandant's wife.

Laurel shivered, her eyes following Nathan as he made his way through the required handshakes and introductions. His presence seemed to fill the room. And it wasn't only his size. It was his striking, dark coloring and his heart-stopping smile, which, when it appeared, was in startling contrast to his brooding, preoccupied manner. It was also his completely unabashed self-confidence, untainted by any hint of arrogance. She noted again the marks of fatigue etched into his face, but she had to admit it would take more than a few lines to lessen the impact he made. He was astonishingly handsome. And so wonderfully big.

And she was in love with him. The thought had occurred to her at least a hundred times since their encounter that afternoon. Exactly what she was going to do about it was a question to which she had no answer. She could scarcely say to Nathan, *I've discovered I'm still in love with you, but I don't want to be. So, would you please go away and leave me alone?* She didn't *want* him to go away. What she wanted was... Well, what she wanted didn't matter. She couldn't have it, and to go on wanting it was the worst kind of foolishness.

But how did one go about falling out of love?

"You knew he'd be here?" her father asked, bringing her attention back to the present.

"I met him this afternoon when I drove out to the Landing," Laurel explained, her eyes never leaving Nathan. "He's staying there this month."

"I see," James replied carefully.

Laurel did not have a chance to respond because, suddenly, Nathan was beside her.

"James," he said, extending a hand to her father. "It's been a long time."

"It's good to see you, Nathan." The Admiral smiled, clasping the younger man's hand in both of his in a gesture of the sincere affection and respect that had always existed between the two of them.

Turning to Laurel, Nathan's eyes coasted over her, taking in her pale blue linen dress in a thorough sweep. "You look lovely this evening, Laurel."

His tone sent warmth rushing through her, and she mumbled a thank-you, trying not to react to the disconcerting way he continued to stare at her even after her father began speaking.

"I was sorry to hear about Jonathan," James said quietly.

Nathan's gaze made one last tour of his ex-wife's blushing face before he turned to reply. "Thank you, sir. It was hard, losing him so suddenly, but I'm grateful he didn't suffer any prolonged illness."

The older man sighed. "I wish it had been that easy for Catherine."

Laurel saw the shock register on Nathan's features, and she cringed inwardly. His eyes flashed to hers.

"Catherine is dead?" he breathed.

James glanced briefly at Laurel before replying to the stunned inquiry. "Why, yes."

Slowly, Nathan shook his head. "I didn't know." The words he did not speak were leaping out at Laurel from the depths of his fierce look. *Has it really come to this? Why? Why didn't you tell me?*

Laurel started to offer him some excuse, but there was nothing she could say that wouldn't betray how confused her feelings about him were. She let her eyes slide from his as her father explained the facts.

"She died almost two years ago, but you know she'd been suffering with cirrhosis for years."

"James, I'm sorry," Nathan said in belated condolence. "I had no idea."

"Well, it's been over for a long time." Clearly not wanting to dwell on the subject, the Admiral continued. "Tell me how you've been. I've been hearing astounding things about your work with that new hospital ship. Are they any closer to scheduling a launch date for her?"

"No, sir," Nathan replied. "But she'll be worth the wait when she's done. I'm convinced we've designed the most sophisticated shock trauma clinic possible. Now it's up to the contractors to get it off the drawing board and make it happen.''

Laurel listened as Nathan and her father talked on about the ship and about Nathan's career. Although Nathan did not elaborate on his success, the facts spoke for themselves. She hadn't known how much of a shining star he'd become, though the fact that he had did not surprise her. He was a brilliant doctor—he was a brilliant man. Having finished both high school and his undergraduate studies at Johns Hopkins in three years each, he had been accepted by the country's top four medical schools. Choosing to stay at Hopkins, he'd had great plans to become a thoracic surgeon. He had achieved that goal and added to it a residency in trauma medicine. But the last place anyone who'd known him might have expected him to be now was designing hospital ships for the U.S. Navy. Noting once again Nathan's Captain's bars, Laurel concluded that, at least the Navy was aware of what a valuable commodity it possessed. She wondered, though, with all this planning and designing they had him doing, how long it had been since he'd had the opportunity to practice the art he had gone to such lengths to learn.

"So, what will they put you to work on next?" James inquired when Nathan had finished his enthusiastic report about the ship.

"I've been assigned special duty for two months in the Antarctic," Nathan answered. "I'll be running training courses. After that, it's back to Jacksonville.''

"I'd wish you the best of luck or offer you some sage advice about how to cope at Project Deep Freeze, but—" James's quick grin was accompanied by a discreet glance at the younger man's shoulders "—it doesn't appear as though you need any luck *or* advice from me. Undoubtedly, your commanding officer has said this, Nathan, but I'd like to say it again. We're truly fortunate to have you. I know your father would be proud of you. And I'm sure Jonathan took great satisfaction in having had a hand in raising one of the finest doctors the Navy's ever claimed."

Nathan cleared his throat as though the praise embarrassed him, and his roughly mumbled "Thank you, sir" could have passed easily for humility. Laurel knew better, though. Uncle Jack had been anything but proud of either Nathan's dream to be a doctor or the fact that he had sought to realize the dream with the help of the U.S. Navy.

Noting that people were moving toward the dining room, James suggested they follow suit. When they reached the archway to the dining room, Nathan hung back to speak quietly.

"Laurel, I wondered if we might talk. Would you let me walk you to your hotel after the reception?"

Laurel shot him a slightly startled glance, an unreasoning spark of pleasure flaring inside her—right alongside a spark of fear. What did he want to say to her? The possibilities weren't good. Yet she had a growing need to prove that she could carry on a conversation with him and not come undone.

"I'd be glad to walk with you," she replied in a tone that matched his for casualness.

Then they were swept into the dinner crowd and had to separate for the prearranged seating.

Laurel toyed with her dinner while pretending to listen to the serious young man from Columbia University sitting beside her. All the while she was fantasizing about what she would say to Nathan if the world were not such a hard and unforgiving place and if she had even the slightest hope that anything would ever be different between them: *I miss you. I miss you so much. Are you still angry with me? Do you have any feeling left for me at all? Oh, Nathan, I don't know what to do about loving you!*

The delicate fragrance of lilacs clung to the night air in the narrow back streets of Annapolis as Laurel and Nathan strolled along the cobbled sidewalk. Many of the houses they passed were more than two hundred years old, and at night, when the tourists had gone and there was no traffic clogging the streets, a timelessness settled over everything. There were no harsh sounds of honking horns, no glaring streetlights or flashing neon signs, only the muffled echo of footsteps on the gently sloping sidewalk and the soft glow of lamps from front parlor windows.

In contrast to the quiet peacefulness of their surroundings, the tension between the two who walked so slowly along Prince George Street was a tangible thing. Neither of them had spoken. Nathan's hands were shoved deep inside his pockets. Laurel clutched her purse and she stared at the sidewalk in front of her.

Finally, unable to stand the suspense any more, she gathered her courage and asked, "Was there something in particular you wanted to talk to me about?"

As though he had been waiting for the go-ahead, Nathan came back quickly, "I'm sorry about your mother, Laurel. I wish I'd known."

Not, she noted, *Why the hell didn't you tell me?*

"I'm sorry, too, Nathan," she replied quietly. "I should have asked Aunt Louise to contact you."

"I would have come to the funeral."

"There wasn't any need for that."

"But I would have come."

She started to say *I know.* It was automatic. But the truth was, she hadn't known if he would come, and she hadn't wanted to risk finding out he would not.

"You know there wasn't much left between my mother and me," she said, offering him a piece of the truth. "For Dad's sake and Lilly's, I should have seen to it that you knew when it happened. For mine, well, it was upsetting, but hardly devastating."

Nathan went on almost doggedly. "All during dinner tonight, I kept trying to imagine what I would have done when Uncle Jack died if I hadn't known Aunt Louise called you. It seems impossible that I wouldn't have let you know—wouldn't have found some way to get in touch with you." His stride lengthened. "I mean, I realize you probably didn't know where I was, but we both know I could have been found pretty easily."

"I said I was sorry."

"Dammit, Laurel, I can understand you hesitating, what with things between us the way they were...are. But doesn't the death of a parent constitute enough reason to put aside differences for a couple of days?"

"We hadn't spoken in over a year."

"If I thought something might happen to your sister or your Dad—or to you—and that I might not find out until years after the fact—"

"I *said* I was sorry, Nathan. What more can I say?"

The stress in her voice brought him to a standstill. His head jerked around, and his eyes locked with hers.

"God, Laurel, I—" He broke off, his breath catching in his throat. "I'm sor—"

"Please don't say you're sorry again."

"But I am. I'm not really angry."

She raised one skeptical brow.

"I'm not," he insisted. "I'm confused! And I am sorry."

Laurel rolled her eyes and sighed.

He didn't seem to notice. "That's what I wanted to talk to you about in the first place."

Something in the tone of his voice brought her gaze back up to his. While she waited in cautious silence, he trained his eyes on some point over her right shoulder and spoke quickly.

"I wanted to tell you that I was sorry for what I said that morning at Subic Bay about you and...and the Landing and your reasons for marrying me. I was angry. It's not a good excuse, but it's the only one I've got for saying things that I knew weren't true."

There was a heavy moment of silence. A couple of midshipmen, late for curfew, ran by. The bell atop St. Anne's church began to toll eleven o'clock. But the Annapolis street seemed to fade away as Laurel and Nathan were transported to another city and another time. It was as though the years in between had not happened.

"You don't love me. You never loved me. You loved St. John's Landing. And you thought you'd get it by marrying me. Well, I've got news for you, lady. Right now, I'd burn the Landing to the ground before I'd ever see you living in it..."

"It's all right, Nathan."

His gaze met hers, and Laurel watched as her quiet statement rocked through him. Obviously he hadn't expected it to be this easy, and as the initial shock wore off, she saw that he couldn't quite believe her.

In a way that told her this was vitally important to him, he said, "I understand you love the Landing, but I also understand you've never confused your feelings

for it with your...your feelings for me. And I want you
to know I wouldn't do anything out of spite to hurt you.
I'm not asking you to forgive me for what I said—only
to believe what I'm saying now."

Laurel lowered her gaze from his. "I believe you.
And I forgave you a long time ago. Let's not talk about
it any more."

He started to interrupt her, but Laurel added with a
hint of impatience, "And let's not apologize for another thing tonight! We've both spent the whole day
being sorry for one thing or another, and I'm afraid if
we don't quit, we'll wind up apologizing for things we
did to each other when we were in grade school! Like,
you could be sorry you told Warren Johnson I threw up
the first time Uncle Jack took me sailing, and I could be
sorry I dumped your favorite tackle box overboard.
And you could say you never meant for me to break my
finger taking the mouse trap out of my hair, and I could
apologize for all the times I deliberately mispro-
nounced your middle name and called you Nathan Saint
John instead of Nathan *Sinjin*. And pretty soon, it'd be
sickening how sorry we both are, and we'd end up dying
in Aunt Louise's proverbial pot of taffy. So, could we
stop now? Please?"

Nathan stared at her in amazement, as though the
notion of levity between them were completely unique.
Then, slowly, his lips began to curve in the first genuine smile Laurel had seen from him in a very long while.
She returned it instantly. And if it was not actually a
full-blown grin they exchanged, it was at least a start.

"You didn't break your finger," he grumbled. "You
sprained it."

"Well, it *felt* broken!" she insisted, waving a hand in dismissal as she began ambling along the sidewalk once more.

Strolling beside her, Nathan continued, "Speaking of Aunt Louise and her pot of taffy—you realize she knew we'd both be here this week."

"I figured that one out."

"Are we going to let her get away with not telling us?"

"I've already planned several speeches, one of which I'll deliver when I call to make arrangements to visit."

Nathan was silent for a moment, and Laurel glanced over to see a frown cross his brow.

"I'm going to her house for lunch tomorrow," he announced. "If you're free at noon, you're welcome to come with me."

She realized immediately that he was offering more than an olive branch. They had cleared the air a little, exchanged all obligatory condolences and apologies. He didn't have to extend this invitation, and, in doing so, he was saying he wanted to spend time with her. The question was, why?

It didn't matter. She simply could not find the will to refuse the pleasure of his company while she had the chance to enjoy it—a chance that might never come again. And lunch at Aunt Louise's seemed as safe a way to see him as any she could imagine. "I'd like to go with you," she told him. "I'm moderating a round table in the morning, but I'm free from eleven-thirty until two."

For a moment she thought Nathan looked surprised—as though he hadn't thought she would say yes and wasn't entirely happy that she had.

"I mean, if it's convenient for you," she said in a rush, suddenly frightened of the step she was taking.

"You'd have to pick me up. Dad has a luncheon and will want the car, I think. Maybe you'd rather not..."

They had reached Clarkson's Lodgings, and when their steps slowed to a halt, Nathan turned to face her.

"I'll pick you up at a quarter of," he said in a tone that sounded as though they were planning a trip to the cemetery.

She searched his familiar features, wishing there were some guarantee she hadn't made a mistake. "I'll meet you here, in front. So you won't have to park."

"I don't mind finding a spot."

"No, it's all right. I'll meet you here."

"If you're sure, then..."

His words trailed off, and they were left staring at each other for a long, silent moment. Then Nathan's gaze skittered toward the town house door.

"Well..." he said.

"Yes, well..." she echoed.

Neither of them moved. His eyes met hers again, then began wandering oh, so slowly over her. Laurel feared her own eyes were returning his caresses all too readily. When he spoke, his voice was soft, almost tender.

"I'll see you tomorrow."

"At eleven-forty-five."

"Right."

"Will you call Aunt Louise and tell her I'm coming?"

"Let's give her a dose of her own medicine and surprise her."

"We're not really going to yell at her, are we?"

There was a drawn out pause before he answered.

"I'm not angry.... Are you?"

Very slowly, she shook her head.

And for another impossible space of time, fire-lit brown eyes held smoky gray ones captive.

"She'll be happy to see you," he said.

"It's been a long time since I've...since I've seen her," she replied.

"Hmm. Yes, it's...been a long time."

Laurel's breath caught, held for an instant, and came out in a thready whisper. "I'll see you tomorrow, then."

"Laurel..."

He was going to kiss her. Right there in the middle of the street. Laurel felt it in her bones. She felt the warmth of his gaze burning her skin, the heat from his great, strong body infusing her with a thrilling and familiar desire. Her lips parted of their own accord when his eyes came to rest upon them. In another second, he was going to take a step toward her. Then he would reach up and remove his hat, tilt his head slightly and bend down to let his mouth settle...

"Good night, Nathan," she managed in a panicked tone.

He stared at her for a moment, then blinked, as though coming out of a daze. Abruptly, his face changed, his eyes losing their hungry look and his expressive mouth hardening into a grim line.

Taking a step back, he nodded once. "'Night, Laurel." Then he turned and strode off the way they had come.

Laurel stared after him. She was aware of the lingering sensation of heat throughout her body and the aching heaviness down inside her. She was also aware of the tendrils of fear curling along her spine. Did she really believe she could spend an afternoon with Nathan and not lose what pitifully little control she had left? Did she truly hold out hope that, someday, the mere sight of him wouldn't turn her into warm jelly? Could she actually imagine a time when her heart would not be filled with a deep longing and an abiding love for him?

Damn her! Damn her for ever taking a single breath! And damn him, too, for ever wanting to breathe the same air she breathed.

Nathan quickened his pace, eating up the sidewalk beneath his feet in long, angry strides that took him back to the Academy in less than half the time it had taken the two of them to walk the same distance.

Driving home, he became impatient with the traffic and reached to turn the radio on full blast, tuning it quickly to a popular oldies station. But even Springsteen's hard-driving rhythm could not match the pace of his furious thoughts.

What in the hell was the matter with him? Talking with Laurel this evening had been a marginally intelligent act for which he'd had a valid excuse; inviting her to go with him to see Aunt Louise had been sheer idiocy for which he had no excuse. Except one: He had to be with her. Every nerve in his body was jumping with tension from seeing her that evening. Every inch of him ached with unfulfilled arousal. And every bit of sense he possessed told him that he was making an enormous mistake. But some completely irrational part of him was obsessed with the need to see her, to hear her, to talk to her. The fact that he couldn't also touch her filled him with almost violent rage.

Dammit, he had been touching Laurel all his life! When they'd been children, he had tugged her hair and pulled her along as they ran through the apple orchard at the Landing. He had carried her on his shoulders and pushed her on swings. And Lord knows how many hours they had spent lying on the dock, swabbing each other's bodies with suntan lotion. He had kissed her on Christmas mornings. And later, when they were falling in love, he had kissed her on lots of other mornings, too. They had snuggled in hammocks and necked in the kitchen pantry and petted each other into near frenzies of frustration. And after they were married—well, to think his body had been *inside* her body, but that now— *Now*, there was a piece of paper lying in his safe-deposit box that said he had no right even to expect he would ever again hold her hand.

Yet he had to be with her, simply because he knew he could be. She didn't love him—no, she had made it exceedingly clear that she did not want to be his wife or his lover or even his friend. And he didn't have forever, only tomorrow and maybe a few days after that. At the end of the week she would be gone. But until then, he was going to spend as much time with her as she would allow—and worry about forgetting her *next* week.

In the end, it did not require any great intelligence to understand why he was willing to put himself through such an ordeal. It only required honesty. Three years, a divorce decree and a string of now-faceless women hadn't changed the most important fact of his life: Given a choice, there had never been a place on earth he would rather be than with Laurel.

Chapter Four

Gracious, child! How could you go and scalp your-self like that? Why, I don't know what gave me a bigger start when I opened the door—seeing you standing there beside Nathan, slim as a willow stick, or looking at all that bare skin on your neck!'' Louise Halliday set a second plate of cookies on her kitchen table, where Laurel and Nathan were seated, then went about making a pot of tea.

With her mouth full of butter almond cookie, Laurel was temporarily unable to defend her dramatic haircut. A glance across the table at Nathan found him studying her hair as he munched away at one of his own homemade favorites, walnut raisin. His afflicted expression made it clear she held the minority opinion on the issue of her abbreviated coiffure.

Resisting the impulse to stick her tongue out at him, Laurel reached for another cookie and began breezily,

"Cutting my hair was easy, Aunt Louise. I walked into the nearest beauty salon, sat down, closed my eyes and didn't open them again until it was over. Nothing to it. I should have done it years ago instead of wasting my time taking care of a rat's nest."

"Hmph!" Louise snorted. "I wish you'd done it years ago, too. Then, *I* wouldn't have wasted *my* time brushing and braiding that rat's nest!"

Laurel opened her mouth to speak, thought better of it and reached for her glass of milk instead.

"Always were itchin' to do something drastic to your person, weren't you?" Louise went on. "I recollect the time I caught you in the third-floor bathroom at the Landing, shaving your legs with a bar of soap and Nathan's razor."

Laurel's glass slammed back onto the table as she choked. Nathan handed her a napkin, then burst out laughing.

"I never saw such a mess," Louise clucked, reaching for the whistling teakettle to pour boiling water into the waiting pot. "Fourteen years old you were and didn't know the first thing about taking proper care of yourself. Didn't know the first thing about a lot of things, as I remember. Shameful it was, perfectly shameful. But we fixed that quick enough. Taught you a few things that day, didn't I, girl?"

"I seem to recall one or two," Laurel mumbled, one hand resting on her forehead, shading her eyes. She didn't dare look at Nathan, who was fighting a losing battle to control his enjoyment of these embarrassing revelations.

"Yes, indeed," Louise continued, depositing her slight form in the chair at the head of the table and pouring tea into her cup. "The Coltranes didn't have any girl-children during my years with them. There was only Jonathan—and Curtis, until he left for the Academy. And then Nathan. So few children for such a big house! Having you with us, Laurel, well, it was always a real pleasure for me." With a sigh she looked down at her tea. "I'm getting old, and with the kind of life you're leading, only the good Lord knows if I'll be around the next time you find your way back here."

"Aunt Louise, no!" Laurel reached for the older woman's hand. "It won't be so long next time. I promise."

"You can't promise that," Louise insisted. "And I want you to know I enjoyed those times with you. A fine and gracious lady, you turned out to be—and a real beauty, too. I like believing I had something to do with that."

"Oh, Aunt Louise." Laurel felt her throat grow tight. "There are times I don't know what I would have done without you."

"Sliced your legs to ribbons, I expect." The old woman chuckled, then waved her hand in Nathan's direction. "Or found your way to the altar with this one even sooner than you did—and knowing more about him than any bride ought to know about her husband before their wedding night!"

Laurel's involuntary gasp and Nathan's groan of discomfort did not deter Louise.

"Yes," she drawled, "it gave me satisfaction to know I got you out of the nest in one piece, with a good head on your shoulders for facing life and solving whatever problems came your way. In fact—" She stopped short, her forehead wrinkling in puzzlement. "Seems to me, from what you tell me in your letters, it's only lately you've been acting like you haven't got good sense."

This is it, Laurel realized, searching madly for some distraction, certain that Aunt Louise was about to voice her long-withheld opinion about the split between her two "children."

Louise's dark eyes were trained on Laurel's apprehensive ones. "I always thought you wanted a home and a family."

"I did. Do!"

"Going about it in a mighty peculiar way, aren't you?"

"Now, Aunt Louise, wait a minute." Nathan leaned forward to rest his arms on the table. "Laurel isn't—"

"You let the girl speak for herself." Louise hushed him with a look that, once, would have had him cowering.

He wasn't cowering anymore, but he did shut up, his eyes telling Laurel he was sorry, that he would not have brought her here if he had known they would be forced to speak about the unspeakable.

With measured care, Laurel asked, "Are you asking me to tell you why I left Nathan?"

"Goodness, no!" Louise straightened in her chair, "I had that figured long ago. What I want to know is, if you're so all-fired anxious to settle down and have some babies, why've you been pussyfooting for over a year with George Ackerly?"

Laurel's eyes flew like magnets to Nathan's.

George Ackerly! he ricocheted back at her. *The* George Ackerly? *The one who could never keep his eyes—or his hands—off you?*

She clamped her mouth closed and swallowed hard.

"Really, child," Louise fussed. "That's a powerful long time to keep a good man waiting when you've promised to marry him. It doesn't make sense— Nathan, if you can't sit still and keep quiet, leave the room. It doesn't make sense that you keep putting off doing what you say you're bound to do."

"Aunt Louise—" Laurel cleared her throat and tried again. "I'm, uh— That is, George and I are—" She closed her eyes. "I'm not engaged to George anymore."

Louise blinked and drew back. "And when did this happen?"

"Several months ago," Laurel murmured.

The older woman's tone was every bit as affronted as Laurel expected it to be. "Oh? And were you planning to tell me you'd given the man his ring back?"

Laurel started to reply, then hesitated, unwilling to admit the whole truth. Finally, she waffled. "I knew I'd be seeing you this week."

Louise fluttered one arthritis-gnarled hand. "Well, the important thing is, you aren't keeping that poor man waiting for something he's never going to get. And he did sound like a fine man, too. Can't understand why you'd want to let him go when, from what you've written to me, he was exactly what you're looking for. Good, steady job. Big house. Nice family."

"We couldn't agree on politics," Laurel blurted out. It was an outright lie. But the next question would have been, *why* had she broken up with George, and she was not prepared to answer it.

Louise took the hint. There was, however, the trace of a smile on her lips that Laurel thought looked awfully smug.

Nathan, on the other hand, was scowling ferociously. She hadn't wanted him to know about her engagement to George, whom she had met in grad school and later worked with at ACDA. And, she admitted,

George had been a bit overzealous in those days, offering her rides or helping out in any way he could when Nathan, who was doing his residency at the time, was busy at the hospital. Nathan had often grumbled that he thought George wanted to take over his own role in Laurel's life. Now he had proof that, indeed, this had been true, and he was absolutely, furiously jealous.

Laurel met his flashing eyes with an indignant look. He had no right to be jealous. He didn't own her. He didn't even love her. Why should she feel guilty because she had sought to fulfill her dreams with another man?

She shouldn't. But she did.

"Nathan, how much longer are you going to let the Landing sit there empty?"

Nathan was so caught up in the riot of emotions inside him that he barely heard Louise's question. When the words sank in, he felt his stomach lurch.

Louise wasn't waiting for him to recover. "The way I figure it, your debt to the Navy ought to be paid sometime in the next year. Are you going to go on chasing after your father's footsteps or come home where you belong?"

"I'm not chasing after my father's footsteps." Nathan's reply was automatic and, he assuaged his conscience, not entirely dishonest. At least, that wasn't what he was doing anymore—and it had *never* been quite the way he had looked at it.

He cast a quick glance at Laurel. She avoided his gaze, but he could see she was every bit as uncomfortable as he with the turn of the conversation. He could only hope she had believed his apology the night before—because he did not see a way out of answering Aunt Louise's question.

"This isn't the time to argue about what your being in the Navy has to do with your father," Louise muttered. "But you and I both know it has a lot to do with what passed between you and your Uncle Jack. You're not going to let all that keep you from taking your proper place are you? You're the only Coltrane left, the only one to look after your family's name and take care of the things they meant to keep."

"The brokerage is running smoothly, and the rest of the interests are intact," Nathan answered evasively, feeling as though he were walking through a mine field. "I get a detailed report every month."

"And what about the Landing?"

"Is there a problem with the way the Historical Society is caring for it?"

"To my way of thinking, there is," she declared. "It was meant to be lived in, the way it's been for the last three hundred years. So, are you coming home when your time's up or not?"

Tilting his chair back on two legs, Nathan toyed with the edge of the gingham tablecloth. "Aunt Louise, I've told you about the hospital ship that's under construction and how important it is to the Navy." He shot her a quick look, knew it was pointless, but continued anyway.

"This ship will give us every advantage in delivering quality care in emergency situations. You see, right now we have to airlift wounded men to facilities that are sometimes hundreds of miles away. This ship will mean that the most up-to-date equipment and operating theaters and facilities will be more readily available if, for instance, there's another terrorist attack on a Marine barracks, like the one in Beirut. God forbid that anything like that will happen again, but if it does, the ship

will mean we're better prepared to meet the situation."
Lifting his gaze to face Louise's stony silence, he finished, "I've invested more than just time in this project, Aunt Louise. I *care* about making sure it's built the way we intend it to be built."

Louise studied him and then concluded flatly, "You're not going to quit."

Nathan held her gaze steadily. "I've been offered a three-year contract that will begin in January. I'm going to sign it."

"And you're going to sell St. John's Landing."

He did his best to ignore Laurel's whimper as he confirmed Louise's suspicion with a slow nod.

There was a moment of tense silence.

Then Louise sighed. "I never thought I'd live to see the day, but I have to say it. I'm disgusted with you, Nathan Coltrane. Disgusted and disappointed."

Nathan's head dropped toward his chest for a moment, but when he raised it again, all he said was, "I'm sorry, Aunt Louise. The Landing is important to me. But my work is more important. I've got too much invested in it to give it up. And you know I always follow through on something once I start it. I won't be able to work with a clear mind until the issue of property is resolved."

"It isn't right," Louise came back. "No man can will another man the right to sell off three hundred years of tradition. St. John's Landing doesn't belong to you, boy, any more than it belonged to your uncle. The land that St. John and Elizabeth Coltrane settled is a trust. A responsibility. Not something you can hand over to a real estate agent and sign away on a piece of paper."

A troubled frown darkened Nathan's brow. He started to speak, but Louise went on.

"If you're so anxious to be rid of it, give it to Laurel. Unless, of course, you're only interested in what you can get for it."

Laurel had listened in silence as long as she could. "Aunt Louise, no! You're not being fair—"

Nathan cut her off. "I don't care about the money. I don't need it, and I don't even want it. But I don't think Laurel wants the Landing, either. If I had any notion that she did, I'd give it to her. Instantly." And his eyes met Laurel's for the first time since the discussion had begun.

"Is that right, child?" Louise asked. "You wouldn't want it if Nathan gave it to you?"

Laurel couldn't speak. Her astonished gaze was locked with Nathan's. She realized now why it had been so important to him to apologize for accusing her of marrying him for St. John's Landing. Offering to give it to her was a total capitulation on his part. And for a single wild moment, she considered saying yes, she did want it. If she had it, he wouldn't be able to throw his heritage to the winds, and maybe someday he would remember that his roots were important and that home meant something more than four walls and a bed to sleep in. But she couldn't take the Landing. She didn't want it as long as Nathan was not in it, and it would only be a way of hanging on to her futile dreams that, someday, he might be and that he would want her there with him.

Her eyes held his as she answered Louise's question. "No, Aunt Louise. The Landing isn't mine. It's Nathan's. He has to do with it as he sees fit."

"I can't believe it," Louise mumbled. "I thought you loved the place. So why are you saying no when it could be yours?"

Laurel had to drop her gaze from Nathan's to reply. "I do love it. But I don't want it."

Louise sighed heavily. "Well, I've had my say, and I did my best to change your mind, Nathan. But if you're bound and determined to do this thing, I won't fight you over it. I'm not going to badger you like your uncle did, until you stop writing or calling and don't ever come to see me because you know the visit will only wind up in a fight. I don't want that between us."

"Neither do I, Aunt Louise," Nathan replied with heartfelt sincerity. But his dark countenance took on a brooding quality that lingered until it was time for Laurel and him to leave.

The ride back to town began in tense silence. Nathan's fingertips tapped a sporadic rhythm on the steering wheel. Laurel twisted the thin strap of her purse between her fingers and stared out the passenger window. Neither of them spoke, both afraid of risking an explosion.

Finally Nathan burst out, "Laurel, I didn't mean for you to hear about my selling the Landing like that."

"It's all right."

"You still believe what I told you last night, don't you? This doesn't have anything to do with—"

"I believe you, Nathan. You've never lied to me."

He fell silent again, and Laurel had to resist the impulse to ask the natural question: why on earth *was* he selling his ancestral home? She couldn't accept that it was only a matter of his work being more important to him. The two did not have to be mutually exclusive. Fleetingly, it occurred to her to wonder if he was suffering from the same problem as she. Did the place hold too many memories of their life together for him, too? But no, that was impossible. An action this final, this dramatic, demanded more feeling behind it than she knew he had left for her.

Pain sliced through her, but along with it came an aching sadness. She glanced at Nathan, sitting so stoically silent beside her, and thought about how alone he was and how tired he looked. And in that instant, Laurel knew she had to at least ask him about the awesome decision he had made. She had no idea how she would begin such a conversation, and her awareness of her own vulnerability to him was acute. But they had been friends long before they had been lovers, and she simply couldn't bear the thought of walking away, knowing he might need someone to talk to. Someone who was not "disgusted" with him for doing what he felt he had to do.

When they reached Clarkson's Lodgings at the foot of Prince George Street, Nathan stopped to let her off. When she didn't get out right away, he draped his left arm over the steering wheel and half turned to face her.

Laurel's gaze was directed at her lap. "Nathan, I was thinking..."

When her words trailed off, he urged quietly, "You were thinking what?"

"I was thinking, I'm only going to be here a week, and, well, I'd like to see you again. If you want to, I mean."

When she got no response, she lifted her gaze to meet his. His eyes were questioning and frankly defensive. There was a brittle, uncertain quality about him she couldn't remember ever having seen before, and she had a sudden desire to reach out and let her fingers smooth the lines that had formed in a downward sweep at the corners of his mouth, to let her palms rest against his cheeks, which somehow looked too hollow. She couldn't touch him, though—not when he might misinterpret the gesture. Not when she might, having gone that far, want to offer him more.

The most she could do was ask, "Can we have dinner tomorrow? I'm free after four-thirty."

Nathan's look of wariness increased. "Before I agree, I'd like to have some idea what I'm in for. I've had my quota of surprises in the last twenty-four hours."

Laurel glanced away. "I promise, no more surprises. At least none you might find—" she hesitated "—unpleasant."

"No more deaths I don't know about?"

"No."

"Major physical changes?"

He was looking at her hair again. Laurel knew it as she gave her head a shake and muttered another denial. Then she added, "Lilly has two children now—you knew she was pregnant with the first—and there'll be a third one along sometime in the next couple of weeks." She met his gaze with the barest hint of a smile. "But we don't think of any of them as either unpleasant or a surprise."

One dark brow shot upward.

"So, do you want to go to dinner with me?"

"Yes."

"Good. I'll let you tell me how much you hate my hair."

"I don't hate your hair."

"Yes, you do."

"I don't. Really."

They stared at each other for a long time before Nathan said softly, "I'll pick you up at five-thirty."

Laurel nodded her agreement; a few seconds later, though, as she stood at the curb watching him drive away, she had the feeling she had just baited a hook with her own name on it.

Chapter Five

"Why, Nathan! Hello!"

Nathan turned from his study of an antique bottled clipper ship on Mrs. Clarkson's mantel to see James Randall entering the cozy parlor of the bed-and-breakfast where he and his daughter were staying. "Hello, James," Nathan greeted his ex-father-in-law. "How's the conference going?"

"Very well, I think," the Admiral replied, joining Nathan in front of the fireplace. "I suppose I ought to say something foolish, like, what brings you here? But I'd rather simply ask if you're waiting for Laurel."

One of the things Nathan had always liked about James was the older man's eloquent way of making an awkward situation seem part of the normal course of events. He smiled. "And I'd rather answer the question you wanted to ask. Yes, Laurel and I are having dinner together."

James hesitated a moment. "I was sorry the other night for the shock I gave you—in speaking of Catherine's death, that is. I hope I didn't cause any, uh...trouble for you and Laurel."

"Not at all," Nathan returned quickly. "I was only sorry I hadn't known sooner."

Looking somewhat relieved, James still sounded uncertain. "I didn't know... Well, I assumed you and Laurel had maintained some contact with each other."

Nathan shook his head.

"She didn't call you when Jonathan died?"

"I understand she was in Geneva. Aunt Louise talked to her."

James took in this piece of news. Then, speaking softly, he said, "I can hardly believe it. Yet, I don't suppose I ought to be surprised. Laurel hasn't communicated very much with anyone these last few years, from what I can gather. She never did talk much to me, but even Lilly has noticed. And that, as I'm sure you can appreciate, is saying something."

The sting of jealousy—fueled by a night spent pondering images of Laurel lying in another man's arms—was fresh in Nathan's mind. Without thinking, he growled, "She's probably been doing her talking to Ackerly."

James drew back a little at Nathan's tone, but his own reflected only dry speculation as he murmured, "I wonder. Somehow I doubt she talked very much to George, either." He shot Nathan a quick glance. "I shouldn't be saying these things, though. It's disloyal of me."

"There's no disloyalty in being concerned." Nathan tried to sound reassuring, all the while wondering if, indeed, James had real cause to worry about his daughter. Then, struck by the irony that he was as ignorant as the other man of Laurel's true state of mind, he snorted softly. "I have to say, James, if you're looking for advice about how to get Laurel to talk, you're asking the wrong person. The only thing I can tell you is, if you've got something to say, don't wait for her to ask to hear it. She's got her own ideas about what's important, and she'll finesse you every time if you let her."

James offered him a look of male commiseration. "Unfortunately, I've known that for years and have yet to find a way around it. Perhaps we should take heart from the fact that, if *we* can't get past her, the Soviets probably won't, either."

The remark was meant to lighten the mood, and though Nathan didn't feel the least bit consoled, he forced a crooked smile. The older man gave him a paternal clap on the shoulder at the same instant the object of their discussion walked into the lobby.

Laurel came toward them, looking a little breathless. Offering her father a quick greeting, she turned to Nathan. "I guess I get to be the one who's late this time. I was moderating a mock negotiation, and the students playing Soviets were remarkably skilled at stonewalling. If it'd been real, we'd be reading *Pravda* and eating borscht for dinner tonight!"

While James chuckled at her suggestion, Nathan merely looked smug. "You're not late," he said. "I want you to note, please, that I was early." He saw Laurel's mouth curve into a smile of acknowledgment, but he was more interested in the dark circles under her eyes. Apparently she hadn't slept any better than he.

Saying goodbye to James and guiding Laurel toward the door, Nathan repeated the vow he'd made to himself not to bring up the subject of George Ackerly. It galled him beyond belief that, while he had been unable to forget her, finally deciding to sell St. John's Landing in a last-ditch effort to do so, she'd been breezing around Washington with a man he frankly loathed. Clearly, *she* hadn't found it too difficult to forget *him*. But he didn't want Laurel to know he was jealous, any more than he wanted her to know the real reason he was selling St. John's Landing. After a lifetime of sharing everything with her, it was damned hard to hide his feelings, but self-preservation dictated that course. Quite simply, she had the power to destroy him. Which made him wonder what on God's green earth he was doing, asking her where she wanted to have dinner.

"Let's walk to the Market House and get carryout," Laurel replied to his query. "I've been inside all day and don't feel much like sitting in a restaurant."

"Besides which—" Nathan winked at her "—you're dying for fried oysters."

Laurel laughed as they crossed the street and headed toward the City Dock. "Since this was my idea, I *was* going to treat you to scallops, but if you're going to be a smart aleck about my oysters—well . . ."

Nathan got his breaded scallops and Laurel her oysters, and they ate the Maryland delicacies out of cardboard cartons as they strolled leisurely along the wharves amid a carnival-like atmosphere. There were people everywhere—students and families and tourists and lovers—enjoying the final hours of daylight along the busy river. Gulls screeched as they dived for bait tossed away by fisherman, and an occasional burst of raucous noise emerged from the nearby restaurants whenever a door opened.

The pleasant commotion did little, however, to settle Laurel's agitation. Nathan didn't help matters, either, as he walked so close beside her that their arms brushed and the heat of his body seemed to touch her all over. Every breath she took was filled with a familiar scent that was partly soap and cologne but mostly him. A careless gesture of the hand, a light smile, the habitual, unconscious swipe at the lock of dark hair that fell over his forehead—she was aware of every move he made. All at once she felt aroused and in love—and terrified of being either.

She tried to remember that her purpose in seeing him had been to get him to talk about his plans for the Landing. Her attitude should be one of casual, friendly interest. But by the time they had finished their dinner, she was incapable of maintaining the facade. They had walked to the end of a long pier, where Nathan stopped to lean against a piling, when Laurel's patience ran out and her curiosity bubbled over.

"Nathan, why are you selling the Landing?"

His gaze, which had been trained on a lovely gaff-rigged sailboat coming into the public marina, snapped to hers.

She went on in nervous haste. "I heard what you told Aunt Louise about your commitment to the hospital ship, and I can appreciate why you'd want to finish the project. But that doesn't really have anything to do with selling the Landing, does it? I mean, couldn't you go on doing your work and keep the property? The Society would take care of it, and Ted Gilliam would see to the finances, and Aunt Louise would let you know the minute something went wrong. There's some other reason, isn't there? Something you didn't want to tell Aunt Louise."

Noting Nathan's taut expression, Laurel realized that, yes, there was another reason, but it was something he didn't want to tell her, either. Abruptly, her courage deserted her. "I'm sorry," she murmured in a tiny, flustered voice. "I wasn't trying to pry. I only wanted—"

"Why do you think I'm selling the Landing?"

The rough timbre of his voice brought her gaze back to his.

"I don't know," she said, searching his features. "I thought perhaps— Well, I wondered if there was some trouble with finances you didn't want Aunt Louise to know about."

He shook his head, his eyes never leaving hers. "There's no problem. The profits from the brokerage have been supporting the Landing for years, even without the other investments Uncle Jack made. Everything's in good shape."

Laurel took this in. She also noted that he was answering her questions, not rejecting them. Or her. At least, not yet.

Recklessly, she plunged on. "I was worried you and Uncle Jack might have had a fight before he died, and that he'd said something— Well . . ."

"Something that's made me want to get rid of his home." Nathan's tone was strangely sardonic. He looked away, and a long moment passed before he mused bitterly, "In a roundabout way, I guess you could say my decision is the result of something Uncle Jack once said."

Laurel's quiet reply reflected her worry. "I knew one day he'd go too far. I knew all his preachings about the hallowed family ground eventually would make you hate it."

"I don't hate it."

She paused before asking, "Will you tell me what happened?"

He glanced at her as though the question confused him. Then, blinking a little, he gazed back out over the water. "It was nothing, Laurel. Nothing worth remembering."

"Oh, Nathan," she murmured, "I don't believe that. I remember plenty of things he said—and they weren't nothing! You didn't used to think so, either. Lord! I remember the night at the dinner table when you told him you were going to take that summer job, pumping gas at the marina. And he said that if you were a *real* Coltrane, you'd learn that your responsibility was to prepare yourself to oversee the family interests, 'not,'" she intoned, "'to behave like a common laborer and stand in line to collect a paycheck at the end of the week.'"

Nathan arched a brow in her direction. "You *were* paying attention, weren't you? Those were his exact words."

"Could you have forgotten them?" she asked sadly. "I know he wasn't trying to be cruel, and it was only that his values were antiquated. Still, he all but said outright any number of times that your duty to the Coltrane name was more important than any duty you had to yourself. Dear heavens! Remember when you told him you wanted to be a surgeon? You'd have thought you'd announced you were joining the circus! He went on for hours, saying things about your father's *mistake* in wanting a career—as though it were a dirty word—and how the only career you were ever going to need was protecting the family's interests."

Caught up in the memory, Laurel shook her head with a long sigh. "I swear, Nathan, as good as he'd been to me, that was one time I came awfully close to telling him what I thought of his stupid notions of how a right-thinking aristocrat manages his life. I never understood how you went on speaking to him afterward."

When Laurel noted the sudden tightening of the muscles in Nathan's neck and the whitened knuckles of the fists he pressed into the tops of his thighs, she expected him to acknowledge that, indeed, something ugly had passed between him and his uncle that made him think he had to be rid of St. John's Landing. She watched as he stubbed the toe of one Docksider along the edge of the pier. He was staring at it, fixedly, when he spoke.

"I'm not selling the Landing because I'm angry with Uncle Jack."

Puzzled, Laurel frowned. She had run out of feasible explanations.

Nathan's careless shrug was both uncomfortable and reluctant. "Before he died, we...we talked. There are things we'd never have agreed on, but he didn't die with a quarrel between us. What I told Aunt Louise is mostly true. I've gotten too tied up in my work to be bothered with the Landing. It used to mean something to me, but, well, it just doesn't anymore."

"Nathan," she whispered, "you can't mean that."

"I'm a doctor, Laurel," he announced flatly.

Her expression went from horrified to bewildered. "And a doctor can't own St. John's Landing?"

"That's not the point. Uncle Jack loved the Landing. He loved being a member of Annapolis society and playing the benefactor. Being a Coltrane was his life. He didn't need any more to make him happy. But my father did. And so do I."

"But, Nathan," Laurel argued, "you don't have to involve yourself in Annapolis society the way Uncle Jack did to be a Coltrane! You're a Coltrane by birth! St. John's Landing can give you something you won't find anyplace else in the world. It gives meaning to your name beyond what you'll give it on your own." She had never heard Nathan talk this way, and she didn't know whether to think he was voicing some long-withheld belief or deliberately lying to her. Either way, he didn't sound anything like the Nathan she remembered.

He sounded even less so as he waved one arm broadly and declared, "Well, maybe I don't want to be remembered as Nathan St. John Coltrane, thirteenth heir to a long line of faceless Coltranes. If I'm remembered at all, maybe I want it to be for what I've done that's worthwhile."

"Worthwhile?" she cried. "Your family's been doing worthwhile things for centuries! Dear Lord, you've done enough on your own to carry the name along for at least another hundred years! If that's what you're after, you've more than proven the point—a Coltrane can make a valuable contribution to society through his own skills and hard work. And if you keep trying to prove it the way you have been, I think you ought to seriously consider keeping the Landing—if for no other reason than that you're going to need a place to go when you collapse from exhaustion!"

Her laugh was ironic. "And I thought my father was dedicated! To have made Captain already, you must have raised your hand every time the commanding officer asked for a volunteer. I've never known a man who was so driven!"

Nathan shot her a penetrating look. When he spoke, his tone was deadly quiet. "That's funny. I've been thinking the same thing about you."

She stared at him for an instant, startled at the anger she saw in his eyes. "What are you talking about?"

"Only that if we're listing achievements, it seems to me you're about as driven as a person can get. What point are *you* trying to prove?"

"I'm not trying to prove anything."

Pivoting slowly to face her, Nathan began a thorough and surprisingly clinical perusal of her tall, model-thin form. Laurel squirmed, finding this cold assessment far more uncomfortable to endure than one of his bold, lustful looks. Finally, his gaze returned to her face, and that, too, got close scrutiny.

"I don't know, Laurel," he remarked coolly. "It looks to me as though the climb up the ladder of success is taking its toll."

Laurel gasped. "Nathan Coltrane! That's rude!"

His gaze was unrelenting. "You've lost weight. You're too pale. You look like you haven't slept in a week. And you've been biting your nails. You're also as nervous as a cornered cat, which I might have believed is due to, uh, shall we say, the stress of the moment, except all the other things were also true when I saw you Sunday afternoon. So I have to conclude that whatever it is that's got you strung out has been going on for some time."

Laurel resisted the impulse to hide her hands behind her back as she tried to glare at him indignantly. The look was somewhat diluted by the fact that she knew he was right. Her reply was huffy. "I'm sorry I don't meet your standards these days."

"Come on, Laurel. I'm only stating the obvious. And besides—" his gaze bore into hers "—I listened to your questions about my selling the Landing. Don't I get the same privilege?" Without waiting for her answer, he went on. "I find it very strange, your being so committed to a career that obviously doesn't agree with you health-wise and that keeps you from having any sort of home life. And we both know it does. Tell me, when was the last time you were in D.C. for more than a few weeks?"

In silence, Laurel stared at a boy fishing off the end of the dock, two piers away.

"Three months ago?" he prodded. "Six? Eight? How long's it been, Laurel?"

Her reply was muttered through clenched teeth. "A year."

"A year!" Nathan drew back. "For a lady who wanted a place to call home, you sure picked a peculiar career."

"I didn't pick it. They gave me the promotion without my asking for it." She shot him a look. "And you tell me how I could have said no. It would have been like your saying no if they'd offered you the position as Director of the National Institutes of Health. The job's challenging and fascinating. But it *is* a job to me. Not a career."

"Well, the end results sure look the same," Nathan returned. "I guess I don't see the difference."

"A person is committed to a career."

"And you're not committed to the negotiating team?"

"Not in the way you are to medicine." She gave an impatient shrug. "Oh, of course, I'm interested in world politics. And it matters to me that there are people trying to make the world a safe place to live. But you know how the government works. I've got the training and the background. They trust me. They'll have me on call forever, probably. But being a negotiator, the actual job itself? I'd give it up tomorrow.''

"For what.''

She met his gaze. "You know as well as I do what it would take. I haven't changed that much, Nathan. I want the same things I've always wanted. A home and a family—and a white picket fence I get to live with long enough to have to paint.''

Laurel felt the impact of Nathan's next question before he asked it.

"So, tell me why you passed up the chance to have it all, when George 'give-me-a-call-and-I'll-be-there' Ackerly was handing it to you on a silver platter?''

Steeling herself against the pain, she took refuge behind the only protection she had. "It's none of your business why I passed up the chance.''

"What happened?'' he persisted. "Didn't good old George have the right ingredients in your recipe for personal happiness?''

She squeezed her eyes closed.

"Come on, Laurel! Let's have it! Why the hell are you racing around the world on ACDA's treadmill? Why aren't you married to Ackerly and living in his nice big house and raising nice fat babies and painting your *damned picket fence*?''

Because I want your fence and your babies, and nobody else's will do. The effort it cost Laurel not to say the words shattered her already broken heart into a million pieces. Before she could stop herself, before she even realized it was happening, she burst into tears.

Nathan's eyes widened, and he drew a sharp breath. The tears running down her cheeks doused the anger that had been blazing inside him, and the resentment he had been feeling began to taste like regret. With a muttered oath of self-derision, he moved close and put a gentle hand under her arm, his tone reflecting only contrition and a rough sort of tenderness as he spoke.

"Come on. Let's go someplace where a little noise won't scare the fish."

His ridiculous comment brought Laurel to her senses, making her realize how public a scene this private conversation had become. With her eyes downcast, she nodded, swiping at her cheeks with her hand as she allowed him to lead her to his car.

Chapter Six

By the time Laurel realized where Nathan was taking her, her tears had dried. He hadn't asked, but the choice seemed right, and she leaned back in the seat, relishing the bittersweet flavor of coming home. The sun was sinking low as they drove up to St. John's Landing and parked. Nathan hadn't spoken since they left the City Dock, nor did he speak when he came around to meet her on the passenger's side of the car. Rather, he slid her hand into his with an ease that put to rest any question of his right to do so, and they walked together toward the forest path. When they got to the place where the path forked, neither of them hesitated but continued downhill to the banks of the river.

Their shoes clattered on the planks of the small wooden pier. When they reached the end of it, Nathan let go of Laurel's hand, and she dropped down to sit with her legs dangling over the edge. The tide was at ebb, the water level low on the dock's thick pilings. Nathan sat down with one foot planted on the dock, his knee drawn up, and the other leg hanging beside Laurel's.

The sun was nearly touching the tops of the trees on the opposite shore; its light angled sharply across the river, turning the smooth surface into a glittering mirror. The sailboat and the small motor boat, tied on opposite sides of the dock, rode motionless at their moorings.

There was a strange peacefulness in being in this spot, Laurel thought. So much of her life with Nathan could be cataloged here, both inconsequential and momentous occasions: first kisses, first declarations of love and a proposal of marriage the memory of which almost brought a smile to her lips....

"Nathan, don't tell me you weren't out with Suellen Johnson last night. I saw you when Alyce and I came out of the movie."

"For Pete's sake, Lauri, I told you I went to the Ice Cream Parlor alone. I was sitting there, minding my own business, when Suellen came over and plopped herself down. What was I supposed to do? Tell her to leave?"

"Hmph! The least you could have done was make her sit on the other side of the booth and keep her greedy hands off you!"

"But Suellen acts that way with all the guys."

"Not with my *guy she doesn't! Not if she expects to live."*

"Don't you trust me?"

"I trust you just fine. It's Suellen I'm worried about."

"Hmm, I see. Well, would it make you feel like I was, uh, better protected from flesh-eating females if we were to get engaged?"

"What?"

"I mean, I don't want to think you're walking around, worrying I might get snatched out from under your nose."

"Are you asking me to marry you, Nathan Coltrane?"

"No, not really."

"What?"

"I didn't think I had to."

"You've got about ten seconds to explain yourself."

"Now, don't get mad. I was asking if you wanted to make it official. Our plans to get married, that is."

"W-what plans?"

"What plans? The ones we've been making all our lives! You know, Lauri, you can be really idiotic sometimes. Who else did you think I'd marry but you...."

Who else, indeed? Laurel wondered unhappily.

"Laurel, I'm sorry for pressing you about Ackerly. I swore to myself I wasn't going to bring it up, but— Well, I had no right."

Nathan's voice was a dark rumble so unlike the spirited tone of his younger self echoing in her mind that Laurel turned to stare at him in shock. His head was hung low, almost resting on his bent knee, and his fingers were tracing the cracks between the boards of the dock. Was this the same vibrant youth who had been so confident of her love? This dejected man who felt he should be penitent when he forgot that she had stripped him of the rights he had once claimed so boldly? As Nathan raised his head to find her watching him, his expression undid her completely. Sorrow. And a well of regret. His eyes were shadowy reflections of her own torment.

Suddenly the pain and longing twisted inside her with such intensity, that it was all she could do not to scream. Instead, to her horror, she began crying once again.

Guilt hit Nathan hard. Seeing Laurel cry twice in the same night was bad enough; knowing his angry, thoughtless questions had been the catalyst was too much. Reaching into his pocket, he pulled out a handkerchief and scooted around to face her, turning her head toward him with a large palm against her cheek. After a few gentle attempts to dry her tears, he gave up. "Laurel, I'm sorry. I didn't know it still hurt so much. But whatever happened, it's over. Do you hear?"

Laurel shuddered and raised enormous, wet-lashed eyes to stare at him in agonized silence. Then her face crumpled again, and she was off on a fresh wave of sobbing.

For a moment Nathan trembled with outraged disbelief that he had to be the one to heal her heartache over another man. But the need to comfort her was more compelling, and as he ran the tip of one long finger down her cheek, the resentment drained out of him. "If you want to talk about it, I'll listen," he said. "Tell me what happened. Did he hurt you?"

"Stop! Oh, Lord, Nathan, please stop! You're killing me!" Gulping, choking on every word, Laurel reached blindly to cover his mouth with her hand. But somehow, once her fingers discovered the firm line of his lips and the warm, rough texture of his jaw, she was too weak to prevent her arms from flinging themselves around his neck. "I didn't break the engagement!" she sobbed. "George did! I didn't love him. I was only using him to forget you, and he knew it! Oh, Nathan, don't you see? I'm not crying because I loved George! I'm crying because I still love *you*! And I'm not *supposed* to love you anymore, but I do! Oh, God, I do!''

Pure astonishment and raw need plowed through Nathan with stunning force. Without thinking, he wrapped his arms around her and pulled her fully into the warmth of his embrace.

With a heartsick moan, Laurel buried her face against his throat. And as unwise as she knew it was, nothing could have prevented the words from pouring out. "It hurts so much, loving you! Because nothing's changed! Nothing! The things you said to me at Subic Bay were true. I do hate the Navy, and I think I always will. I'll never stop being afraid of what it can do to people. And I'll never stop needing a place to call my own that nobody can take away from me. Oh, Nathan!'' She hiccuped on a great gulp of air. "After all those years of your working to make it right for me—all the things you went out of your way to do, trying to make me happy— I couldn't let you keep trying when it was never going to work! It made you so angry! I was afraid if I stayed you'd . . . you'd end up hating me, and I couldn't bear it. I can hardly bear it now, knowing how you must feel. And I know I shouldn't be telling you I love you, because it only makes everything worse. But I couldn't let you go on thinking I was crying over another man when the only man I've ever cried over—the only man I ever *loved*—is you!''

The only man I've ever loved is you. It was like sunrise on the ocean. It was like nothing Nathan had ever felt before to hear Laurel say he hadn't killed her love for him. The spark of hope he had been trying so hard to extinguish flared brightly, warming him with its revitalizing force.

In the next moment, however, it died to an ember as he realized that, besides saying she loved him, Laurel had also made it clear she didn't *want* to love him. And what use was love without the commitment to keep it alive?

Nathan tensed as the conflicting emotions inside him tangled in a web of confusion. He did not accept that it was as hopeless as she believed it to be, but he couldn't erase the scars that made her afraid. He couldn't go on waiting for her forever, but neither could he let go of the conviction that love this powerful should be able to conquer anything. His strong arms tightened around her slender form as his eyes closed and he absorbed the sweet agony of holding her again like this. What in the name of God could he do or say that might ease her lonely suffering—or his own?

The answer was clear and urgent.

Releasing her, Nathan pried Laurel's hands away from her face. And his fingertips trembled over the tear-drenched smoothness of her cheeks, his dark gaze penetrating the painful bewilderment in her eyes, as he told her the simple truth.

"Lauri, I love you, too."

For an instant Laurel's tortured countenance was transformed into something quite different—something radiant and almost hopeful. And for a moment the world seemed to stop, as though it were waiting for them to catch up. For one heartbeat, they hung, teetering on the edge of taking the only step that separated them, of closing those last few inches between their parted lips and their pounding hearts, and holding on as the world spun off once more on its timeless whirl into the dazzling brilliance of a star-filled universe.

But they had taken that step once before, long ago when innocence had guarded them from pain, and it had come as a dreadful shock to discover their universe had limits. They had crossed the boundary line only to find it not so dazzling or star-filled but a wasteland, and the truth was, neither of them was prepared to live through that disillusionment again.

The step back from the edge was long and agonizing, but they took it, Laurel dropping her gaze first, Nathan letting his hands slide down over her arms until they rested on his own thighs. Sighing, he turned to stare out across the water.

Somewhere in the past half-hour the sun had sunk below the trees on the opposite shore, turning the sky into a palette of rose and orange hues and the trees into silhouettes.

"If it helps at all," Nathan began in a tone oddly lacking in emotion, "I don't think our divorce decree says anything about us agreeing not to love each other."

Laurel was crying again, a quiet sound in the otherwise silent evening, but she stopped to listen to what he was saying.

"I don't know how not to love you," he continued. "I don't think about you every day and wonder what you're doing or if I'll ever see you again. And I don't plan my life on some vain hope that you'll come back to me. But nothing I've told myself has stopped me from loving you, and I'm not sure anything ever will. I think I might as well try to stop breathing."

"Oh, Nathan," Laurel whispered. "I didn't know. I thought you couldn't possibly still—" She broke off, then rushed on. "But we've got to stop loving each other this way! Don't you see? It's never going to work out the way we wanted it to. I'm never going to be able to stand being a Navy wife, and you've come too far to give up your work. I can't face the rest of my life, knowing I can't have you but that I can't have anyone else, either! And I can't stand the thought of you hurting like I hurt inside! We have to let go of each other! Otherwise, we're both dooming ourselves to a life of no love at all!''

A minute passed. Laurel had to clench her fists in her lap to keep from touching him again.

"So—" he began in a ragged, halting voice. "So, where does this leave us?"

She took a deep, shaky breath. "I don't know. I've been so confused, so upset, but I was only thinking of myself. I had no idea— Well, I didn't know *how* you felt, but I hardly expected you'd even want to be—to be my friend, when what you wanted was to—'' She had to leave the sentence unfinished as the bonds around her heart squeezed yet tighter.

"I've missed you," she breathed, lifting her face to the twilight sky. "I've missed you so much. I hate not seeing you, not being able to call you or write to you. I hate not knowing what you're doing—or even where you are!''

Nathan watched as Laurel fought off another wave of painful emotion and thought about how incredibly empty his life had been without her. The urge to hold her again was fast becoming overwhelming, and he guessed a stronger man would get up and walk away. The farthest he was able to make himself go was a couple of feet to sit, cross-legged, at the edge of the pier, and even the bit of space he'd put between them felt like oceans. The thought of there actually being oceans—and years of emptiness—was, at that moment, unbearable.

He spoke quietly. "I don't know, Laurel. I honestly don't know if I could ever be simply friends with you. I don't know if I could promise not to grow resentful again that...well, that things can't be different for us." He paused, then uttered a short, dry laugh. "One thing's pretty clear. My head may be confused, but my body's sure as hell not. I want to make love with you again."

His bald statement—which was no more than an acknowledgment of the desire that had been simmering between them these last few days—brought Laurel's gaze flashing to his. Their eyes held in the growing darkness, and the air between them was suddenly charged with a tingling sexual awareness. Nathan's look was wholly carnal, and Laurel felt her skin grow warm...and then hot.

Her lips burned as though he had kissed them; her breasts ached as though he had touched them. There was a fluttering in her womb and a liquid rush of tremors, as though her body were preparing for his possession. And it required no imagination at all to know what that possession would be like. She had felt it—deep and hard and so breathtakingly powerful that, at times, she had wondered if she would ever be separate from him again. There had been moments when it had frightened her to think he would take not only her body but her soul, as well. And perhaps he *had* taken it; for after all this time of not having so much as talked to him, she was melting with readiness merely because he had looked at her and said he wanted to make love.

She could be no less honest than he had been. Lowering her gaze, she spoke in a tremulous voice. "I want to make love with you, too. Very much."

"I don't think that's going to change for either of us," he warned. "Do you think you could live with that? Knowing that every time I see you, I'm going to be thinking how much I want you? Do you think you could stand knowing it's never going to happen? Because it won't, you know. Our lovemaking meant too much to me to settle for it on a casual basis."

"I wouldn't want it that way, either," she answered, though a part of her was not quite sure it wouldn't take whatever it could get of love as she had known it in Nathan's arms.

Then, overwhelmed by a sense of futility, she shook her head. "But it's pointless to be talking about this. I don't have any idea, either, if it would be possible for us to be nothing more than friends. But I do know it isn't fair to ask you to settle for a friendship when what you wanted was a marriage."

Nathan frowned. "Why isn't it fair? Do you think I've been any happier than you've been? Do you think I've missed you any less than you've missed me? We can't go back to being children, but maybe we can go on from here. Hell, Laurel, three days ago if somebody had told me I'd be having this conversation with you, I'd have said they were crazy. But I'll be damned if I want to stop talking now that we've started—the devil with whether it's fair or not!"

She didn't want to stop, either. The possibility of having him be a part of her life again was irresistible—which was the very reason she should resist, the voice of wisdom warned her. She appeased her conscience with the notion that surely it would not be so hard to fall out of love with him if she knew, in doing so, she would not be losing everything.

When she spoke, her words were filled with all the fearful expectancy of a blind person who's been offered the gift of sight. "Do you mean it? You want to be friends again?"

Nathan's mouth twisted sardonically. "I won't tell you it can't hurt to try, when we both know it could hurt like hell. But I want to try, anyway. If you do."

"Yes," she answered. "Oh, Nathan, yes, I do."

They studied each other a moment longer. Then, with obvious effort, Nathan smiled. Slowly, Laurel made her own lips turn upward, and before too many seconds had passed, the exchange had become genuine.

"Are you free any time tomorrow?" he asked.

Her face fell when she recalled that she was not in Annapolis for the primary purpose of renewing old acquaintance. Regretfully, she replied, "I've got a full schedule and won't be free until ten tomorrow night."

Nathan frowned thoughtfully. "I've got a meeting with Ted Gilliam in the morning on Thursday."

"I'm free after three o'clock."

"Would you like to go sailing?"

That won him a shaky grin. "You know I'd love to."

"I can get one of the cruisers from the marina, if you'd rather relax and not be bothered with—"

"No," Laurel interrupted. "*The Scallop* will be fine."

"Sure?"

"Positive. I'll meet you here as soon as I can, Thursday afternoon."

The message from her father that awaited Laurel when she arrived back at Clarkson's Lodgings lifted her spirits another notch and sent her racing to her room. Falling onto the bed, she reached for the phone and dialed the hospital where, it seemed, her sister was currently residing.

"Laurel! Daddy said you'd probably call. How are you?"

"How am *I*?" Laurel exclaimed. "The question is, how are *you*? And how's my new niece?"

"We're both wonderful," Lilly assured her. "Rebecca was born at four this afternoon. I've had a shower and a nap and haven't stopped eating since I woke up. I'll probably be awake half the night."

"I'm so happy for you, Lil," Laurel returned, visions of tiny pink fingers and toes dancing in her head. "Did everything go okay?"

"Everything went fine," Lilly replied with the casualness of a woman who'd had three children. "I can't sit down, and my knees are rubbery—nothing unusual. But, Laurel, from what Daddy says, it sounds like *you've* got some unusual things happening. Nathan's there?"

Laurel blinked, disconcerted. "Yes, he's at the Landing on leave."

"Have you talked to him?"

"Some. We had dinner this evening. Lilly! For heaven's sake! You had a baby today—two weeks early, no less! How much did she weigh? Who does she look like?"

Almost distractedly, Lilly replied, "She weighs eight pounds, and thank God she didn't wait another two weeks. It's way too soon to say who she looks like. But Laurel—" Lilly broke off, hesitating. "This is the first time you've seen Nathan since your divorce, isn't it?"

"Uh-huh."

"How does he look?"

"Fine."

"Is he very upset about his uncle's death?"

"He seems to have handled it okay."

Laurel knew Lilly was waiting to hear that, having met serendipitously, she and Nathan had immediately fallen into each other's arms and decided to walk off once more into the glorious sunset. When the silence stretched on and Laurel failed to support the fantasy, Lilly sighed in disappointment.

"I thought maybe if you spent an evening with him— I suppose it's something that you're speaking to each other."

"Of course we're speaking," Laurel replied.

"Well, I didn't know."

"But we're not about to get back together. So, let's not talk about it. Okay? Tell me how Stan is. And for heaven's sake, tell me about this baby! I know you've had three, but there must be something special about Rebecca that makes her the most wonderful baby you've ever seen—along with Christopher and Leslie, of course."

With another long sigh, Lilly complied with Laurel's request, relating the details of her new daughter's birth as well as a fuller description of her growing family's busy life. The conversation ended with Laurel confirming her plans to visit as soon as she had checked in with the agency the following week.

Laurel prepared for bed, grimacing in the bathroom mirror at the sight of her puffy eyes and tear-splotched complexion. She was certain she would sleep better than she had the night before, simply because she was physically and emotionally exhausted. However, she lay awake for a long time, thinking about Lilly and her new baby and her happy family—which included her loving husband, who was a lieutenant commander in the Navy.

Conversations with Lilly always left her feeling strangely out of whack, as though her common sense and her emotions were at odds. She knew she should be delighted her sister had made a satisfying life for herself, but she couldn't shake the disquieting belief that all was not what it seemed.

How could Lilly be happy when she'd had to move three times in the course of seven years of marriage? How could she be happy knowing that what she had to look forward to was three years at the most before she would have to pack up her household and her three children, say goodbye to whatever friends she had made and start over again somewhere else? Most of all, how could Lilly have watched the agony their parents had gone through as their marriage slowly disintegrated and not be terrified the same thing might happen to her own idyllic union?

Laurel could not accept that, with their shared background, her sister had succeeded in finding happiness under the same circumstances in which she herself had failed. Lilly had always been so trusting of people, so ready to believe good things would happen to her as long as she expected them to happen. What if they stopped happening? What if Lilly's dream come true became a nightmare?

Exhaustion eventually drugged Laurel into sleep, but not before she'd had the chance to consider the potential for nightmares developing in her own life: what if it turned out to be an enormous mistake to have told Nathan she still loved him? Would he accept what she was able to give, or would he ask for more? Could she trust him to be sensible and cautious, or would he move with characteristic speed in the direction he wanted them to go, pulling her along and, like as not, failing to

let her know where they were going? Lord Almighty!
What would she do if he set out to convince her—
again—that *their* dreams could come true, too, if only
she'd believe his love was all she'd ever need to make her
happy?

Nathan fared no better than Laurel with sleep that
night. At 3:00 a.m., a loud noise brought him bolt up-
right in bed, his chest and back glistening with sweat.
His eyes were wild with panic as they searched the
darkness surrounding him. When he realized where he
was and that the shout he had heard was his own, his
breath rushed out in a low groan, and he fell back onto
the bed to lie staring at the snowflake pattern of lace
above him, waiting for his heart to stop racing, waiting
for the knot in the pit of his belly to go away.

His thoughts were thoroughly self-deprecating. God,
what a joke. The great Dr. Nathan Coltrane, whose
hands never shook when they were bathed in blood,
who could find his way into the most mangled body and
make it work again. Where was this paragon from the
Navy Medical Corps? Why, he was lying in a pool of
sweat, trembling with terror. And the cause of his dis-
graceful condition? Nothing more lethal than a woman.
Well, not just any woman. Oh, no. Only in the presence of a certain woman did the fearless Nathan Coltrane turn into a puddle of melted butter. The one
consoling factor in this humiliating state of affairs was
that it seemed he had a similar effect upon her. And a
fat lot of good it did either of them.

The dream that had awakened him was simple and to
the point: *No! Don't leave me. Don't leave! Don't!* In-
terspersed with flashes of warmth and closeness, of
bodies touching and lips whispering *I love you*, the

image of him alternately pleading and thundering at Laurel not to go took on the bizarre quality of a real nightmare. The knowledge that the nightmare had come true once and could easily do so again made Nathan question his sanity, and for a minute or two he practiced telling Laurel he'd had second thoughts about this business of being friends.

He would not tell her, though. Not when he was nearly delirious with joy over discovering he hadn't lost his most cherished treasure. Not after the way she had poured her heart out to him that evening. He was in awe of the courage it must have taken for her to say she still loved him, believing all the while that he did not love her.

But then, he recalled, Laurel had never lacked for courage. It was her inability to remove herself from the past, her abiding sense of hopelessness—a kind of cynicism, almost, that things would ever be any different than she had known them to be—that stood in her way. He, on the other hand, had always possessed enough hopefulness for both of them. Or so he had once thought. And that, in essence, was the lesson he had tried to learn from this whole sorry mess: you could not *make* somebody believe in the future, though he had fought hard enough and long enough to do exactly that. He should have realized he was fighting against impossible odds. It wasn't as though he hadn't had enough warnings....

"I hate it! I hate everything about it! Uniforms and ships and moving! Especially moving! And I don't care if you think I'm wrong."

"Hey, come on, Lauri. I didn't say that." The lanky youth draped the towel he had been using to dry his hair around his neck and dropped down to sit beside the girl,

whose bare legs were folded close to the edge of the dock. He tried to put his arm around her shoulders, which were also bare but for the thin straps of her wet bathing suit, but she shrugged him away. "I didn't mean I thought you were wrong to feel the way you do," he tried to explain. "But I don't think it has to be that way."

"Just because your parents' marriage didn't fall apart doesn't make it right, what the Navy does to people," she snapped, her voice thick with unshed tears. "And how do you know, anyway? You were only ten when they got killed. Maybe they hated each other and were better at hiding it than my parents are."

"They didn't hate each other," the boy insisted. "Look, I know you're upset over your Mom, but she's been drinking too much for years. It's nothing new. You've got a month away from her now, so try not to think about it. Maybe it won't seem so bad by the time you leave in July."

"Oh, Nathan." The girl's head fell forward, and a curtain of long, wet hair hid the tears she could not prevent from escaping. "You don't have to live with it. I can hardly stand the thought of going back to Norfolk, knowing I'm going to have to listen to my parents yelling at each other and my mother yelling at Lilly and me. I'm so tired of being worried all the time about . . . about things."

"Things like what?"

When his question was met only by silence, the boy lifted a finger to his pretty companion's chin to turn her face toward his. "Like what, Lauri?" he prodded.

She turned her head away but could not resist when his finger lingered to stroke her cheek. Suddenly she burst out, "Like whether or not Mom's going to be able to get Lilly off to school in the morning. Or if I should go to chorus rehearsal and risk coming home to find out that Mom's asleep on the couch and Lilly hasn't been picked up from her friend's house—or if anyone even knows where she is!'' And with that admission, her control broke and the tears flowed unchecked.

The boy frowned. "Has your mom's drinking gotten that bad?"

She nodded, swallowing hard. "It's awful. This last sea tour of Dad's has been the worst ever. There were times when... oh, Nathan, I've been so scared." Somehow her hand found its way into his and their fingers laced together in a familiar pattern.

"You should go to somebody," he told her. "You know that's what the Navy Family Counseling Program is for. It's their job to help families who've got troubles like yours."

Shaking her head quickly, she replied, "If Mom found out, she'd kill me. It already seems like we fight constantly! She criticizes my friends and the way I dress and says I'm a disgrace to my father. And how will it look to Admiral So-and-So's wife if she's got a daughter who's a hippie—just because I hung a Lovin' Spoonful poster on my wall! She dresses Lilly and me up like dolls and carts us off to those meetings where the officers' wives talk about the next tea dance to raise money for some charity. The way she trots us out, you'd think we were her front-line offense—like she's the one gunning for these stars and stripes instead of Dad. When we get home, she collapses in a chair with a martini and tells us how bad our manners are and how we'd better shape up, because Dad's career depends on it and he'll be furious if we don't toe the line. I'm so tired of hearing that! Oh, I wish he'd resign! I wish he could be a...a schoolteacher or anything where he wouldn't have to move. Maybe Mom wouldn't get so nervous then. Maybe she wouldn't worry all the time that we're going to do something wrong. Maybe...maybe she wouldn't want to drink.''

The boy's gaze dropped to study the slender hand he held. ''Have you talked to your father about it?''

''How could I?'' the girl cried. ''He's been at sea for the last six months! He got home two days ago, then I got on the plane to come here. And I don't ever want to go back!''

''So, don't,'' he returned instantly. ''I'll ask Uncle Jack to talk to your parents. You can live here at the Landing.''

''Oh, Nathan, I couldn't do that.''

''Why not?''

''Well, just because I couldn't!''

''That's silly. You know Uncle Jack and Aunt Louise would be happy to have you.''

''Nathan, I—I can't. It wouldn't be right.''

He smiled a little. ''You mean, because you're afraid I might want to... well, get too involved?''

An innocent flush of pink touched her feminine features, already kissed by the day's sun.

''I promised I wouldn't push you, Lauri,'' he said gently. ''I know you're only fifteen. I'd never ask you to do anything you weren't ready to do.''

''If I lived here, you might.''

''I wouldn't.''

''But you might, and...and I'd probably let you. I can never say no to you for long.''

''Lauri, I—''

''But that's not the reason, anyway,'' she murmured past her embarrassment. ''I can't leave Lilly. Besides, *when I go home, I've got to help pack. Dad finally got accepted to that duty assignment he's always wanted at the sub base. We're moving to Connecticut."*

The boy's look brightened. *"Hey, maybe that'll help. You said your Mom hates Norfolk."*

"You'd think it'd help, wouldn't you?" she replied with a bitterness far beyond what her years should have allowed. *"But after Dad told us, Mom got really drunk and went on and on about how hard it's going to be at the top, having to be on duty alongside her husband every single minute."*

"What did your Dad say?"

She laughed harshly. *"He told her he was glad to see it made her so happy. It was like he was rubbing it in! They hate each other, Nathan. And I swear, it's the Navy's fault!"*

A speedboat pulling a skier raced by on the river, stirring up the glassy water. The boats moored at the small dock bobbed wildly, bumping against the pilings, while along the thin ribbon of beach, two sandpipers chased an incoming ripple of waves.

The boy spoke quietly. *"When are you moving?"*

"In October."

"A month after school starts. That's rotten."

The girl shrugged. *"Mrs. Murdock wanted me to try out for the cheerleading squad, but I guess there's no point in bothering. I don't mind so much—I'm sort of used to it by now—but Lilly's just starting to make friends, and it's going to be hard for her."*

The boy's hand tightened on the smaller one it held. *"Look, if you're really set against coming to live here, at least call your Dad and see if you can stay the whole summer instead of only a month."*

"I don't know..."

"We could sail Uncle Jack's Laser in the Severn Sailing Association races. I was, uh, going to ask Sophie Michaelson to crew with me, but you know I'd rather have you." He gave her ribs an affectionate poke. *"If we win, I'll give you half of* The Scallop.*"*

She swatted weakly at his teasing fingers as her gaze dropped to the new Rhodes 19 sailboat he'd been given for high school graduation. *"Oh, Nathan, I couldn't let you do that."*

"Sure, you could."

"Well . . ."

"It's a long time until Christmas vacation."

"I don't know, Nathan. There's so much to do to get ready to move."

"It'll all be there waiting for you when you get home. Come on, Lauri. It'll be good for you. Besides—" he nudged her hair aside to place a fleeting kiss at the base of her neck *"—I want you to stay."*

His head rose, and their eyes met.

"I love you," he said.

Her gaze fell to her lap, and she whispered, *"You know I love you, too."*

"Yeah. You've been telling me since I was ten and you were eight. I kinda got the idea."

"You also know I'd rather be here, with you, than anywhere else."

"So, stay with me. There's nothing stopping you."

She shot him a sideways glance, and he offered her a grin that was full of exuberance and adolescent innuendo.

She hesitated another instant, then, slowly, her lips curved into an answering smile. *"All right. You win. I'll call Dad tonight. . . ."*

As Nathan relived that long-ago summer, he remembered thinking he had won that battle. In the same way, he had thought he'd won the day Laurel approved his plan to apply for the Navy scholarship. But he had been wrong each time. It had been a mistake ever to believe that her choice to be with him meant she had overcome her feelings about the Navy. She hadn't overcome them; she had simply stopped talking about them. And she had spent every day of their marriage waiting for her worst fear to be realized—waiting for their relationship to fall apart the way her parents' had.

It had been a self-fulfilling prophecy. Every time he had been transferred, every time his duties had conflicted with their plans, Laurel hadn't complained, but she had withdrawn a little further into herself. And as the years had passed, there had been a bigger and bigger part of her missing from what she gave to him.

His reactions had run the gamut from frustration to panic and, finally, to rage as he had tried in every way he could think of to make her happy so that she might surrender that part of herself again. Arranging their moves, doing most of the housework, seeing to it they entertained frequently in the hopes that she'd make friends. Once, he'd searched for hours to find her a real Christmas tree in Yokosuka, Japan, where pine trees were virtually nonexistent. To this day, he didn't fully understand his nearly frantic need to reclaim all of Laurel's love; he knew only that it seemed to go beyond any reasonable need a man ought to have. And he had surely gone to *un*reasonable lengths to achieve the goal.

But nothing had worked. When it came down to it, at night, when he would take her in his arms and make love to her, he would find her passionate and willing to give him everything—everything except that one small part of her heart he had wanted the most. The one part he hadn't had since the last time they had made love on the very bed upon which he was lying. The one part he *still* wanted and would never quite be able to accept that he could not have.

So why, Nathan had to wonder, was he jumping at the chance to have Laurel back in his life? Clearly, the kindest thing for both of them would be to say a polite goodbye and walk away, before they wound up hurting each other all over again.

Rolling to his side, he looked at the empty pillow beside him, its pristine whiteness gleaming starkly in the darkness. His hand slid across the bed, and his fingers touched the pillowcase. No, he could not let Laurel go. Not now that he knew she loved him. Not, he feared, as long as there was a breath of hope left in his body that she might ever be entirely his again.

Chapter Seven

"Well, good morning, Grandpa!"

James Randall grinned as Laurel walked into the cheery dining room of Clarkson's Lodgings, planted a kiss on his cheek and slid into a chair across the table from him. The room was filled with plants and red wicker, and the French doors opened onto a patio behind the town house. Honey Clarkson was chatting with other guests at a nearby table, and the single waitress rushed forward with a hand-printed menu for Laurel.

"I take it you got my message," James said.

Laurel nodded, offering him a bright, if slightly brittle, smile. It had been a rough night, but she figured she could face the day as long as she went on smiling and concentrated on maintaining world peace between her teams of youthful mock negotiators; those overly eager pseudo-Soviets needed to learn that creating an impasse had serious repercussions.

The waitress took her breakfast order—coffee, black. Then Laurel turned back to her father. "I called Lilly when I got in last night. I'll be going down there, probably on Tuesday."

"Oh?" James set his coffee cup in its saucer and gave her a puzzled look. "I thought they'd hired a woman to help out."

"They have. But a stranger's not the same as a sister, Dad."

"Besides which," he added with a knowing grin, "you're itching to get your hands on that baby."

"Aren't you? Come on, now. Lilly's told me how much time you spend playing with Christopher and Leslie when you visit. Imagine!" Her hands flew up in horror. "James Randall, U.S. Navy, cavorting on the floor with a brown shag bathmat on his back and a stuffed sock tied to his nose, hollering, 'Hi, Big Bird! It's Mr. Snuffelupagus. Can you come out and play?' Mercy! How *will* he explain it to the Joint Chiefs of Staff?"

"He'll plead guilty." James laughed. "But he won't embarrass his fellow grandfathers, who may have engaged in similar subversive activities, by offering an explanation!"

"But he will stop teasing his elder daughter about claiming a couple of days of aunthood!"

James's smile was warm. "I'm not teasing you, honey. Nothing pleases me more than seeing the way you and Lilly care for each other. In fact—"

When he failed to go on, Laurel's gaze was drawn to him. He was tracing the rim of his empty coffee cup, a frown creasing his brow.

"'In fact' what?" she urged.

Haltingly, he began, "Since your mother's death, I've thought about a lot of things, Laurel. It's natural, I suppose. The death of someone close to you changes your perception of mortality." His gaze flickered to hers briefly. "You and I—we've never really talked much, I know. And maybe someday we'll manage to be in the same place at the same time with nothing else to do, so we can, well, simply be together."

When he paused, casting what Laurel recognized as a hopeful look toward her, she smiled sincerely. "I'd like that."

He straightened in his seat, clearly encouraged by her response, and continued less hesitantly. "There's something I want to say now, though, that I guess the new baby and talking to Lilly has made seem more immediate to me. I want you to know how much it means to me that you love your sister. That you've always loved her."

Laurel's lips parted slightly in mild confusion. "Of course, I love her. Is it so strange that I would?"

James shook his head. "It's not a bit strange, but the *way* you love her is quite special. Frankly, Laurel, I don't think it's too much to say that the major credit for Lilly growing up happy and well-adjusted goes to you."

"Dad, no, I—"

"It isn't that your mother and I didn't love you both," he went on, insistently. "We did. Very much. And I think, in our separate ways, we did the best we could to show that love. But—" he sighed "—our best wasn't always good enough. More often than not, it was you who saw to it that meals were on time and that Lilly's hair got brushed before she went to school. And when she had nightmares, it was you she called for—not me or your mother. You've picked up the pieces and filled in the gaps in her life so many times. And I realized, talking to her last night—hearing how thrilled and happy she is—I didn't want another day to go by without telling you how proud and grateful I am that you're my daughter.''

Laurel felt tears well up in her eyes at her father's unprecedented declaration, and it was only the shock of how truly defenseless she had become in the past few days that won her a measure of control. ''I don't know what to say,'' she murmured.

''I'm not trying to embarrass you, honey,'' he added. ''It's simply that— Well, I hope you're able to share in Lilly's happiness. You deserve to reap some of the rewards for the love you've sown.''

Laurel didn't trust her voice not to give away her doubts on the topic of her sister's happiness, so she tried to smile and reached quickly for her coffee.

Either her father did not notice her discomfort or he was simply bent upon waxing sentimental this morning. ''Do you remember how upset Lilly would be whenever you'd come to visit Nathan?'' he asked.

Laurel remembered. Only too well.

''She would cry for days after you'd gone,'' he went on. ''If I hadn't known how important it was for you to have your holidays in Annapolis, I might have kept you home.''

Laurel grimaced. ''I think you've found the limits of my love. As much as I care about Lilly, I'm not sorry you didn't give in to her tears.''

''There wasn't any danger of that happening,'' he assured her. ''It always gave me a good feeling to put you on the plane. I tried to encourage your friendship with Nathan partly, I guess, because you had to give up friends so often. I wanted you to know it was possible to keep a friendship alive, even when physical space separated you."

Laurel's eyes grew wide with wonder. The fact that her father recognized one of the chief difficulties in being a Navy brat had never occurred to her. Nor had she ever considered that his willingness to let her spend summers and holidays with the Coltranes had been motivated by anything more than wanting to protect her from her own home environment. And he soon confirmed the latter suspicion.

"It's an awful thing to say," he continued, "but I suppose sending you to visit Nathan appeased my conscience somewhat. I knew that as long as you were at the Landing, you'd have a chance to be what you were—a child. It's a little late for such things, but I've always been sorry you had to grow up so fast. And I don't mean only in how you took care of Lilly. Your mother's drinking—when it was bad, which was often enough—was a terrible burden for you in so many ways, and I'm sorry for that. But there simply wasn't anything I could have done about it."

You could have resigned your commission. The forbidden words came so quickly to her mind that, for a moment, Laurel was afraid she had spoken them aloud.

"I tried hard to get your mother to seek help." His brow furrowed in both consternation and sorrow. "She wouldn't admit she had a problem—and besides—" his lips twisted in a cynical smile "—what would the other officers' wives have said if they'd found out she was in treatment? It was so sad. All she ever really wanted in life was to get to the top and wear my rank as her own."

Laurel drew back, unable to believe her father understood so little about the woman he had married. "Dad, I think you must be wrong," she said in a carefully controlled tone. "Mom hated the Navy. I remember how she'd cry whenever you'd get a new duty assignment."

James shook his head. "Your mother cried a lot on almost any excuse, but it wasn't the Navy that was the source of her troubles. If that had been the case, don't you think I would have resigned my commission?"

The assurance with which he asked the question, as though it were a foregone conclusion, told Laurel that he was absolutely serious. And she was astonished. "I don't know, Dad," she stammered. "Would you have?"

He shocked her further by saying, "I offered several times."

A feeling of unreality crept over her. It was as though they were discussing a different family, not the one she had been a part of.

"What did Mom say?" she asked weakly.

"Catherine swore she'd leave me if I ever breathed a word about resigning to anyone. She liked the prestige and the feeling of belonging it gave her. If I'd resigned, she would have lost everything that was important to her."

Laurel was speechless. She could not accept what her father was telling her. Yet he never lied, and with her mother dead, he certainly had no reason to do so. It occurred to her that he hadn't spoken of these things before because, in his code of ethics, it would have been disloyal to talk in less than positive terms about his wife while she was alive. But what a time he had picked to air the family linen! A time when her own emotional energy had already been taxed beyond its limits.

"You're very quiet, Laurel," her father noted.

"I'm sorry. I guess I'm a bit shocked," she admitted. "It's strange to hear you talk about giving up the Navy. I thought— Well, you always seemed so dedicated."

James's reply was tinged with bitterness. "A man gets that way when there's little else in his life that matters. Oh, it's true, I was eager enough when I started out. As the son of a West Virginia coal miner who'd never seen the ocean, I found the prospect of making a career in the Navy extremely appealing. When I met your mother, I was certain I was in love. Catherine was charming and poised and always knew exactly what to say to people to make them feel comfortable." He grimaced in dry self-mockery. "In other words, she represented everything I thought I lacked and had always envied. It seemed like a godsend that the notion of being an officer's wife delighted her. Neither of us realized that we'd fallen in love not with each other, but with what the other could give us. I'm not saying we didn't genuinely care for each other, but it wasn't the sort of love that sustains a good marriage. By the time I realized that, it was too late to do much about it. And I suppose, in the long run, we both got what we asked for. Catherine was the supreme hostess and diplomat. And for her, I became an Admiral."

It was such a sad scenario, Laurel wasn't sure she wanted to hear the answer to her next question, for fear it would get worse. "If you didn't love Mom," she asked hesitantly, "why didn't you leave her? Why did you stay in a marriage that sounds as...well, as cold as the one you're describing?"

James was silent a moment before replying. "If I'd left your mother, I would have lost you and Lilly, too. In those days, mothers got custody with rare exceptions, regardless of the facts. Her drinking wouldn't have been an issue. I couldn't bear the idea of not seeing you for months on end—it was bad enough when I was at sea, knowing there was a limit to how long I'd have to be away. And frankly, Laurel, I was afraid of what would happen to you if I weren't *ever* there to keep some control on your mother's drinking. It was an awful situation, and I'll probably never be able to apologize enough to you or to Lilly for subjecting you both to it."

For a minute, Laurel was again afraid she might cry. She had to fight off the tightness in her throat to speak. "Dad, I'm sorry. I didn't know. I never dreamed what it was like for you."

"You had no way of knowing," he said simply, absolving her of any guilt. "Now, I've gone on long enough. We're both going to be late if we don't hurry." He reached across the table to give her hand an affectionate squeeze. "And I promise, I won't bore you with any more maudlin ramblings this week. We'll stick to pleasant things and save the soul-searching for that future date when neither of us has anything else to think about—a time that I hope won't be too far off."

"We'll plan it before we leave on Sunday," Laurel promised, wondering how he could possibly think she was bored by his astonishing revelations.

As they left the hotel, James asked, "By the way, how did your dinner with Nathan go last night?"

Laurel's reply was delivered with a studied casualness. "Oh, fine. We're going sailing tomorrow afternoon."

There was a pause before her father remarked pleasantly, "That's nice. I hope you have good weather."

* * *

At three o'clock on Thursday, Laurel rushed from the conference to the guest house to shimmy out of the silk dress she had worn all day and pull on a pair of white shorts and a tank top. Visions of blue skies, gulls soaring overhead, bright-colored spinnakers snapping in the breeze—and Nathan—made her hurry. It had become critical to prove to herself that she could be with Nathan, even loving him and knowing he loved her, and keep her priorities and goals in mind. She needed to know that she did not have to be a victim of her own emotions—or of Nathan's extensive talents in the art of persuasion. Besides, the adoring, almost worshipful love she felt for him might have been excusable in a nineteen-year-old, but in a woman nearing middle age, it was thoroughly inappropriate. Indeed, it was high time for her to stop playing the innocent and, in short, grow up.

Although her logic may have been sound and her intentions the best, Laurel could not prevent the breathless feeling of happy anticipation that rippled through her as she left her room. When she reached the front door of the guest house, her heart was tripping at a light, swift pace and her eyes were sparkling. When she opened the door to discover Nathan walking up the sidewalk, she reacted to the sight of him with an enormously delighted smile.

"Well, how about that!" He tossed her a crooked grin, his eyes skimming over her long, bare legs in thinly disguised approval. "I'm right on time!"

Laurel laughed nervously. "Actually, you aren't supposed to be here at all. I was driving out."

"I didn't get through with my meetings until late. Thought I might as well wait and pick you up." Motioning toward his car, he added, "The weather reports are for clear skies, and *The Scallop*'s set to go."

Laurel noted the frequency with which he was stealing glances that held something more potent than friendship. She also noted the delicious way her body responded to those glances. She went to leave a message for her father, telling him their car was there if he needed it, but as she did so, she knew that the wisdom of this experiment was in serious doubt.

On their ride to the Landing, Laurel shared the good tidings about Lilly's new baby.

"God, I can't believe it! Lilly with three children!" Nathan's pleased exclamation hinted at nostalgia. "Seems like yesterday you were helping her plan her wedding. Where's Stan stationed now? And how come you haven't hopped a plane to go help out?"

Laurel gave him a mildly indignant look. "I can't very well leave in the middle of this conference."

"You mean there are some things that take precedence over your sisterly duties?"

"Hey, now—" she began in protest. But the defensive words died unspoken under his gentle grin. Nathan had always been an awful tease, but never a cruel one.

A smile played across her lips as she admitted, "Lilly needs me like she needs a fur coat in July. Stan's stationed in Norfolk and has a week's leave. They've also hired a mother's helper, but I'm going, anyway, as soon as the conference is over."

Nathan flashed her a grin. "I couldn't picture you being an absentee aunt. Tell me about the two older children. What are their names?"

"Christopher and Leslie," Laurel replied. "They've both got dark auburn hair like my mother's and huge blue eyes like Stan's. Christopher's an exceptionally even-tempered three-year-old. And Leslie's a classic holy terror at the tender age of eighteen months and far too clever for anyone else's comfort."

Nathan chuckled. "In other words, your advice to the newest addition will be to watch out for her big sister!"

"We're all holding our breath to see what happens." Laurel laughed, too. And throughout the rest of the ride, she related stories about her niece and nephew, making it obvious that, in spite of her busy life, she managed to spend time with them and loved them a great deal.

Nathan listened, smiled in the right places and made appropriate comments, but he had to fight off a wave of sadness that it wasn't their own children upon whom Laurel was lavishing her love. He had wanted so badly to raise a family with her. At first the delay had seemed reasonable. Money and time had been tight; while he was in medical school and doing his residency, Laurel had been finishing her studies and doing public relations speaking tours for ACDA. As time had passed, though, and things had gotten better for them, her excuses had seemed weaker. And he had become worried that, left up to her, the time was never going to be right.

He had tried gentle persuasion. He had tried subtle hints. And he had tried a few hints that were not so subtle—like the couple of occasions he had brought home orphans to spend holidays with them, in the hopes of encouraging Laurel's maternal instincts. She had enjoyed the children, was always sad to let them go, but she hadn't wavered once in her resolve not to start their family.

Nathan could look back now and see that the notion of Laurel having his baby had eventually gone past any simple, genuine desire for a child of his own and had become symbolic of a much larger issue. It was as though in refusing to allow him to impregnate her, she was withholding final judgment on their marriage—and on him. Her unwillingness to come to him unprotected and vulnerable had hurt. Badly. It had also heightened his growing panic at the thought that he was losing her.

For some reason, it had been this issue that had most tried his patience, which had worn extremely thin by the time Laurel had turned thirty. So thin, in fact, that in a rare moment of desperation, he had entertained some wildly uncontrolled fantasies about swapping her birth control pills for harmless, ineffective placebos. In these corrupt scenarios, she never discovered the truth. He could have found a way to do it. And maybe a baby would give her something to think about besides how much she hated Navy life. Of course, he never would have actually done it. Besides it being a gross violation of professional ethics, he could not have deceived Laurel in such a contemptible manner.

Yet Nathan wondered bleakly if sabotaging the pills could have been any worse than what he had done that horrible morning at Subic Bay when his patience had finally run out. For after ten years of not a single angry word, he had said every last one of them in the space of ten minutes. The explosion had cost him everything. And here they both were. He without any family. Laurel using her sister's children to compensate. How sad, he thought. How incredibly unnecessary. And how utterly foolish it was for him to be wondering, still, how Laurel's slender, white-skinned body would look swollen with his child.

When they arrived at the Landing, Laurel went directly to the boat while Nathan stopped at the cottage to change. By the time he joined her, Laurel had clipped the jib to the forestay and attached the halyard to the bow.

"That's what I like to see," Nathan said jauntily, as he jumped aboard. "An efficient crew."

"Crew, my foot," Laurel retorted, securing the tiller. "You gave me half of this boat, Nathan *Sinjin* Coltrane, the summer we won the Severn Sailing Association race."

Nathan laughed. "Oh, I did, huh? Funny, but all I remember is how mad you were when I invited Sophie Michaelson to come to the barbecue we had afterward."

"Ha!" Laurel snorted and turned toward him, a flip comeback poised on her tongue. Then she went hot all over and completely forgot what she was going to say. He was half turned away from her—which was a good thing, because she couldn't unglue her eyes from the sight of him, dressed in a tight white sleeveless sweatshirt and a pair of black gym shorts.

As he reached forward to unhitch the bowline from the cleats on the pier, Laurel swallowed hard. Lord, he looked good! All height and shoulders and brawn—rich bronze skin sleeked over hard, well-defined muscle, and a good portion of it sprinkled with nearly black hair. With a shiver of pure sensual awareness, Laurel remembered her friend Linda's comment upon seeing the photograph she had kept on her dresser—the shot of Nathan dressed in swim trunks, standing on this same boat. "Good grief, Laurel! He's huge! And—and hairy! Doesn't he scare you to death?"

No, she thought, there had been moments when she had wondered if she might die from *pleasure*, but never from fear. Besides, even if the mere sight of him hadn't turned her on like wildfire, how could she have been scared of someone she had first met as a little boy with a missing tooth? She could even remember when she had been taller than Nathan, before puberty had hit them almost simultaneously and she had filled out while he had soared upward. She had been there the Christmas his voice had begun to drop from a smooth tenor to its present, sonorous baritone. She had seen his chest when it had been in the throes of growing swirls and swirls of silky hair. And the summer they had whiled away perfecting the art of openmouthed kissing, she had been altogether fascinated by the mysterious changes that went on beneath the zipper of his jeans whenever he held her close.

Yes, it seemed to her that Nathan had turned out perfectly, and she felt oddly, ridiculously proud of the fact, as though she had somehow had a hand in it. Staring at that virile body, Laurel was overwhelmed by a sudden rush of feeling, the touchstone of which was a single word: *mine*.

But he wasn't hers. And the sooner she accepted that, the better off they both would be.

They pushed away from the dock, and Nathan started the outboard, steering *The Scallop* to the mouth of the river. Once there, Laurel raised the jib; Nathan shut off the motor and raised the mainsail. In the next instant the sails filled and the boat took off across the water, running before the wind. Soon they were headed across the open waters of the Chesapeake Bay.

Laurel let her eyes close as she leaned back and dangled her arms over *The Scallop*'s side. Her blissfully mindless state was only slightly disturbed by Nathan's comment.

"Whatever you're thinking looks pleasant."

Her lips turned up a tad. "I'm thinking that this is exactly what the doctor ordered. Or should I make that 'what the Captain ordered?'"

She heard the smile in his voice as he replied, "I won't argue semantics with you as long as the medicine is working."

"Hmm. It's definitely working. I can feel my nails growing already."

He chuckled, and she went on to ask, "If I promise not to accuse you of working too hard, will you tell me more about what you had to do with this amazing ship they're building?"

"I'll tell you even if you don't promise," he answered, and then proceeded to do so.

Laurel had always loved hearing Nathan talk about his work, but on this particular occasion she could not prevent her thoughts from wandering back to what her father had told her the previous morning. *A man gets that way when there's little else in his life that matters.* Nathan had always been a dedicated physician, but he had never been a career Navy man in his heart. Was he now? Had that been what her leaving him had accomplished? The thought was too painfully ironic to consider.

"My Dad's quite impressed with you," she remarked when Nathan had finished relating the details about his part in the floating hospital.

"I'm glad to hear that," he replied. "And I don't mean because of his position. I have a lot of respect for your father and how he's handled his career." Curiously, he added, "I wonder if he's started thinking about retirement. Do you know?"

Laurel's eyes opened, and her brows drew together in a deep frown. Two days ago, she would have uttered a brusque denial that the word *retirement* was even in her father's vocabulary. Now she was not so sure. That realization brought a sardonic laugh to her lips.

Nathan misinterpreted her cryptic response. "Whoops. Guess your father's career comes under the heading of topics not to be discussed, huh?"

"No," Laurel replied, shrugging a little, nervously. "In fact, I've spent a lot of the last two days thinking about it. Dad and I— We had breakfast together yesterday. He was feeling good about Lilly and the baby, and somehow we started talking about how I've always looked out for Lilly. He thanked me for it, and—" She broke off, then went on in a rush, "And he apologized for things having been the way they were and for not being able to do anything about them."

"God Almighty, Laurel, you didn't tell him he could have resigned!"

Nathan's horrified tone made her blush guiltily. "No, but the strange thing was, I didn't have to say it. Dad told me that my mother wouldn't *let* him resign. He said he offered, if it would help her to stop drinking, but she swore she'd divorce him and take Lilly and me with her if he did. She wanted to be an officer's wife. So he stayed in because he was afraid of what would happen to us with Mom, by ourselves."

She stole a brief glance at Nathan and found that he was as stunned by the news as she had been. Somehow that reassured her and gave her the courage to continue.

"I felt awful," she admitted. "And confused! I still can hardly believe it. I grew up thinking my mother hated the Navy—it's what she *told* me, for heaven's sake! I thought she loved Dad, too, but he says they never really loved each other—not in any true, lasting sense. He says they were both guilty of having ambitions and using each other to achieve them. It was so sad. I felt so sorry for him."

Nathan spit out a short, explicit oath. "If I were you, I don't think I'd be feeling sorry for anybody but myself. It must make you angry as hell to find out that all your life you've believed a lie."

Laurel nodded. "Yes, there's that, too. I can't help wondering what it would have been like if Dad had resigned in spite of Mom's threats. Or how I would have felt if I'd known the truth from the start." She gazed out over the water, as though trying to envision the different life she might have led *if . . .*

Then, with a frustrated shake of her head, she concluded, "But what's the use in wondering? Mom's gone, and Dad's an Admiral. It's pointless to go back and speculate about how things might have been."

But it's not pointless, Nathan longed to shout. He wanted to take her by the shoulders and shake her until the fragments came together and she saw what was so plainly before her. It wasn't easy to keep quiet when the tiny spark of hope he had labeled foolish two nights before had jumped into a small but steadily burning flame.

Suddenly, crazily, something *had* changed! After years of believing that her mother's drinking was caused by her devotion to a military man who was callous and insensitive to her needs, Laurel had discovered that this was not the case at all. How long would it be, he wondered, before she put two and two together and realized that her own hatred of the Navy was based on the same lie? How long would it be before she realized that, if her father's uniform did not make him an ogre, then neither was he himself likely to become one, simply because he wore the same uniform?

Shifting uncomfortably on her seat, Laurel grumbled, "I feel like I've been positively myopic about this. I should have realized the truth years ago."

"Dammit! Don't you blame yourself," Nathan came back quickly. "If your father hadn't told you the truth—and he's a little late getting around to it, if you ask me—you might never have known. You've been acting on the basis of the only information you had, and I'd say the conclusions you reached were completely logical. You had to survive, Laurel. Don't hold it against yourself how you went about it."

And with that, Nathan realized that he no longer held it against her, either. He had thought understanding her problems had been enough. But understanding was not the same as forgiveness. And until that moment, he hadn't truly forgiven her for allowing her fears to determine the outcome of their marriage. The realization washed through him, bringing instant and towering relief from a burden he had not been aware he was carrying.

Laurel stared at Nathan, fully aware that she had just been absolved of all the blame he had heaped upon her at Subic Bay. Did he realize what he had said? His face reflected as much surprise as she herself felt, but as she watched, his features relaxed, losing not only the look of surprise but some of their tired grimness. His eyes, instead of being filled with sadness and regret, held a fiercely tender expression, and Laurel knew that, yes, he had understood what he had said. And he had meant it,

Then, before she could even think of a response, Nathan's look changed again as his gaze shifted from hers to focus on something off in the distance. The next instant, he was moving.

"Here." He shoved the sheet line in her direction, and she took it automatically. "Hang on to this. We've got trouble coming."

Laurel straightened instantly and turned to look over her shoulder. Her eyes widened as she saw the eerie black thunderheads hanging over the western horizon. "Some clear skies," she muttered.

Nathan snorted as he dropped the sails. "Guess we've both forgotten how fast the weather can change on the Bay."

"Mmm," Laurel replied. "Guess we're about to be reminded."

Chapter Eight

It would have been stupid not to be scared. A storm in a twenty-foot sailboat was no laughing matter. And it had been years since she had sailed; this was hardly the time to test her rusty skills. But there wasn't any choice. Nathan would need her help.

They had the sails down and the motor started in a matter of minutes. Laurel pulled two life jackets out of the cutty at the front of the boat, tossed one to Nathan and put hers on. With the outboard at full throttle, they were headed for the mouth of the South River, but neither of them believed they had any chance of making it before the storm hit. Thunder rolled, ominously close. The wind had shifted out of the northwest and was blowing with dramatic force, churning the dark waters into choppy, white-capped wedges. It was pitch-black above them, but mysterious patches of sunlight streaked through clouds to shine like spotlights on the sails of other boats that were trying to get to safety. Across the water they could see the murky gray curtain of rain getting closer.

They were a long way from their own dock when the rain hit, pelting down with a force that stung as badly as any needle. Only it was thousands of needles, and all of them were cold. Within seconds, they were drenched to the skin.

When the first streak of lightning blazed across the wicked-looking sky, Laurel and Nathan both shuddered, exchanged one look of mutual worry and fear— and then laughed. It wasn't that either of them was foolhardy; they were well aware this was a life-threatening situation. But they could not make the boat go faster, they both trusted the other to do everything humanly possible to ensure their safety, so what was left but to enjoy being terrified together?

It required every ounce of his considerable strength for Nathan to hang on to the tiller and keep them on course, yet the effort he was exerting did not prevent him from offering Laurel a devilish and thoroughly wet grin. "I'd offer you a refund on your cruise," he shouted above a clap of thunder, "but I'm fresh out of small change!"

"Keep your money!" Laurel scoffed, somehow managing to look dignified as she crouched in the bottom of the rocking boat, clutching the side with one hand and bailing water with a bucket held in the other. "Nobody's going to call *me* a fair-weather friend!"

His tone became more serious. "Are you cold?"

"I'll live!" she hollered. "Besides, there's not much we can do about it."

He looked down at his own sodden clothes. "Nope. The shirt off my back wouldn't be worth much!"

No, but being wrapped in your arms would be worth a lot, Laurel thought, though she could not have said whether it was cold or desire that aroused in her the almost overwhelming urge to scoot over beside him—to heck with whether they capsized or, for that matter, what he might think of such an overture. But the moment that had passed between them before the storm hit had left her a thousand times more vulnerable than she had been before; as long as she thought he still blamed her for not trying hard enough to make their marriage work, she'd had some defense. Now there was none.

She tightened her hold on the boat and applied her attention to bailing so that she would not see either of the dangers before her: the storm or Nathan.

The storm lasted ten minutes, then blew itself off as quickly as it had come, leaving the sky an ominous, muted gray and the air smelling like salt and sea grass. It also left a breeze that was not as balmy as the one that had been wafting over the river a while before. Nathan accepted the towel Laurel handed him from her bag, but by the time they had both mopped their hair, the towel was soaked. And Laurel was shivering.

Nathan did not even consider raising the sails. They were a mile from the mouth of the South River; with the wind blowing against them, they would have to tack to get there. And the sky did not look promising. Noticing how silent Laurel had become, he cast her a concerned glance. She was sitting in the bottom of the boat, her beautiful long legs drawn up toward her chest and her arms wrapped around them. Her hair was starting to dry in the wind and fluttered around her face in wispy curls. When she caught him watching her, she offered him a tremulous smile. She was cold and wet and shaking with the aftershocks of the scare they'd had. But even under such circumstances, Laurel remained, as always, completely herself: She didn't panic, she didn't complain or whine or throw out pointless recriminations. Instead, she looked at him with her heart in her eyes and smiled.

Nathan's own heart was hammering against his chest. What would she say, he wondered, if he told her their new arrangement was not going to work? Not by a long shot. He wanted her heart as open to him as his was to her. He wanted her body as hot and aroused as his own was becoming, watching her. He wanted her friendship *and* her love. And nothing less would do. When he'd agreed to try to be friends, he would not have given two cents for his chances of convincing her to give him anything more. But what about now? He was starting to wonder.

Laurel's teeth were chattering when they reached the Coltrane dock, and Nathan quickly secured the boat.

"Come on," he said, wrapping his hand firmly around hers to pull her up onto the pier beside him. "Let's go get dry."

Laurel hung back, her eyes wide and a little scared as she cast her gaze up the forest path. She understood that he intended to take her to the cottage, not back to the guest house. And she knew the air between them was laden with far more intimacy than her weak defenses could handle. But she was freezing, and so was Nathan; it would be absurd to insist he drive her to town.

Her eyes met Nathan's in a searching look, and in the depths of his steady gaze, she found questions but no answers. But there was reassurance there, too. And a great deal of love.

With an uneasy nod, she agreed to his plan and let him lead her up the bank over the rain-washed path.

The sky was darkening again when they reached the small clearing where the cottage was nestled, and under the protection of the trees, its interior looked dim.

"My robe's hanging behind the bathroom door," Nathan said, releasing Laurel's hand to switch on a lamp as they entered. Then, without giving her time to think or react, he gave her a gentle push toward the hallway. "Take a shower, and don't worry about using up the hot water. I'll be fine once I dry off."

"Are you sure—" she started to ask, acutely aware of his hand on the small of her back, guiding her.

"Positive," he interrupted. "Go on. Get warm."

And then the bathroom door was closing behind her, and Laurel was alone. Quickly, her hands shaking, she peeled off her wet clothes. A shower had been installed inside the claw-footed tub with a circular curtain that hung from the ceiling. She turned on the water and stepped into it, drawing the curtain around her. Instantly, she was enveloped in clouds of blessedly hot steam and spray. She closed her eyes, groaning in relief, and let the hot water pour over her chilled skin.

All the while, she was thinking about what she would do when the hot water did, indeed, run out. She had set out that day to prove she could be friends with Nathan without giving in to her longing for him. She hadn't planned on a trial by fire. She hadn't planned on discovering that the fierce and boundless love she'd once had from him, the love that had made their honeymoon in this cottage magical for her, was once more within her grasp. It had been so long since she'd felt that love, untainted by any trace of anger or resentment. She wanted desperately to reach for it and had no idea if she would be able to resist doing so.

Her panic rose sharply when she stepped out of the shower. She tried to remind herself that the years and her imagination had surely exaggerated the ecstasy of the lovemaking she and Nathan had shared in that wonderful old bed. No two mortals could possibly have achieved such a heavenly state. It was time to give up living on dreams and memories and to realize that lovemaking, like the rest of life, had its moments of both pain and pleasure, disappointment and fulfillment. It was childish to want to go back. It was foolish to wonder if it could ever be that special again.

But, oh, she did wonder.

And the wondering made her tremble when she reached for Nathan's black terry-cloth bathrobe off the back of the door and hung the towel she had been using in its place. The robe swallowed her, as she had known it would. It was cozy and soft and smelled of Nathan, and as she triple-cuffed the sleeves and wrapped the belt twice around her waist, she tried futilely not to think about the masculine body the robe last had hugged.

There wasn't anything she could do about her clothes except wring them out, hang them up and pray they dried enough to put back on in the hour she mentally allotted herself to stay. When she left the bathroom, she plastered a bright smile on her face, but it was totally ruined by the frightened look in her smoky eyes.

Her arrival in the great room coincided with Nathan's emergence from the bedroom. He smiled and came toward her, wearing nothing but a pair of old jeans that fit snugly across his thighs and narrow hips. Without a belt, the jeans rode low, the snap grazing his navel, where a whorl of dark hair shot upward in a line that fanned out to encompass the whole luxurious expanse of his chest. His bare chest. His feet were bare, too, like hers. And his hair was still damply ruffled.

Laurel's helpless gaze skittered over him, taking in all she could see, trying not to think about what she couldn't see, before rising to his face, which was shadowed by stubble and the growing darkness outside. The expression in his eyes, as they roamed over her dishabille then snapped up to meet hers, was softer, somehow, than before and so incredibly hungry.

Outside, the distant rumbles of the second, fast-moving storm rolled across the river. Laurel buried her hands deep in the robe's pockets and decided that, wet clothes or not, in an hour she was going to have Nathan drive her back to town.

"Feeling better?" he asked, coming to stand directly in front of her, lifting his hand to lay it against her cheek. "Hmm. Definitely warmer."

"I'm fine," she replied, wondering why he was standing so close—and why his fingers were lingering so long on her cheek. Wondering what they were doing there at all!

"Are you hungry?" he asked.

She shook her head. She could not have eaten a thing.

"I made you a cup of tea."

His hand left her face but managed to get caught straightening the collar of her robe. The backs of his fingers, brushing her collarbone, sent lovely sensual messages throughout her body, rousing memories of what those same capable fingers could do to other, even more sensitive parts of her. Parts of her that were, at that moment, responding in an extravagant fashion.

"Tea—" she began hoarsely. "Tea sounds good."

"It's in the kitchen." With obvious reluctance, he drew his fingers away, then slid his hands into the back pockets of his jeans.

The action stretched the faded denim taut across his loins and was, for Laurel, a fascinating and stirring reminder of precisely what it was she had been missing. Suddenly, it became imperative to move.

"The kitchen," she gasped. "Right! I'll, uh, go get it!"

She whirled to dash into the small galley kitchen at the back of the cottage. A flash of lightning lit the room briefly before she switched on the light, and her gaze zeroed in on the mug of steaming tea Nathan had left steeping on the counter. The fact that she had given up drinking tea over a year ago in favor of black coffee somehow slipped her mind as she went about squeezing out the tea bag and dumping in several spoonfuls of sugar. She was stirring with a vengeance when Nathan spoke from close behind her.

"We're liable to lose the lights."

"Oh? Oh, well—"

"I guess I ought to go check out the car. I had some trouble with it the other day when it rained."

"Really?" Laurel's shaking fingers wrapped themselves around the handle of the hot mug as she asked apprehensively, "What sort of trouble?"

"It won't start when it's wet."

Her tiny sound of distress accompanied the crash of her mug on the counter. She started to jump back, but Nathan's arms were around her, lifting her out of the way before the mug had bounced off the counter and onto the floor, where it shattered.

He carried her quickly out of the room, away from the broken china, and set her down in the living room, asking, "Did it burn you?"

"No." Her reply came out in a croak as her hands fluttered against his chest and shoulders, trying to make herself push him away. She thought it had worked until she realized he had only dropped down on one knee in order to lift her foot for closer inspection. "I'm okay!" she insisted, groaning inwardly at the feel of his gentle hands on her calf and instep. "I'm all right, Nathan. Really!"

But he had to be sure, it seemed—although the strong, sensitive fingers that were now exploring her hands and forearms did not feel the least bit clinical. Desperate to stop him before the examination went any further, she nearly screamed, "Nathan, I'm *all right*! I'm not cut or burned. I'm sorry, I didn't know you were so close behind me and—and I—" She whimpered.

"Laurel, it's only a broken cup. You're shaking like a leaf. Did it scare you that badly, or was it the storm?"

At that very second, the light flickered and a clap of thunder shook the house.

Laurel shuddered almost violently. "I'm not scared! I'm only—"

"Only what?"

"Only...hold me, please. Oh, Nathan, just hold me."

"I'm right here."

"It's not the storm. It's— Oh, Lord, I'm afraid I—"

"It's okay, sweet— Laurel . . . ? God, Lauri, *don't*!"

With her fingers splayed deep in the furry mat on his chest and her lips nuzzling through it to taste the warm, musky-scented skin beneath, she mumbled brokenly, "I can't help it. Oh, Nathan, it was a mistake to come here.

It was a mistake to think I could be with you like this,
because if I don't kiss you, I think I'm just going to
die!''

His hands slid up her back to hold her head still, and
Laurel heard in his ragged breathing and the racing of
his heart beneath her ear the effort it was costing him to
keep passion at bay.

"If I kiss you, I'm going to make love to you," he
rasped. "I'm going to carry you into that bedroom and
make love to you on that bed. Every night this week I've
lain there, wondering. I want to *know*, Laurel! I want
to know if it was a dream or if it was really as wonderful as I remember it being.''

"I've wondered, too!" she cried, her words muffled
against his throat. "I've wondered for so long! But I'm
afraid to find out!''

Hearing her terrible ambivalence, Nathan tilted her
face toward his, and Laurel's knees weakened as her
eyes opened to meet the raw need and longing she found
in the depths of his turbulent gaze.

"Make love with me, Lauri," he whispered, watching her lips as his thumb grazed over them, tracing their
contours as they trembled open for him. "Make love
with me because you're as crazy as I am to be free of all
this damned wondering.''

"I want to," she breathed, her hands moving, un-
bidden, in a sensuous pattern back and forth over his
ribs. "I want to make love with you so much, but I
don't know if I could stand how bad it would hurt. I
don't know if I could stand hurting you again, afterward, when I have to...to go.''

"Listen to me, Laurel." His hands framing her face
tightened, and his eyes compelled her to hear his words.
"I want you to think about what I'm saying. We're both

hurting about as badly as a person can hurt. The worst has already happened. And neither of us has a single thing left to lose.''

But what could they possibly have to gain? Probably nothing. Perhaps a great deal. And she would never know if she wasn't willing to risk everything to find out.

Suddenly, in a quicksilver moment of the sort of stuff that faith is made of, the fear of discovering that her memories were lies was eclipsed by the intriguing prospect of creating a *new* memory—a present reality, a vibrant, living thing that contained all the possibilities for the future she and Nathan could breathe into it, together. The dread that she would be trapped once more by her all-consuming love for him paled beside the completely unique idea that there might be a different kind of love to be found here. A love that could last them a lifetime. And if it turned out that there was no future and that their lifetime together had, indeed, reached its end? Well then, at least she would know the full extent of what she was leaving behind. Yes. When she said goodbye on Sunday, when he sold St. John's Landing and this cottage along with it, let them *both* know exactly what it was they had lost.

Sensing her growing certainty, Nathan drew her pliant body against his until her senses were engulfed by the pounding of his heart, the trembling of his body. Her own body melted on a moan of pure yearning when his hands brought her hips into the cradle of his thighs and she knew the glorious, bold demand of his sex pressing against her.

"Lie with me," he urged softly. "Let me touch you and be inside of you. Let me feel you come apart in my arms, and hold me when I come apart in yours. Make love with me, Lauri, because, honest to God, I don't think I can let you go.''

"Don't," she whispered, gliding her hands behind his neck. "Don't let me go."

Her words and the promise inherent in them kept breaths and heartbeats in abeyance for the space of a few rapidly ticking seconds as they stood motionless, their gazes locked. Then, with nearly excruciating slowness, his head lowered until his parted lips touched hers.

In the next instant, their mouths melded in an explosion of need so violent that it tore groans from deep inside both of them. Their eyes closed, their mouths slanted, opening to join fully, both of them knowing that, at last, their wondering was at an end. The knowledge—the incredible, awesome relief—washed through them, bringing with it tears and a few breathless words.

"Again. Yes, kiss me again..."

"Oh, God, it's been so long...so long..."

Far too long. And the headlong way they went about making up for the time they had lost proved it. The kisses she scattered over his face were feverish and moist. His hands were nearly frantic as he fumbled to loosen the knot in the belt of her robe. The sounds they made were utterances of love—and one thickly muttered oath of satisfaction as the robe hit the floor and she was warm, bare flesh in his arms. His eyes raked over her, scalding and possessive, draining the strength from her legs. She wilted against him.

The distance to the bedroom was traversed in a few long strides, where he stood her beside the bed. Then her fingers became the clumsy ones as they opened the snap and unzipped his jeans. There was nothing clumsy,

though, about the way she slid her hands inside the
waistband and, finding nothing but denim between her
nakedness and his, leaned forward to press her breasts
against his chest as she pushed the jeans off him, drawing her fingers back up the length of his thighs.

Dark skin, white skin. Hard muscle, soft round
breasts. Trembling hands reaching out to touch, to
arouse, to slake a never-ending thirst to know the other's glowing flesh. And kisses—so many hungry, suc-
culent kisses. Lips that tugged and caressed, tongues
that reveled in a familiar and cherished sweetness. Two
beautiful long-limbed bodies, wrapped in each other's
arms, chest to breast, thigh to thigh, aching with a passion they could not hold inside.

White lace. White lightning. And a throaty, feminine sigh as he lowered her onto the bed and followed
her down, searing a path from shoulder to breast with
a mouth that was open and hot and carnal. Plucking,
teasing, nuzzling a nipple that puckered and tingled beneath his lips. Ravenous, devouring suckling of a nipple that swelled with pleasure inside his mouth.

White sheets. Black thunder as the lights blinked out
and questing, slender fingers grazed over a flat abdo-
men, traced a trembling course along an arresting length
of satin-sheathed steel, which pulsed and strained
within her grasp. His sharp, gasping intake of breath
was made against the smoothness of her throat. His
husky, dark words of eroticism were breathed against
her breast, her belly, the softness of her thigh and the
glistening, quivering folds of her womanhood.

White rain. White heat. Lightning blazing across the
sky as he lowered his body into her waiting arms.
Thighs opened and cradled lean hips. Hard male flesh,
heavy with need, parted the entrance to her welcoming

depths. And there came a moment of perilous wonder as eyes met and breath stood still. But the moment passed to the next, his name becoming a whispered prayer and hers a rumbled groan, when in one sure thrust, he brought them home.

Sweet tears. Salty kisses. Quiet, panting sobs of joy. Hands holding tight through the storm, as the rhythm of love began. This was the way it was meant to be. This aching, shuddering need. This trembling vulnerability. And the breathless, surging desire to surrender their bodies to the other—not to *make* love, but to let love be made between them until they were both possessed by it wholly. And all the years had not been wasted in wondering or waiting, for this was everything—and so much more—than any memory they had ever lived before.

Slow, knowing movements brought a keen, voluptuous pleasure. Long, smooth glides made their bodies slick and their pulses race. Hard, deep thrusts took them quickly to the limits of breath and strength and will. Then there was no will or thought or awareness beyond the moment. And the only words to be spoken were two lovers' names being chanted in the darkness, as their bodies dissolved in the act of becoming one.

One breath. One heartbeat. One hot, enchanted place where all sensation begins and ends. Where promises are kept and life is made. And where love binds two souls into one.

Chapter Nine

Morning brought with it countless golden sunbeams. They poured through the cottage window and across the snowy-white sheet that covered the two bodies entwined in sleep. Nathan stirred as the bright light teased his eyelids, causing them to squeeze shut, flicker indecisively and finally, reluctantly, open.

As his sleep-hazy eyes gradually focused, they came upon a sight that was both precious and beautiful, and thus he was rewarded for the small annoyance of being awakened so soon after having fallen asleep. With a guttural sound of contented lethargy, he shifted to bring his cherished feminine companion fully into a back-to-front embrace. She murmured faintly, and one fine-boned hand fluttered, as though to fend off the intruder, before settling in a light caress on the back of the larger hand that now engulfed the swell of her breast.

Nathan smiled, rubbing his face against the softness of his beloved's silky curls, breathing deeply of the musky-sweet scents that filled the room and anointed his body and hers. Yet he knew this was a stolen moment, one that had slight chance of lasting beyond the next heartbeat, and that tempered his pleasure a little. Enough, anyway, to make him glance at the bedside clock.

"Mmm...Nathan?"

"Hmm."

"What're you doing?"

"Waking you up."

"I'm so tir—"

"Lauri, it's time for breakfast."

"Hmm? Uh-uh. Had Breakfast. Eggs 'n' bacon. 'S good."

"That was supper, sweetheart. At midnight."

"Oh, well, you go ahead. I'll just...sleep. Oh, love... Oh, Nathan, that feels so good."

The easy sound of his chuckle buried in the curls behind her ear sent a shiver of warmth down Laurel's neck, across her shoulder and downward to her breast, where Nathan's fingertips enhanced the sensation a hundredfold. Arching her sleepy body against his hand in languid abandon, Laurel became slowly aware that her back was pressed against him from his chest to his thighs. A tiny smile formed on her lips as she snuggled deeper into his embrace. And then the smile softened into an expression that was purely sensual when she realized her movement had brought a certain easily sensitized part of her into stunning contact with the part of him that was so extraordinarily good at sensitizing. His hips moved suggestively, letting her know how fully prepared he was to take advantage of the situation.

She drew a shallow breath. "Nathan?"

"I want you again, Lauri. Now. In the daylight, when I can see you. But it's seven o'clock. When do you have to be at the conference this morning?"

As she turned slowly within the circle of his arms, Laurel's lashes fluttered open and her clear gray eyes gazed adoringly at him. His hair was sleep-tousled, his face heavily shadowed with a full day's growth of beard, and his chocolate-colored eyes were warm and glowing with the reawakened embers of passion. With the memory of the night past fresh in her mind and the pleasurably aching awareness of it lingering in her body, Laurel knew to the bottom of her soul that, for better or worse, she would be in love with Nathan Coltrane for the rest of her life.

"There's time," she said softly. "I don't have to be anywhere until nine."

Nathan lifted a finger to brush a stray curl off her cheek and tuck it behind her ear. "Are you sure? We were up most of the night."

For an answer, Laurel slid her thigh over his hip, arched her body and, with breathtaking ease, drew him into her. His eyes melted into pools of black; his hands guided her hips, and he pressed into her with a deep, unhurried deliberation, as though he might claim the stolen moment and hold it for eternity.

"God, I love you," he breathed.

"And I love you," she returned.

The sun continued to sketch lacy patterns on the lovers who watched each other's countenances change as passion grew... and peaked... and slowly receded.

Their morning greeting left time for hurried showers but no breakfast. When Nathan pulled the car to a stop in front of Clarkson's Lodgings, Laurel leaned across the seat to give him a quick kiss goodbye, but he was having none of it. Instead, he pulled her to him for a lusty farewell that left her breathless and eager for more.

"Mmm, that feels different." She nuzzled her cheek against his jaw. "No whiskers."

Drawing back, Nathan lowered his gaze to her chin and grimaced. "I guess I ought to apologize. You're probably going to spend the next twenty-four hours powdering your face and treating brush burns on at least ninety percent of your body."

"You're excused," she replied magnanimously. "Only remember, the next time a woman who adores you falls into your arms and says she going to die if she doesn't kiss you, tell her she'll have to wait while you go and shave."

"Yeah," he drawled. "I'll do that—right after I get this woman who adores me to promise she'll come back tonight and let me kiss her some more."

Laurel smiled, touching his lower lip with the tip of one finger. "Any woman who'd turn down an offer like that is a fool."

Nathan drew a deep breath, as though in relief, before he kissed her again. Laurel made no effort to resist, but she experienced a moment of uneasiness. Had he thought she would say no? *Should* she have said no? They had not talked about the rest of the week, much less what would come after it. But knowing she needed her attention focused and sharp for the day's activities, she was trying not to think about exactly what last night had meant—or what she was going to do about it.

"You have no respect for time, Nathan Coltrane," she whispered when their lips parted and her eyes opened slowly to meet his. "Besides which, you've ruined my morning discussion group. I'll be lucky if I can put two words together that make sense."

He grinned. "Keep looking like that, and you won't have to say anything. They'll know exactly what you're thinking."

"Oh, Lord," she groaned. "My reputation will be ruined. Let me go—quick!"

Still grinning, he released her, and she slipped out the door, leaning down before closing it to tell him, "I'll be through at five today. Shall I drive out, or do you want to pick me up?"

"I'll pick you up," he said. "I'm going to take this car back and get one that works. I'll call and leave a message about what time I'll be here."

"Okay." She tossed him a breathless "I love you" before closing the door and turning, prepared to race to her room.

The sight of her father standing at the guest-house entrance brought her to a dead halt. His head was tilted thoughtfully to one side as he took in her rain-wrinkled clothes, then looked at Nathan's car, which was pulling out into traffic. When his eyes met hers, his brows arched in question, she decided that circumstances spoke rather eloquently for themselves.

James cleared his throat with a pointed glance at his watch, and Laurel went into motion once more. "I know, I know," she mumbled, "I'm going to be late."

"Have lunch with me?" he asked.

Laurel nodded her agreement before rushing through the door, leaving her father staring pensively after her.

If there had been a happier morning in his life, Nathan could not remember it. He tried, halfheartedly, to refrain from feeling overly optimistic, but it was useless. His step as he walked down to the Landing's dock was far too buoyant. His movements as he unfurled *The Scallop*'s wet sails were too quick, too sure. And his whistle was much too bright as it bounced across the water and broke the peaceful stillness of the Landing's wooded banks. Indeed, the world seemed a thoroughly delightful place that morning for one reason alone: Lauri—*his* Lauri—had found her way into his arms last night. And he had absolutely no intention of letting her go, ever again.

The things Laurel had learned about her family left nothing to stand in their way. She had no reason to fear the Navy any longer, no reason to think of it—and, therefore, of him—as the enemy from whom she must protect herself in all ways and at all costs. And after last night, she would have to realize how unimportant geographical permanence was compared to a lifetime of love.

What would it be like, Nathan wondered, to be married to Laurel and not feel he was forcing her to endure a life she hated, without even being able to tell her why? Just imagining such a state was enough to make him feel as though he had finally lived down the transgressions of his youth and was standing at the brink of an entirely different future. Amazingly, he found he was able to think about the onerous conditions under which he and Laurel had begun their marriage and, for the first time ever, not experience a stab of guilt.

He had told her Uncle Jack had refused to pay his tuition. He had told her that if he didn't want to lose his place at Hopkins, he had to move quickly in asking the Navy for a scholarship. And those things had been true, in greater or lesser degrees. What was also true, but what he hadn't told her, were the things Uncle Jack had said the day he'd cut off his tuition support. And he had no intention of ever telling her.

Picking up a bucket, Nathan jumped into the run-about moored beside *The Scallop* and began to bail out the collected rainwater. As he worked, the memory of the words that had determined the last fifteen years of his life swam in his mind . . .

Dammit, Nathan! This is Laurel's doing. She's the one who encouraged these crazy notions of you being some damn lackey with a stethoscope around your neck. I truly thought a year of it would cure you, or I wouldn't have wasted the money. But I can see the girl's got you so bowled over, you're losing sight of who you are and everything I've taught you. I swear, boy, this could be thirty years ago, Curtis standing there where you are, telling me he's decided to seek a commission in the Navy. At least your mother had the common sense to try to talk him out of it, even if she did go off with him after all. But your Laurel hasn't had the advantages your mother had. And if you're going to take a woman from a lower class and try to make her fit into our way of life, you've got to know what's bound to happen. Those people are ambitious, and they're all out to prove their worth. But you're a Coltrane! You don't have to prove anything to anybody! Curtis, now, he let the idea of wearing a uniform and sailing the seas seduce him away from his proper future. Instead of staying here and helping me save the family from financial embarrassment—and things weren't so easy in those days—he had to go chasing off after rainbows. Now you want to do the same! A doctor! Bah! Dreams! That's all Curtis's exotic ideas were, and that's all yours are, too. Nothing but irresponsible, adolescent fanta-

sies. *Well, I'm not having it. I won't sit by and let you
make the same mistake your father made. You'll stay
here, where you belong, and put your mind to keeping
our interests productive. And you'll straighten out that
girl you married so she knows what's expected of her.
That's a big order, boy, and I expect if you apply yourself to it, you'll be too busy for daydreams about cutting and sewing on other people's body parts.''*

Thus the fight had begun and ended. Nathan wondered whether anything Laurel could have said to him
after Uncle Jack had made that speech would have
made a difference. He doubted it. At twenty-one, his
pride had demanded satisfaction. Jonathan Coltrane
had taken his last shot at his brother Curtis without
Curtis's son doing something about it. And the newly
wedded Nathan St. John Coltrane, thirteenth heir of the
grand old Annapolis family, was not about to let anyone insult his beloved bride. It had taken him about five
minutes—the time he spent stalking from Uncle Jack's
study at the big house to the cottage—to calculate the
precise way in which his honor could be satisfied.
Which, as Aunt Louise had noted, was to follow in his
father's footsteps.

It had seemed the perfect solution—join the Navy
and get them to send him to medical school. It had been
a way of demonstrating his allegiance to his father. It
had also been a way of removing Laurel from Uncle
Jack's presence and protecting her from ever finding
out that the man whose hospitality she'd enjoyed all her
life thought of her as nothing more than a self-seeking
social climber. Not incidentally, it had also been a way
of achieving his own goal; and when he had looked at
the matter objectively, there really *didn't* seem to be any
other way to do so.

It had taken perhaps another year—until the first time he'd had to go off on Naval Reserve duty—to realize what a mistake he had made. Why hadn't he been less impulsive? Why hadn't he tried to reason with Uncle Jack? Even if he hadn't been able to persuade his uncle to give him the money, there might have been other ways. Inconvenient perhaps, but not impossible. He could have waited a year and tried to get a scholarship from Hopkins. He could have tried to get one from some other medical school. He could have tried to persuade a bank to overlook his lack of collateral and his uncle's objectives and lend him the money. But by the time all these convoluted plans had formed in his mind, it was too late. He had committed fifteen years of his life to the U.S. Navy.

It was a hard way to grow up, learning to live with one's mistakes. He had done it by deciding that if he was going to be in the Navy, then, by God, he was going to make the best of it. And, by God, he had. The hardest part, though, had been bearing the burden of the truth alone, not being able to share with Laurel why it was they were living a life neither of them wanted. But even if he hadn't been sure it would have hurt her to know, he hadn't seen how it could help their disintegrating marriage to tell her he had let the ravings of a self-centered old bigot push him into bargaining away their future.

But now, thank God, Laurel would never have to know. It was history and sooner left forgotten. Uncle Jack was gone, and the cruel words he had spoken no longer held any power.

Nathan grinned. This was a new day, a new life. After January, he would no longer be in the Navy because he *had* to be but because he *wanted* to be, because he had made a place for himself that was as gratifying as any he could have hoped to make elsewhere. There was some pride in having accomplished so much in the face of the odds. He had given the Navy his best, and they had treated him well in return. He had no cause left to regret what he had done. Not anymore. Not now that he knew he had not lost Laurel and, in fact, could have another chance at loving her.

Tossing aside the bucket he had been using as a bailer, Nathan vaulted out of the boat and began striding back along the dock. When he reached the edge of the bank, though, he slowed to a stop. And there he stood for a moment, his feet spread wide, his hands planted on his hips, his gaze wandering over the woods, the quiet water—the splendor of the land gracing his home. It was with characteristic determination—but a great deal more pleasure than he had felt upon viewing the same scene several days earlier—that he began to formulate plans to secure his and Laurel's future. It was a future that was looking brighter with each passing second.

Laurel picked halfheartedly at her seafood salad as she listened to her father talk about the conference. The only thing on her mind was what to say to him when he asked her about Nathan; it was almost a letdown that he had not mentioned the topic, even in passing. And finally she could not stand the waiting any longer.

"All right, Dad." She dropped her fork, placed an elbow on the table and brought her forehead to rest on the back of her hand. "Are you going to ask me if I spent the night with Nathan or not? The answer is, yes."

When a full thirty seconds passed and her father had not responded, Laurel lifted her head to find him staring at her. His gaze was clear and unwavering as he spoke.

"I wasn't going to ask."

"I know."

"Do you want to talk about it?"

"I'm not sure."

"It's not over, is it?"

She could only shake her head.

He sighed. "I knew it the minute Nathan walked into the reception on Sunday."

Laurel's brows drew together in a frown. "You did?"

"Honey," her father began with an indulgent look, "it's been years since I've been in the same room with you and Nathan, but I haven't forgotten a moment of the experience. It was at Lilly's wedding, and I recall standing by the bar and noticing that people were watching the two of you with as much, if not more, interest than they were the bride and groom. 'My, what a magnificent couple,' they all said. And I thought I would burst with pride, because they were right. What they didn't say, but what was clear in their envious looks, was how obviously in love the two of you were. But then," he smiled a little, "that was no surprise to me, because I'd seen you together many times in the past. And, Laurel, that's what it was like Sunday evening—stepping into the past. Nathan walked into the room, the two of you looked at each other, and I suddenly felt as though I were standing in the back of the church on your wedding day, preparing to walk you down the aisle toward him."

Laurel felt a telltale blush creep into her cheeks, and she knew if she tried to speak, her voice would be a whisper.

James shook his head, not expecting a reply. "I'm certainly no expert on love, but a person would have to be blind not to recognize the love you and Nathan feel for each other. It's always been that way. When we left Spain you cried until your mother and I worried you'd be sick. I think Jonathan Coltrané and I shared the opinion that it would have been inhuman—immoral, almost—not to do everything we could to allow your friendship to continue, because Nathan talked of nothing but seeing you again from the day he arrived at St. John's Landing."

Toying with his coffee spoon, James concluded slowly, "When you left Nathan, I knew one of you must have done something truly devastating to the other. But whatever it was, it didn't kill the love, did it?"

Astounded once more by her father's keen observation, Laurel stared at him. "No," she murmured. "No, it didn't. We love each other very much."

Silence hung between them for a moment.

Then James said, "I always wondered how you felt about Nathan going to medical school on a Navy scholarship."

Laurel knew instantly that his words had been anything but casual—and that the time for pretense was past. Nevertheless, she had to drop her gaze as she answered. "I didn't have a lot of choice in the matter."

There was another flash of silence before James burst out, "Don't tell me he took the scholarship without telling you?"

She shook her head quickly. "No. It wasn't like that." Staring at the napkin she was methodically folding and unfolding on the table before her, she explained, "You remember, we were married during

semester break, my second year of college. Nathan was
halfway through his first year in medical school. Two
weeks afterward, we were getting ready to go back to
Baltimore for the spring semester. Nathan went to say
goodbye to Uncle Jack, and the two of them had a
quarrel."

"Was that unusual?" James asked. "I understood
their relationship to be somewhat stormy. Jonathan always struck me as a rather rigid individual, set in his
ways."

"That's putting it politely," Laurel replied dryly.
"And the older Nathan got, the more the two of them
fought. Honestly, Dad, most of the time I couldn't
blame Nathan for losing his temper with Uncle Jack.
You can't imagine how pious the man could sound
when he was instructing Nathan on his responsibilities
as a Coltrane—or saying how he didn't want Nathan to
grow up to be *footloose*, like his father." She frowned.
"You know, sometimes I think Nathan went into the
Navy for no other reason than to prove he *was* his father's son."

James's voice was shocked. "Curtis? Footloose?
Jonathan couldn't have been serious! I remember Curtis as one of the most dedicated, hardworking individ-
uals I've ever known. In many ways, it's true—Nathan
is like him."

"Believe me," Laurel returned, "Uncle Jack was serious. He thought it was a dreadful mistake his brother
made, going into the Navy instead of upholding the
family tradition, so to speak. But it's purely speculation on my part as to whether his attitude had anything
to do with Nathan taking the Navy scholarship."

"So, if that's not the reason, why *is* he in the Navy?"
James asked, perplexed.

Laurel let out a sigh. "Because as a result of the fight I mentioned, Uncle Jack refused to pay his tuition. We'd always known he didn't want Nathan to be a doctor. He thought it was frivolous. Unnecessary. He wanted him to stay at the Landing and take over the yacht brokerage. But he paid the first year's tuition, and we naively thought he would keep paying it."

She paused, shaking her head slowly. "Whatever the two of them said to each other that day must have been the last straw. It was February. Too late to apply to Hopkins for a scholarship. And there wasn't a bank in the world that would have loaned Nathan money, given the clout his uncle had and the fact that Nathan himself had no collateral. The deadline for applying for the Navy scholarship was March first, and it seemed the only thing left to do. I couldn't have lived with myself if I'd stood in his way and he'd been forced to give up his plans."

"That would have been a real tragedy," James agreed. "But those were terrible circumstances for having to make such an important decision."

"Yes, they were," Laurel conceded. "Yet, I suppose if I'd ever believed it would really happen, I might not have let Nathan convince me so easily."

At her father's puzzled look, she explained, "I was certain that Nathan and Uncle Jack would mend their fences. But when the tuition bill came, they were barely speaking. I begged Nathan to let me talk to Uncle Jack and try to get him to change his mind, but he refused. Absolutely. Said there was no way he'd let me fight his battles—that no *man* would allow his wife to go begging for money, especially from the person who'd refused it in the first place."

James shot a look heavenward. "Ah, the foolishness of male pride."

"Well," she put in dryly, "he might have been foolish, but he wasn't the only one. I didn't think I had any choice, either. I'd agreed to his applying for the scholarship, so I had to let him accept it."

"Only to find you couldn't live with the decision."

Unconsciously, Laurel's hand clenched into a fist around the napkin that was, by now, becoming frayed. But rather than reply to her father's conclusion—which was, so obviously, the truth—she let a sardonic note creep into her voice. "Oh, Nathan was certainly bright and breezy about it. I can still hear him saying, 'You'll see, Lauri. It'll be fun. Traveling is an adventure. We'll make it work!' And he certainly did *his* best to make it work—arranging our moves even though he hates details and paperwork, helping me study even when he was exhausted. I don't have to tell you what it was like—you know as well as I do. And Nathan wouldn't let me do *any* of it. It got so that I felt . . . well, almost like another piece of baggage. Useless! But he was so wonderful and enthusiastic, I thought I must be crazy not to be happy! When a man does ninety percent of the housework, then hires a housekeeper to take over while he's on sea duty, how do you tell him you'd rather have hired her yourself, or even done the work yourself—but most of all, that you at least would have liked to have been consulted?"

Laurel shook her head. "Nathan kept saying it was going to be okay. But, Dad, it wasn't okay, and both of us knew it. I left him because I was certain we'd all but destroyed each other trying to *make* it be okay, when it was just never going to be."

Laurel fell silent, wondering what use there was in dredging up the past. Her father could not solve the problem. Neither could she, yet she felt an almost desperate need to try. Having realized that nothing would ever stop her from loving Nathan, she was having visions of her life stretching out before her, long and empty.

Her father's next comment indicated that he, too, understood her dilemma, although the solution he suggested was the last one Laurel would have expected to hear from him.

"Nathan's payback time must be about up."

Her eyes riveted on his. Slowly, she nodded. "He's got until January. But he's planning to accept the contract they've offered him."

James grimaced a little. "I can't believe I'm saying this, but have you considered asking if he'd be willing to change his mind?"

Laurel did not say how many times the thought had occurred to her that morning. She offered her father the same argument she had been offering herself. "How can I, Dad? I'd feel awful asking him to give up his career at this point." Her lips tightened. "He didn't want to be in the Navy, but it's clear he's become quite committed to it."

"And you think he's become so committed that he wouldn't give it up if he knew he could have you back?" James raised one dark brow. "Perhaps you're underestimating your own importance, Laurel."

With her eyes fixed once more on the napkin, which she had succeeded in mutilating, Laurel spoke in a tiny voice. "I guess I'm afraid to find out. He chose the Navy over me once before."

"Come now," her father admonished gently. "Isn't that being a bit childish? The man did what he thought he had to do."

She blushed. "Maybe. Sometimes I do feel like a child—or at least an adolescent—around Nathan. It's like I got stuck at the point in time when we married and haven't been able to move past it. I guess I never understood how he could have loved me and yet asked me to do something he knew I . . ."

"Hated," James finished for her.

It was foolish to deny it. They had been talking around it for the past fifteen minutes. "Please, don't think I'm blaming you," she said.

"It wouldn't surprise me if you did." He shrugged. "But I'll take whatever absolution you're willing to hand out."

"Actually," Laurel began in a bitter tone, "after our talk the other morning, I think the blame more appropriately rests on Mom and my own childish fantasy. I hated the Navy because she told me *she* hated it and presented it to me as the worst of all evils. And when you get right down to it, it isn't really the Navy I hate. It's moving! Lord, if I never have to do it again, it'll be too soon!"

She shook her head. "But the point is, Nathan *knew* how I felt, yet he let something as silly as a fight with Uncle Jack compromise our future. No matter how I've tried to look at it, I've never been able to accept that. I know he was young—and he's always been somewhat impulsive—but I still don't believe anything they said to each other could have been so awful that it couldn't have been cleared up. He wouldn't even tell me what they fought over! What could it have been that was so irreparable? For heaven's sake, in spite of everything, it was always clear they *loved* each other!''

There was a moment of tense silence, during which Laurel bit her lower lip to keep it from trembling.

"You and Nathan love each other, too," James said quietly. "But you haven't spoken in three years."

Laurel's eyes closed tightly.

"People say and do hideous things to the ones they love," he added. "You know that as well as I."

"I've been afraid to talk to him," she whispered. "Afraid he'd talk me into believing again that it could work out." Her eyes opened, and she met her father's gaze with a pleading look. "Dad, when I'm with Nathan, I don't seem to be able to think clearly. I lose sight of my own needs, because—" She faltered in the effort of trying to put her fears into words. "It seems as though Nathan knows me so well, that he must know what I need as well as I do. When we were children, a lot of the time he seemed to know *better* than I. I've been afraid he'd convince me that our life together could be wonderful if I'd only let it be, when the truth is, I was miserable before. I want—" Her voice broke. "Oh, Dad, I want a home! One that doesn't move at the whim of the U.S. Navy. I know it sounds like a frivolous reason to end a marriage—"

"No, it doesn't," he interrupted. "I lived in the same house until the day I left to go to the Naval Academy. There are things about that kind of security that a service life can't give you, and I can understand why you'd want those things. But have you considered the fact that the worst is over? Nathan's in a very different position now than he was ten or fifteen years ago. It might not be so bad. I know the model you had was far from idyllic. But really, Laurel, not *all* Navy marriages are predestined to fail. Look at Lilly. She's happy as a lark!''

At the mention of her sister's name, Laurel's teeth clenched. Her father immediately noticed her hardened expression.

"You don't believe Lilly's happy?"

She shrugged. "I don't have any reason to think she's not. Yes, I suppose she's happy enough."

James sighed rather disgustedly. "But you're waiting for the ax to fall on her, too. For someone who prides herself on her objectivity, I think you're being awfully judgmental. Have you and she ever talked about any of this?"

Reluctantly, Laurel answered with a little shake of her head.

"I thought not," he remarked pointedly. "You wouldn't dream of burdening Lilly with your troubles or asking for her opinion—or expect her to offer you any thoughts you hadn't already had on the subject."

"Dad, please." Laurel shifted uncomfortably.

Her father was unapologetic. "You might try talking to her. *Ask* her if she's happy. And try believing her when she says she is."

"I probably won't have to ask," Laurel mumbled. "When I see her next week, I'm sure I'll be bombarded from all sides with happiness."

A concerned look appeared on James's brow. "My, how bitter you are. I'm so sorry, honey. I had no idea it was that bad."

Was she bitter? Laurel wondered. She had not been aware of it, but she was beginning to see that hiding her feelings from the world had meant she had hidden them even more thoroughly from herself. It seemed they had all come tumbling out at once, and it was taking every ounce of energy she possessed to survive the violent shifts of the last few days.

Somehow, before she saw Nathan that evening, she had to find her equilibrium or risk repeating history. For as uncertain as *she* might be, one thing Nathan had never been was ambivalent. Chances were excellent that he knew exactly what he wanted. And after last night, she would have to be witless not to know that what he wanted was her. The question was, what else did he want? And could she live with it?

Chapter Ten

Laurel hurried from the Academy to Clarkson's Lodgings that afternoon to find a note from Nathan saying he would pick her up at seven-thirty. With a tiny sigh, she noted that it was only five-fifteen. Telling herself she was grateful for the time to get ready, she spent the better part of an hour "relaxing" in a hot bath.

In fact, relaxing turned into a critical study of her body—a body many women might have envied but that Laurel feared was not what it once had been. She got out of the tub, wondering if Nathan had noticed the changes three years and her dubious eating habits had caused—and if he had found the changes objectionable.

As she stood in front of the mirror applying what little makeup she wore, it pleased her to see that the dark circles under her eyes were gone and that her complexion was looking much rosier—even if her cheeks were a bit too hollow. A glance at her nails, however, sent her scurrying for an emery board and a bottle of polish. Once satisfied with her diligent efforts to improve their appearance, she unwrapped the towel from her head and picked up her hair dryer.

Five minutes later, when she realized that, instead of drying her hair, she'd been staring at it and wondering how long it would take to grow back down to her waist, she knew it was hopeless. She could tell herself from now 'til doomsday that she was a mature, independent woman who was fully in control of her life, but when it came to Nathan Coltrane, she would always feel like a young girl in love for the first time—excited by the thought of him, eager to please him and woefully unable to keep her love a secret from him. Or, apparently, from anyone else.

As she slipped into an indigo denim shirtdress and did up the buttons that ran down the narrow skirt, she decided that maybe it wasn't such a bad thing to feel this way. At least, it wouldn't be bad if she thought there was a chance it might work out, without her having to sacrifice everything else that was important to her.

Could she do it? Could she go back to Nathan if he asked her and learn not only to accept but actually to enjoy Navy life? She was closer to thinking it possible than she ever had been before. But what if it weren't? She could not put them through another divorce!

Flopping down on the edge of the bed to pull on a pair of low-heeled red sandals that matched the big leather belt cinched about her waist, she stopped short to consider an even more frightening question: Did she dare expect that Nathan might give up the Navy?

It wasn't as though he would be giving up medicine. And after all, she was willing to resign from her position on the negotiating team, if it meant they could have a home and family together. Last night, she had *been* home—lying in St. John and Elizabeth's cottage, wrapped in the arms of a man who was the proud issue of their boldest dreams. She knew as surely as she knew she loved Nathan that he belonged to St. John's Landing and that she belonged there with him.

But Nathan thought he belonged in the Navy and that the Landing didn't mean anything to him anymore. At least, that's what he had told her. Had he really meant it? Could last night have changed his mind? Was it foolish to hope that building a future with her might mean more to him than anything the Navy had to offer?

Common sense told Laurel it would be wise to guard against feeling too optimistic as a result of one night of lovemaking, yet the very thing that had made the night so special was that she *hadn't* been guarded—and she did not want to feel as though she needed to be. How long, though, could she go on allowing herself to be so intensely vulnerable to him?

Not long, she knew, before her heart and her conscience would require some commitment between them.

The questions whirled in her head, begging answers she did not have and making her so restless that the spacious bedroom suddenly felt like a tiny box; she thought she would go out of her mind before seven-thirty finally arrived. When the phone rang at seven-fifteen, she snatched up the receiver, praying it wasn't Nathan calling to say he would be late.

"Laurel? Did I catch you at a bad time? You sound harried."

At the sound of her sister's voice, Laurel immediately tensed. "I'm fine," she said. "Is something wrong?"

"Good grief, you *are* harried!" Lilly declared. "You usually wait at least two or three minutes before you ask me that. No, nothing's wrong. Everything's wonderful. I was calling to tell you Rebecca and I are home from the hospital. I guess it feels funny, your not being here with us."

Laurel frowned, knowing as she spoke that she was overreacting. "You're sure everything's going okay? Do you need me sooner?"

"No, of course not." Lilly laughed softly. "We're doing great, but I'm used to you being around for major events like this. You've spoiled me rotten."

"And loved every minute of it," Laurel assured her.

"I'm glad." Lilly sighed. "But you'd think I'd have grown up by now, wouldn't you?"

With her father's words echoing in her mind, Laurel's mouth twisted a little in self-mockery. "I don't think that's the problem," she said softly. "I think you're already grown-up and you've only been keeping it a secret so I wouldn't feel useless."

"Never," Lilly declared. "You're never going to be useless to me. Besides, you'd know in a second if I really felt that way. I've never been able to lie to you."

The remark was too close to being the answer she most needed to hear from her sister, and Laurel could not resist asking, "Lil, that's true, isn't it? You'd never try to hide it from me if something were wrong, would you?"

There was a brief silence. Then Lilly's startled voice blurted out, "Laurel, that's the craziest thing I've ever heard you say. You know darned well you're the first person I run to at the slightest hint of trouble."

"I'm sorry," Laurel said quickly, glad Lilly could not see the color she felt rising in her cheeks. "Forget I asked."

"You realize, you've got it exactly backwards," her sister went on. "You're the one who's always protected me from the harsh, cruel world—and from the dreadful burden of hearing about *your* troubles."

"You think I should give it up?"

"I wish you would."

Laurel was amazed at how easy it was to let go of her picture of Lilly as a little girl who needed her to be invincible and to replace it with one of the two of them as women who loved each other as sisters and as friends. She could only wonder why she had not done it years before.

"All right," she said. And taking the first, frightening step toward this new relationship, she added, "When I see you next week, I swear, I'll bore you to tears with the longest, saddest story of star-crossed lovers you've ever heard."

Her sister wasn't fooled for a second. "You and Nathan?"

"Do you know any others?"

"Oh, Laurel, I knew it was bad," Lilly whispered. "That's why I called, really. You sounded so strange the other night on the phone, I was worried about you. You *have* been seeing him this week, haven't you?"

Laurel glanced at the clock, noted that it read seven-twenty-five and replied honestly, "I'm doing more than seeing him. I spent the night with him last night, and I'm going to spend another one with him tonight—and I'll probably spend tomorrow night, too."

"Probably?"

"Hmm."

"Laurel, are you okay?"

"Of course. I'm fine. I mean, I'm *not* fine. That is—" She sighed in frustration. "Oh, Lilly, I don't know how I am! Maybe I'm wonderful, and maybe tomorrow I'll be the happiest I've ever been in my life. And maybe I'm about to become the most miserable human being you'd ever care to meet. I don't know! But don't ask me to explain it now. Nathan's picking me up, and there's not anywhere near enough time to tell you all of it."

"Laurel!"

"I'm sorry. I guess I should have waited to say anything, but...well, you asked."

It was Lilly's turn to sigh in frustration, but her tone was gentle. "You *will* tell me all of it when you get here, won't you—if I don't die of curiosity before then?"

Laurel smiled. "You'll be too busy taking care of Rebecca and sleeping to even think about it."

"You've got to be kidding. Besides, the woman Stan hired to help out is a dream. I haven't had to— Hey!"

Lilly's sudden exclamation cut Laurel off as she was about to say she had to hang up.

"Why don't you ask Nathan if he wants to come down with you next week? Stan and I would love to see him. Gosh! Christopher and Leslie would go crazy over him!"

"Oh, Lil, I don't know." Laurel's brows knitted in a frown.

"Well, you think about it," Lilly suggested. "If it seems like a good idea, the invitation's open."

Laurel thought about little else as she hung up the phone and walked down the stairs. And she thought about it as she left the guest house and looked up and down the street for Nathan's car. Then, remembering he had said he was going to get a different one, she stopped looking and focused her attention on the possibility of extending her time with him beyond the next two days. She was debating the pros and cons as she stood, frowning at a nail on which she had already managed to chip the polish, and didn't hear the horn beeping two yards away at the curb. The sound of Nathan's voice got her attention, though.

"Sorry I'm late."

Laurel's head snapped up, the butterflies instantly fluttering in her stomach and her frown dissolving into a soft, teasing smile as he came toward her. "You wouldn't want me to think I was being picked up by the wrong man, would you?" she asked as her eyes drank in the sight of him in dark linen slacks and a blue and white striped shirt that was open at the collar.

"Hey, now," he said, his arm encircling her waist to guide her toward the curb. "I've gotten better. Really. I was early the other day, wasn't I? And I was here yesterday in time to catch you before you left."

"Well..."

"I haven't been late for my shift at the hospital once the whole time I've been at Jacksonville."

"You're joking."

"Uh-uh."

"I'm... impressed!" Laurel stopped short, her attention having shifted to the sleek Mercedes sedan to which Nathan had led her. "Don't tell me this is the only car the rental place had left."

"Oh, no," Nathan said, holding the door as she slid in. "But this was all they had in *silver*—and I wanted one that matched your eyes."

Laurel shot him a look that questioned his sanity. Then, seeing the grin flirting at the corners of his mouth, she laughed.

When Nathan had walked around and gotten in behind the wheel, she returned the quick greeting he had planted on her lips, then asked, "Why *are* we riding in such luxury?"

"Do we need an excuse?"

"No, I suppose not."

"But I've got one. I'll tell you over dinner. Where would you like to eat?"

"How about Chinese carryout at the cottage?"

He raised one skeptical brow. "How do you feel about cold egg rolls for breakfast? That's about when we'd get around to eating them."

"You're probably right," Laurel grumbled, her lips curving into a smile that was partly shy, partly alluring and a little uncertain.

"You've already missed one meal today you couldn't afford to miss," Nathan continued. "When did you start losing weight, anyway?"

She bristled instantly. "There's nothing wrong with my weight."

"Nothing that ten pounds wouldn't cure."

"Did you miss them last night?"

The look he gave her was both hot and tender. "Lauri, I'm being concerned, not critical. The only thing I missed last night was sleep, and you know it."

Laurel couldn't resist asking, "Not even my hair?"

"Well..."

"I knew it. You *do* hate it."

"I do *not* hate it."

"Keep saying it, and you might believe it."

Nathan sighed. "I guess you're right. In fact, last night when you came out of the shower wrapped up in my robe, with your hair all full of damp curls that smelled like my shampoo, I thought to myself, 'Hmph. Ridiculous. A grown woman with all those wispy things fluttering around her face.' And I sure didn't like having them tangled around my fingers when I kissed you that first time. Uh-uh. They're just too damned soft." Wagging a finger at her, he turned a corner one-handed and continued. "And this morning? Well! Before I woke you up? When I was lying there, holding you? I spent a long time wondering where those silly, soft curls came from that kept rubbing themselves against my face. You never had curls before." His frown was ominous. "They're awfully ticklish, you know, when you manage to drag them all over my stomach and thighs and... Well, they tickle. That's all. And I don't know if I can stand much of that. And one more thing. I've been thinking a lot about how I'm probably going to hate having those curls get in the way tonight—when my head's next to yours on the pillow. When we're making love, and I'm trying to whisper in your ear... When I'm inside of you... Yeah..." Nathan sighed again. "You're probably right, Lauri. I must hate them. Can't imagine what made me think they were really kind of pretty."

With her lips parted in sensual wonder, Laurel stared across the small distance that separated her from Nathan.

His eyes caught hers. "Convinced?"

Laurel blinked once and nodded, all the looks of horror he'd given her hair evaporating into the ambiguous past. She must have been mistaken. Or, the thought came, he had done it to her again: talked her into believing something that wasn't true.

Embarrassed by her own skepticism, Laurel wondered why on earth Nathan would go to such lengths to convince her that he liked her haircut if he did not. But her cynical side offered an immediate response: He'd do it because he had always adhered to the principle that you could make *anything* be true if you said it often enough and with enough conviction. It wasn't that he lied; he simply thought the way to deal with reality when it was less than desirable was to believe with all your heart that things were, or could become, exactly as you wished.

Laurel couldn't determine if that was what Nathan was doing now, but the very fact that she couldn't worried her. Her hair was a small matter. Their future was not. When the crunch came, would she be able to hold her ground, if it turned out she and Nathan did not agree?

One thing was certain: If his means of persuasion continued to be this provocative, she was in trouble. Even at that moment, wondering whether she had been very nicely conned, her body was alive with response to his erotic verbal foreplay.

In the end, Nathan chose the restaurant, and they went to McGarvey's on Market Place at the City Dock. Laurel discovered that having missed breakfast and, for all practical purposes, lunch, she was ravenously hungry. Nathan teased her when she ordered spareribs and a Caesar salad for two, but that didn't hinder her enjoyment of the meal. And in order to prevent her confused thoughts from driving her crazy during dinner, she kept the conversation light, regaling Nathan with stories about her student negotiators.

Over coffee she asked, "So, are you going to tell me about your new penchant for big, expensive cars?"

"*Big* is the operative word," Nathan replied. "You know I'm not comfortable in anything smaller for more than twenty miles. What time do you want to leave on Sunday?"

It took two seconds for Laurel's pulse rate to shift to high gear. "Around ten. But, Nathan, you don't have to—"

"Do you have to take your Dad to the airport?"

"No, he'll be staying for another week. But, Nathan—"

"I'm curious as hell, you know."

She stared blankly. "About what?"

"About where you're living. Is it an apartment?"

"I bought a condo in Foggy Bottom. But, Nathan, I don't know if this is such a good idea. I mean, I won't really have time to do anything but check in at the office and pay some bills. I promised Lilly I'd be there Tuesday."

He looked at her strangely. "I'm not expecting you to entertain me. How is Lilly, anyway? Have you talked to her since Tuesday night?"

Laurel frowned. His adroit switch in topic could not have been better timed. "She called earlier this evening. Everything's fine."

Nathan shook his head a little, his expression wistful as he picked up his coffee cup. "It's still hard to picture her running after three kids. I remember her at our wedding, trying to act grown-up as your maid of honor. All eyes and giggles and whispers."

"She was only fifteen," Laurel reminded him, realizing she was rapidly losing control of the conversation.

"Were you planning to fly to Norfolk?"

"Uh-huh."

"Do you think Lilly will mind my driving down with you?"

Laurel jerked to attention. "Oh, Nathan, I don't know. She just got home from the hospital—"

He waved off her protest with a casual gesture. "We can call her tomorrow and find out. I'd like to see her and Stan—and meet the angel and the hellion you've told me about, not to mention the new addition. And Laurel—" his gaze locked with hers "—it's a four-hour drive to Norfolk. I want to spend the time with you."

She wanted to spend the time with him, too, but her head was spinning with little, dizzying waves of fear that made her very cautious. He was acting with the best of intentions, she reasoned. It would be peevish—cruel, almost—to argue with him about this. She wanted to argue, though. She wanted to say he had no right to rearrange her life for her. She wanted to say she was not going anywhere with him—not another single step— until she knew she could count on being with him for the rest of her life.

The closest she came to voicing her feelings was to mumble a qualified, "Well, we'll see."

On the ride to the Landing, Laurel decided she was being exceptionally unfair. Even after last night, it was absurd to expect Nathan to change his entire life without giving him a chance to think about it. The world was not going to come to an end in the next two days. It would be good for them to have some relaxed time together after the conference was over. Besides, Lilly had told her to bring Nathan along—a point Laurel was well aware she had not mentioned. She would mention it, though, as soon as it seemed appropriate.

Thus, having rationalized away her anxieties, Laurel started down the path to the cottage at Nathan's side with a growing sense of pleasant anticipation of the night to come. His arm around her shoulders was strong, and the heat from his body warmed her where they were pressed together, sides to hips, as they walked. The silence between them was peaceful, intimate.

When they closed the door of the cottage behind them, Nathan pulled her into his arms for a long, tender kiss, and Laurel gave herself to the moment, and to him, entirely. The kiss ended with a soft, moist sound of parting lips that made Laurel sigh. She rested her head against Nathan's chest, content to hold him and to be held by him. His hand on the back of her waist moved in slow motion while the thumb of his other hand caressed her cheek, his fingers threaded through her hair as he held her head against him. She could hear his heartbeat, strong and clear and steady.

"I've got something to give you." Nathan's voice was quiet in the darkness.

"Hmm." Laurel nuzzled her face against his neck. "Can't it wait until morning?"

She could hear the smile in his reply. "It probably could, but I'd rather it didn't." Then, brushing her hair once with his lips, he pushed her away gently. "Let me get the light."

The room brightened, and Laurel followed, curious, as Nathan crossed to the desk. He picked up something and turned to hand it to her.

"What is it?" she asked, realizing as she took the object that it was a wooden box. She examined its half-octagonal shape and noted, "Its a lap desk—a very old one."

"Right," Nathan confirmed. "Uncle Jack used to keep it in his safe. Since he died, Ted Gilliam's had it, but I got it from him today to give to you."

Laurel ran a hand over the inlaid top of the oak and pine box. "It's lovely," she began a little hesitantly. "But why has it been in a safe? I wouldn't think—"

"Open it."

Not having any idea what to expect, Laurel went to the couch and sat down with the box on her lap. Slowly, she lifted the lid to look inside. At first what she found only confused her further: folded papers—old ones, surely, for some were crumbling at the edges and all were yellowed with age. She chose one of the less ancient-looking ones and unfolded it carefully.

The letter from Captain Jason Coltrane, Army of the Potomac, was dated June 27, 1863, and read,

My dearest Olivia,
Tomorrow we shall begin our march north into Pennsylvania. The men are restless and eager to reach our destination—a small seminary town called Gettysburg...

With an almost mystical feeling of anticipation making her hands cold, Laurel refolded the letter and reached for another. This time she discovered she held an official document, signed by the rector of St. Anne's Church, proclaiming the marriage of Suzanne Curtis Clemmons to Nathaniel Elder Coltrane on the fourth day of September, 1816. Below the rector's signature was a long list of witnesses, all of whom laid claim to the name Coltrane either by birth or marriage.

"I don't understand," Laurel said as she glanced at several other documents marking milestones in the lives of Nathan's ancestors. She started to speak again, but she came to a paper that raised goose bumps on her arms and, for a time, made speech impossible.

The paper was yellowed and the ink badly faded, but Laurel held it closer and was able to decipher portions of the ancient document, which began, "Last Will and Testament of St. John Coltrane, 1703," and which ended, "...for all future generations...this land so loved and dear to my heart...forever, St. John's Landing."

Wide-eyed, Laurel turned to Nathan, who had come to sit beside her on the couch. Her hushed whisper reflected both awe and confusion. "Nathan, I don't— Why are you giving me these things? I know you said the Landing doesn't mean anything to you anymore, but these papers are priceless! Surely, they must mean—"

"It was a lie." He stopped her with a large hand placed over one of hers. "St. John's Landing means everything to me you said it should. It's my heritage. It gives meaning to my name beyond what I'll ever be able to give it myself. And the thought of losing it has been driving me crazy."

"Oh, Nathan, I knew—"

His fingertips pressed gently against her lips. "But it hasn't driven me anywhere near as crazy as believing I'd lost you. The other night, when you asked me why I was selling the Landing, I didn't know you still loved me. I couldn't tell you I was selling it because I couldn't think of any other way to forget you."

"No!" Laurel's cry was horrified. "Nathan, you can't do it! I can't *let* you do it!"

He shook his head quickly. "Sweetheart, I'm not going to do it. I told Ted Gilliam today to stop negotiations with the Historical Society."

"Oh, thank God," she breathed, the tension draining out of her in a tiny moan.

"Lauri, look at me." The backs of his fingers stroked upward along her throat to lift her chin and turn her face toward his. "I came home to say goodbye to my memories of you. But it turned out that, instead of memories, I was faced with the real thing. And instead of goodbye—" his thumb brushed her lips "—it seems like we've been saying hello. Am I wrong, sweetheart? Do you want to say goodbye to me again?"

"Dear Lord, no!" Laurel laid a hand against his face. "Nathan, I never *wanted* to say goodbye to you! I love you so much. So very much!"

His fingers wrapped themselves around her wrist, and he turned his head to place an ardent kiss in her palm. "Lauri." He spoke thickly, his lips moving against her skin. "God, it's been a nightmare without you. The worst was coming home last fall. Everywhere I looked, I saw you. Every room in the house had some memory of you attached to it. And this place! I couldn't even make myself come inside."

With a whimper, Laurel told him, "I'd have died if I'd found out you'd sold the Landing because of me. I wouldn't have been able to bear thinking I'd ruined your home for you."

"You haven't ruined my home, sweetheart. You've made it come alive again." His hand found hers where it rested on the wooden box. "Now I want to make it come alive for you."

Laurel couldn't help the surge of blind hope that made her breath catch in her throat as her gaze dropped to their entwined hands.

"I know how much having a home means to you," Nathan began. "And I know how you feel about St. John's Landing. In a way, the contents of this box represent the very heart of the Coltrane legacy. And since you're the only woman who ever has—or ever could—hold my heart, I want you to have it. I want you to know that as long as this house and this land is here, you'll never be without a home. I swear it. You said Monday you wouldn't let me give the Landing to you, but will you take it now, Lauri? Will you let me give it to you to share with me?"

"Yes! Oh, Nathan, *yes*!" And wondering how she ever could have doubted him, Laurel threw her arms around his neck and began strewing kisses across his face with elated abandon.

Not attempting to hold her off, Nathan still found it necessary to put in, "Do you understand what I'm really asking? Are you saying yes, you'll marry me?"

"Tomorrow! Next week! Tonight would be better!"

With a deep and ragged breath, he hastily put the box aside, then pulled Laurel to her feet and wrapped her in his arms, covering her mouth with his in a burst of relief and passion.

For Laurel's part, the moment could have dissolved into lovemaking without another word spoken, but there were things Nathan felt compelled to discuss.

Dragging his lips across her cheek, he confessed, "I was afraid you'd want to think about it. Or at least wait until I got back from Deep Freeze. I didn't think I'd be able to stand being there without knowing you'd be waiting for me in Jacksonville."

Laurel leaned back enough to lock her gaze with his. "I'll be there," she whispered.

"We'll need a bigger place than the one I've got now," he told her, his eyes alight with enthusiasm. "It's a one-bedroom apartment and ugly as sin. We'll look for a house with a yard."

"If you really think we need to bother, I don't mind looking ahead of time."

"No. I don't want you having to do it alone. We'll work it out when I get there. Oh, Lauri—" he hugged her tightly "—Jacksonville's not a bad assignment. It'll be a wonderful place for us to start again."

Laurel laughed softly as she replied, "I'm sure it will be. But it wouldn't matter if it was Rota, Spain."

Nathan grinned. "You know darn well, no Navy wife in her right mind wants her husband assigned to Rota."

"Oh, I don't know," she scoffed. "Spain was pretty good to me. It gave me you. And besides, as long as I know the Landing is here waiting for us, I can stand anything for six months."

The light in Nathan's eyes flickered with a hint of uncertainty. "Six months?"

Instinctively, Laurel responded to his tone, her own voice becoming hesitant. "Yes. Until January. When your payback time is up."

She knew the instant the words were out of her mouth that the past five minutes had been a dreadful mistake. The look on Nathan's face alone was enough to make her stomach clench into a sickening knot.

"Laurel—" He swallowed, hard. "I haven't changed my mind about signing the contract. Did you think I had?"

Chapter Eleven

Laurel's answer to Nathan's question was written in the ghostly pallor of her skin and the wounded look in her eyes.

His voice pierced the cloud of disillusionment and pain that had descended over her.

"Lauri?"

"I don't understand." She spoke in a hoarse whisper. "You just gave me... You told me you wanted to share your home with me. Now you're saying we aren't going to live in it?"

"God, I didn't realize..." Nathan's voice trailed off, his fingers digging into her shoulders. "But the Landing will be here! Don't you see?"

She shook her head. "No, I guess I don't. How is its being here going to make a difference to me?"

"It will if you let it!" Shaking both of them in his urgency, he went on. "It's always made a difference to me. That's why I never cared where the Navy sent me. I always knew the Landing was here if I needed it. And I knew someday it would be mine and that I'd live here again. I carried it in my heart, and it didn't *matter* what house or what city—even what country—I was living in. This was home! Oh, Lauri, I couldn't give it to you before, when it might have helped the most. It wasn't mine to give. But it is now, and I want it to be yours, too.''

Laurel's gaze dropped from Nathan's until she was staring fixedly at his chest, which was rising and falling with the rapid pace of his breathing. "You mean, you want the Landing to be mine to—to think about when I'm feeling lonely or . . . in need of comfort.''

He nodded. "Hopefully, you won't be, but, well, yes.''

"How long is someday?''

"What?''

She raised her eyes to his. "You said you knew you'd live here again *someday*. When is someday going to come?''

Clearly, her question threw him. He cast his gaze around the room. "God, Laurel, I don't know.''

"If the ship isn't finished in three years, will you sign another contract?''

"Yes, but—''

"And another contract—and another project—after that? When are you going to quit, Nathan?''

"I don't know!'' he answered, frustrated and defensive. "But what difference would it make if I wanted to stay in until I retire?''

They stared at each other again, both knowing that the future hung in the balance.

Laurel drew a shaky breath. "So. What you're saying is that, for maybe the next fifteen or twenty years, you want me to carry this box around the world and know that *somewhere*, I have a home."

"The box is only a symbol," Nathan replied quickly. "Home isn't a place, Laurel. It's the people in it. You must realize, the reason you've never felt you had a home isn't because you've moved so much but because your parents didn't love each other enough to make whatever house you lived in *feel* like a home ought to feel."

Laurel's eyes grew cloudy. "You've got no right to analyze my childhood as if you were there, living it for me."

"But I *was* there!" His tone became more gentle as his hands eased their grip on her shoulders. "Not living it for you, no, but *with* you—at least, as much as I could. I'm not blaming you, sweetheart. I'm only saying it would be crazy to think you hadn't formed your impressions of what a home is from a model that was—" he hesitated "—well, faulty, at best."

Laurel's entire body stiffened, but Nathan didn't seem to notice.

"Oh, Lauri, don't you see how different it can be this time? We won't be struggling anymore, financially or otherwise. And I might get a stateside assignment that could last years. Maybe we won't have to move at all!"

"Except that they'll be sending you to every hot spot on the face of the earth, every chance they get."

"For God's sake, don't *invite* trouble!"

"But it's true, Nathan."

"But it might not be. And what if it is? The special duty never lasts long. Oh, sweetheart, we've lived through hell, and I don't know how, but we came out of it loving each other more than ever! Isn't that the most important thing? God!" He pulled her rigid body against him. "How can you even think of letting something like moving stand in our way? It's only boxes and papers and an airplane ride. We'll take our home with us, Lauri. It'll be whatever we make together."

Suddenly Laurel knew exactly what it meant to be so angry, you couldn't see straight. "No," she snapped, wrenching away from him. "It's not fair, Nathan. It's not fair for you to hand me a bunch of papers full of dead people's names and tell me someday I'll get to add my name to the roster. Someday I'll get to enjoy the place these people worked for and loved—the place *you* lived in and loved! How dare you stand there and tell me I shouldn't need or want what you've always had! St. John's Landing is your *home*, and whether you keep it or sell it or—or—" she waved her arm wildly "—or give it to the Salvation Army, at least you've had a choice! That's all I ever wanted, Nathan! A choice!"

Whirling on her heels, Laurel stalked to the door, yanked it open and walked out without so much as a backward glance.

Nathan was right behind her as she strode up the path. "But I'm not trying to take your choice away! I'm trying to *give* you one!"

"That's not how it feels to me," Laurel tossed over her shoulder. "You think it's going to be so different between us, but all I see is that you *still* think you know better than I do what I need. You *still* think you've got the right to tell me what my choices ought to be. And you're *still* trying to convince me that everything is wonderful when it's not!"

"Dammit, Laurel!" Nathan grabbed her shoulder and twisted her to face him before she could start downhill toward the dock. "Next thing you'll be saying I forced you into marrying me! I'm not going to listen to you tell me you weren't responsible for making your own choices."

"Oh, and I had some really fine options, too, didn't I?" Poking him in the chest with one finger, she recalled, "Like the one where I got to choose between leaving you, two weeks after we were married, or living in the Navy." Turning her back on him, she continued toward the water.

"You could have said you wouldn't do it!" Nathan shouted, hurrying after her.

"Ha!" she fumed, her heels clattering on the dock as she intoned with mock gravity, "'Lauri, sweetheart, it's the only way. If I don't apply for the scholarship, I won't finish med school.' What was I going to do, Nathan? Tell you not to be a doctor? *Now* it's, 'Marry me, Lauri, or I'll have to sell the Landing.' That's blackmail, Nathan. Emotional blackmail. And I'm not buying it." Ignoring *The Scallop*, she went directly to the motorboat moored on the opposite side of the dock and grabbed the bowline off its mooring.

"You're twisting things totally out of perspective," Nathan growled, coming up behind her to snatch the line out of her hand and rewrap it around the piling. He gave the knot a violent jerk. "It never entered my mind to look at it that way. It's true I came here to sell the Landing because it hurt too badly to be here, but for God's sake, I'm not *blaming* you for it!"

"Good," she said succinctly. "Then you won't blame me if you change your mind again about selling it because I've decided not to marry you. It won't be my fault if you give it up now—just like it wasn't my fault when you gave it up fourteen years ago to become a damned vagabond!" Turning, she slipped off her sandals, tossed them into the boat and hitched up her skirt to sidle down after them.

With his dark brow deeply furrowed, Nathan watched as Laurel found the keys to the boat and shoved them into the ignition.

"This is crazy!" he barked.

"It's not crazy!" she retorted, swearing under her breath when the boat wouldn't start. "It's the truth, Nathan. I had to live with the mess you made of things with Uncle Jack—not that you ever deigned to tell me what the mess was. But it doesn't matter anymore. Whatever reason you had for insisting the Navy was the only way you'd get to med school, it was more important to you than I was." Banging a fist on the seat in frustration, she gave up on the ignition and twisted around to discover that the gas line wasn't connected to the outboard.

"Oh, I get it," Nathan drawled, his feet spread wide and his hands planted on his hips. "*That's* what this is all about. Talk about blackmail! 'Nathan, leave the Navy so I'll know you love me.'"

"That's not what I'm saying," Laurel countered, stumbling on her way to the stern.

"It sure sounds like it to me."

"Well, maybe I *do* want to know why you won't quit," she declared, shoving the fuel line into place, then flailing for a hold when the boat lurched suddenly under Nathan's weight. "The whole time we were married I listened to you tell me you didn't want to be there but that you didn't have any choice, and now I find you so dedicated you're ready to extend your duty with a patriotic smile!"

She laughed bitterly on her way back to the helm. "You know what I think? I think you *always* wanted to be in the Navy! That it was your way of getting back at Uncle Jack for all the nasty things he'd ever said about your father. And I was just too in awe of you to believe you were capable of something as stupid as revenge!''

Taking hold of the hose Laurel had connected, Nathan gave it a decisive yank the instant before she turned the key in the ignition. Not needing to look to know what he had done, she slumped in the seat.

"It's not true, Laurel," he stated. "I really didn't want to be there."

"So, why won't you quit?"

"Because this isn't *then*—it's *now*! This is my career we're talking about! I've got almost fifteen years invested in it! You can't be serious—wanting me to give up everything and start over!"

"Oh, yes," she said quietly, hitching her skirt high to climb out of the boat. "I am very serious."

"But, *why*? Just so you can paint a picket fence?"

The question hung for a moment above the dark waters of the river before his next words sent it plunging to the bottom.

"I won't do it."

"Fine."

"I'm not going to throw away a satisfying, hard-earned career because you've got it in your head that *I'm* the one who's going to make up to you for everything you missed."

"It's your choice."

"Laurel, for the love of God!" Nathan vaulted out of the boat onto the dock. "I've given you everything I've got to give! What more do you want?"

Tears were streaming down her face as her fingers worked uselessly at the rope that stood between her and escape, but her answer was absolutely clear. "I don't

want your house. I don't want your box. And I don't
want your pie-in-the-sky notions about what happiness
is or should be. I've done all the living I'm going to do
on dreams and promises, Nathan. I'm thirty-four years
old, and I want something that's real. I want a real
home that I get to live in with real children. And a real
husband, who's married to *me*—not the U.S. Navy!
And nothing you say is going to convince me that I
shouldn't want those things or that I ought to settle for
anything less!'' With a thoroughly miserable groan, she
gave up trying to loosen the rope, wrapped her arms
around her waist and stood staring out across the water.

A moment later, Nathan's quiet, bewildered question broke the charged silence.

"What are you trying to do here?"

"Leave!"

"You're going to take yourself back to Annapolis? In
the dark?"

"The boat's got lights. And I do remember the way."

"Lauri, come on," he prodded. "This is ridiculous.
We're not accomplishing anything by making each
other angry. Let's go back to the cottage and talk about
it."

"Are you going to change your mind?"

Her query was met only by the sound of water lap-
ping against the hulls of the two boats moored at the
dock.

"You see?" she noted. "There's nothing to talk
about."

"Maybe that's the problem," he muttered. "We've
been doing too damned much talking." And before she
could twist away, his hands took hold of her shoulders

and drew her stiff form against him. "Lauri, look at me."

She shook her head in quick refusal.

"Sweetheart, I'm not going to let you run away from me again. You already said you don't want to. Let's go back and start over. It's not too late. We can do it right."

She knew it wasn't possible, but the utter certainty that she was going to lose him again was so unbearably painful that she didn't have the strength to keep him entirely away while he was still there. The tight rein on her emotions slipped a little—enough to let him hold her, enough to allow the warm, familiar feel of him to touch her deeply.

The anguish she was suffering was evident in her quietly spoken words. "Nathan, I want to leave now. Please. Before we spoil everything again."

"I won't let you do it," he said. "When you left me at Subic Bay, you did it without telling me any of the things you've said tonight, and I'm not going to let it go."

Her eyes closed as she whispered, "I'm sorry. I'm sorry it's taken me so long, but I didn't understand any of this then."

"Well, I don't think you understand it *yet*," he countered. "And I sure as hell don't, either. But I know something we both understand." His hand moved to the back of her head. "And before this goes any further and we do end up ruining the start we made last night, maybe we could both use a reminder of what this is really all about."

"Nathan, no—" Laurel started to say, her stomach knotting as she realized his intent. But her protest became a throaty moan when his head lowered and his mouth whispered across hers in a breath-stealing caress.

At the first touch of his lips, Laurel died inside, resigning herself to living out the scene she had been desperate to avoid. She tried. She really tried to give him what he was asking of her. But it had been wrong from the start.

And Nathan knew it. Warmth and passion. Coolness and fear. Her answer to his kiss was a study in ambivalence, and the déjà vu feel of it sent shards of panic slicing through him. Her lips parted for his, and she allowed him access to her mouth, but she took no liberties with his. Her body was pliant, but there was no shivering response, no arching to get closer. Her hands resting lightly on his biceps weren't pushing him away, but neither were they clinging; in fact, the slight twitching of her fingertips told him she did not really know what she wanted her hands to be doing. And she was whimpering—tiny sounds of pleasure and agony that tore at his gut.

"Lauri...Lauri, it's all right," he tried to soothe her. "I love you so much."

"I love you, too." She gulped brokenly.

But her lips remained hesitant beneath his, her body accommodating rather than passionate, and he knew her trembling had little to do with arousal. Once, he would have taken whatever she had been able to give. But not anymore. He wanted it all.

With a strangled cry, he crushed her to him, his mouth slanting across hers with nearly bruising force in a desperate effort to catch her before she left him entirely. But the harder he tried to wrest from her the response she had given so willingly the night before, the less of it he got. He knew it was futile, but he went on trying, and in that one kiss it seemed he relived the entire course of their marriage. Frustration, anger, fear, grief. Feelings that were familiar to him and that corresponded exactly to her level of withdrawal. The sure knowledge that no matter what he did, she was not going to surrender her heart filled him with the bleakest despair he had ever known.

With a long, anguished groan, he loosened his hold and ended the kiss, tearing his lips away from hers as though peeling flesh from his own body. When he was finally able to open his eyes, he found her gazing at him, her eyes gray pools of tears.

Laurel's hands flew to cover her face. "Please, Nathan. Please, I—I want to go now."

Everything inside him recoiled. It was wrong. He *knew* it was wrong. But he also knew both of them were physically and emotionally exhausted and that nothing good was going to come of pushing it any further.

Taking one tremendous, racking breath, he gave in. "Okay. We'll talk about it tomorrow."

"No! I don't want to talk about it again. Not ever!"

"Well, that's tough. You're not running away from me again. *Not ever.*"

Her hands fell away from her face, and she raised tortured eyes to his. "I'm not running, Nathan. I'm crawling. Last night I was the happiest I've ever been in my life, and I thought tonight was going to be the same. But we'd only be postponing the inevitable, because I'm leaving on Sunday. Alone."

He stared at her, stunned. His first response was to say *like hell you are*. He could see the old hopelessness settling over her, and he despised it. But he was in no shape to talk her out of it.

Abruptly, he grabbed her by the hand and began striding back along the dock. "Come on. Let's get out of here before I start saying idiotic things I don't mean."

It was not until they reached the hotel that either of them spoke again.

"Laurel, don't leave on Sunday." Nathan's voice was quiet and strained.

She paused, her hand on the car door handle. "There's really no point in my staying any longer."

"I think there is."

"Nathan, don't make this any worse—"

"Please, Laurel." The fingers of his left hand pressed into the bridge of his nose.

Laurel knew if she tried to speak, she would cry. She'd done that already, and it had produced nothing but more pain. Endless pain for both of them.

"I'll call you tomorrow," he said. When she did not respond, he lifted his head and turned his gaze to hers, repeating the statement in a voice that was almost steady. "I'll call you tomorrow."

She was able to hold his gaze for only a fleeting moment—long enough to whisper the hated words one last time.

"Goodbye, Nathan."

And then she was running.

Nathan watched Laurel race away, knowing full well that she thought she had said goodbye to him forever. If he'd had even the slightest notion it could be true, he would have been chasing after her. Instead, he pulled away from the curb, not at all sure where he was heading, except that he knew he wasn't going back to the cottage.

Deep down inside, he understood it was critical that he and Laurel work this thing out before Sunday had a chance to separate them once again. What exactly they were working out was beginning to look a lot more serious than his being in the Navy versus her wanting a permanent home. It seemed she felt he had dictated her entire life.

God Almighty! Wasn't he ever going to live it down? One time! Once in a lifetime of knowing each other he had been guilty of forcing her to make a choice she hadn't wanted to make. But she was never going to let him forget that it had been *his* needs, not hers, that had driven him into the Navy. Or so she thought.

He had been tempted to tell her the truth. The whole truth, of which she'd guessed only a part. Yes, back there on the dock when she'd been railing at him, all righteous and indignant, it almost would have been worth the satisfaction of seeing her face when she learned it had been not only his father but her as well whom he'd been defending in . . . in "making a mess of things," as she'd put it, rather than apologizing to Uncle Jack.

It was the *almost* that had stopped him. He was thirty-six, not twenty-one. He had learned that revenge was, indeed, stupid. And the value of a moment's satisfaction of the sort hurting Laurel would have given him was exactly zero. But you paid for it forever. As he was doing now.

There had to be another way to convince her their life together was not over. There had to be another way to make her see that the past didn't matter, that what mattered was the future. Yet even as he began thinking of ways to change her mind, he could not quite ignore the voice that prodded him to wonder if he, too, was clinging to the past. What buried reason did he have for refusing to admit that her assessment of his motives had been partly right? Was he afraid—or ashamed—to tell her that, yes, it was true: Once, he'd thrown away their future in order to salvage his pride.

Chapter Twelve

Laurel managed to wait until she reached the door of her room before falling apart. Her hands shook badly as she tried to make the key work in the lock, and she kept having to wipe away the tears blurring her vision. When at last she had the door closed behind her, she flung herself across the bed and let the deep, heart-wrenching moans tear through her. A few minutes later she was still so wrapped up in her suffering that she didn't hear the gentle knock on the door connecting her room and her father's. But when gentle became insistent, her head jerked up from the pillow where it was buried, and she swallowed the next sob.

"Laurel? It's Dad. What's happening? Are you ill?"

With a whimper, she grabbed for a Kleenex and rolled to sit on the edge of the bed. She started to say, "I'm fine—" but the words were so ludicrous that she began crying once more in a wave of almost hysterical laughter.

James Randall did not knock again but simply entered through the unlocked door, closing it quietly behind him. For a moment he stood silently, waiting for Laurel to acknowledge his presence. Finally she raised her head and looked at him, every shred of the agony inside her reflected in her eyes.

For an instant her breath caught as she fought a battle with pride and years of ingrained prejudice against what her father represented. But when he held out his hand and said, quite simply, her name, pride received a mortal blow and the object of her prejudice suddenly became her ally. Laurel flew off the bed and flung herself into his arms, offering James the only opportunity he had ever had to hold his daughter while she cried on his shoulder.

She had no idea how long she went on crying, but somehow they ended up sitting on the edge of her bed as she poured out the story in halting bursts. James got the gist of it, and when Laurel's tears subsided to a manageable level, he spoke remorsefully.

"Honey, I'm so sorry. I'm afraid I let you in for this, suggesting that perhaps Nathan might change his mind about accepting the contract."

"No." Laurel pushed away from him to reach for another Kleenex. "I let myself in for it. I was hoping he'd change his mind even before you brought it up."

"And you really can't see your way clear to try the Navy again?"

"Dad, that's not the point!" She dropped her head into her hands, only to lift it a moment later as she jumped to her feet and began pacing. She was trembling from head to toe in the aftermath of her tears, but the tumult of her emotions would not allow her to sit still for long. "I probably could live in the Navy now, without it seeming like the end of the world," she said. "Being with Nathan means more to me than my job or having the same mailing address year after year. But I have to know that I mean that much to him, too. How do you think it feels," she cried, "knowing I was his *third* choice—after medicine and . . . and his infernal Captain's bars?"

"Laurel, really, I doubt Nathan sees it that way."

"He probably doesn't," she conceded, "but that's how it feels to me! He just doesn't understand why he shouldn't be able to have *every*thing he wants!"

James studied his daughter closely. "So, you've made up your mind he's got to learn that some choices are mutually exclusive, the choice between marrying you or staying in the Navy being one of them."

Waving her arms, Laurel groaned. "Dad! You don't understand! I've lived with Nathan! I *know* what it's like, once he's made up his mind to do something—or not to do it. To have it, or not to have it. I swear I can hardly remember a time in our whole lives when he let anything stop him. It's like—" she searched for words "—like being in the way of a typhoon! When you're in the eye of it, the whole world is gorgeous, but Lord help you coming and going!"

James looked askance. "Laurel, are you sure you aren't exaggerating? Nathan never struck me as being that destructive."

She shook her head quickly. "He's not destructive— or cruel or even deliberately insensitive." And with her heart in her eyes, she added, "He's the kindest, most generous, loving man in the world. And I'm sure his utter determination in the face of the worst odds is at least ninety percent responsible for making him so good at what he does. Can you imagine a trauma specialist who believed in being conservative and maintaining a wait-and-see attitude?''

"Hardly." James's mouth twisted in a dry grimace.

"Nathan simply doesn't take time to realize that *his* way isn't the *only* way." Moving to stand by the window, Laurel gazed at the street below and listened to the raucous cries of gulls soaring over the harbor. Quietly, she added, "It's too easy for me to fall into the trap of believing him—because most of the time, his way *is* the best way. And even when it's not, he makes it look so appealing, I feel like a fool arguing with him."

"Do you have the idea that not seeing him again will, shall we say, teach him a lesson?"

She met her father's gaze. "Dad, I'm not trying to teach him anything. I'm trying to survive." Then, turning back to the window once more, she thought about how little concern she'd had for her own survival the previous night. She truly hadn't been out to teach Nathan a lesson by making love with him, although there had been an element of wanting to show them both what was possible between them. Still, if the passion and love of the night they had shared hadn't motivated him to change, there was nothing more she could do. There was nothing left of her that he hadn't had. And, it seemed, it was not enough. Not enough to compensate him for the loss of his Captain's bars.

James sighed. "So, what did Nathan say when you told him you didn't want to talk to him again?"

Laurel felt her face grow warm. "It wasn't what he said, it's what he did. He—he kissed me."

"Oh, dear," James muttered. "Man's ancient cure for everything."

Laurel shrugged, her fingers twisting at the braided cord that held the drapes back from the window. "It isn't that he tried to—to force me. It's that he simply can't understand why the fact that we love each other isn't enough. I wish to God it were...but it's not.''

Regretfully, James had to admit, ''No, you can't use love to cover up problems. Still—'' he paused a moment ''—I'm inclined to endorse the spirit of Nathan's, uh...ardor. Have you considered that you might be forgetting one of the primary rules of negotiation?''

''No matter what, keep talking.'' Laurel spoke the words as though by rote.

''You know,'' James began in a philosophic tone, ''you and I have become jaded, I think, about the whole business of negotiation—what's possible, what isn't. But on a fundamental level, it occurs to me there's potential for a marriage to become rather like the relationship between two world powers. 'I'll give you my missile if you give me your tank.' 'No, but I'll take *ten* of your missiles, and you can have *two* of my tanks.' ''

When Laurel raised a skeptical brow, James smiled. ''It's silly, I know. And I'm not suggesting our international problems can be so simplistically stated—oh, that they could. But if a marriage isn't going to reach the stage of, say, our relations with the Soviets, you've got to be willing to give *all* your missiles—and trust the other person not to take advantage of your defenseless position. If you hold back even a single handgun—just in case—the other side will know it. And resent it. And mistrust you. Then they'll hold one back, too. And you'll think your fears have been realized and so decide perhaps you should have *another* weapon—a bigger one this time.''

''It's called escalation,'' Laurel put in, seeing his point but wishing she didn't.

''Yes, it is, isn't it?'' her father returned. ''Tell me, Laurel, how much honest, straightforward communication would you say could go on across that sort of defense line?''

"You know as well as I do," she murmured. "Very little." And the notion of two people ever loving each other deeply through that same defense line was just short of impossible. She and Nathan had tried it during the years of their marriage, and it hadn't worked. But could she promise never again to feel the need of such protection?

Laurel's forehead came to rest on a windowpane. "I'm scared, Dad. I'm not as ... well, resilient, I guess, as I was when I was nineteen. I don't think I could take it if it didn't work."

"You may not be as resilient," James replied, "but, hopefully, you're a lot wiser, and in many ways, you're stronger. Don't let your fear of being the first to lay down your weapons ruin your chance for happiness. If you wait for Nathan to lay down his... Well, a man's pride is an awesome thing, honey. It mellows with age, but it never really gives him any peace."

Her lower lip refused to remain steady as she whispered, "Am I not allowed to have any pride?"

A long moment passed. When James finally answered, he had ceased to be the sympathetic father and had become instead the man who had begun with nothing and arrived at the top; his tone was direct, firm and unrelenting.

"Well, Laurel," he began, "when you and Nathan are both old and gray like me—when you've spent your life trying to prevent disasters and Nathan has spent his preparing to clean them up—I hope you're both able to take great *pride* in your treaties and your commissions. Because I'm afraid they're all you're going to have to be proud of."

* * *

When the phone beside her bed rang at 7:00 a.m., Laurel knew it would be Nathan. She let it ring four times before she decided she might as well pick it up, because he would only keep trying until she did.

"Good morning." His voice sounded tired and solemn.

"Hello," she returned evenly, rolling onto her back on the rumpled bed.

"Did you get any sleep last night?"

"Some."

"Are you ready to talk about spending more time with me?"

The autocratic note that crept into his voice made Laurel steam. "I'm not going to see you again, Nathan."

"Laurel, this is ridiculous. It started because I rented the sedan, didn't it? You didn't like me assuming—"

"It's not the car."

"Well, what the hell is it then?"

"Where would you like me to begin?"

"How about the beginning?"

"How about San Diego."

That stopped him.

"What?" he asked incredulously.

"You heard me," she snapped. If he insisted they have this conversation, then they'd have it on her terms. "Let's start with San Diego, where we lived for exactly three months in a perfectly satisfactory apartment before you went off to work one day and, on your lunch hour, rented a three-bedroom house that we couldn't afford but that you *knew* I'd love. You convinced our landlord to let us out of our lease and signed a lease on the house, which, you'd decided, was much more convenient for me, since I'd started teaching, than the apartment on the other side of town. *Then* you came home and told me we were moving."

"But, Lauri, you hated that apartment!"

"It needed a coat of paint and the kitchen faucet fixed."

"And you liked the house I rented."

"Mmm. It was lovely."

"And you didn't have to worry about getting to work."

"I never had to take a single bus."

"Well, you sure as hell couldn't have been upset at having to pack boxes again. I packed every one of them myself."

"As I recall, we lost about half the dishes."

"This is crazy."

"Then there was Yokosuka..."

"Japan?"

"...where I first experienced the luxury of a house-keeper."

"Mrs. Sato."

"That lovely lady you took the liberty of hiring to keep me company while you were at sea. She didn't speak a word of English, but she *did* know how to giggle. And she took every opportunity to indulge. I lost count of how many times she walked in on me while I was scrunched up in that dwarf-size excuse for a bath-tub. And did she apologize? Not once. She'd stand there twittering behind one hand and pointing from me to the ceiling with the other, like I was some kind of giant or something!"

"You liked her sushi."

"I often wondered what she would have done if she'd ever seen *you* in that tub."

"You'd probably have found out if you hadn't fired her by the time I got back from maneuvers."

"Oh, that's right. I did, didn't I? That was just before Christmas. You remember, don't you? That was the Christmas Eve I spent wondering until one in the morning where you were and if I should worry that you'd had an accident or if you were just being later than usual."

"I wanted you to have a Christmas tree."

"Chopped personally by you from practically the only forest in Japan? Nathan, I promise, the artificial tree we had would have done the job."

"You said you missed having a real Christmas tree."

"What I *missed* was having a husband who was there to help me with the five orphans he'd brought home to spend Christmas with us."

"Now, listen here, Laurel! Those kids were abandoned! It's a national disgrace, the way American servicemen leave foreign women pregnant and unable to take care of their babies! God! You can't tell me I shouldn't have brought them home. The very least we can do is try to help the poor kids have a decent holiday!"

"I absolutely agree. And they would have had an even better holiday if I'd known they were coming."

"I thought you'd like having them."

"What you *thought* was that it would make me think having a few of our own would be a nice idea."

"Laurel, wait a minute, now—"

"Then there was the night Lilly called to tell us she was pregnant. It was just before you got your assignment for the Philippines. When I got off the phone with her, I walked into the bedroom, and you were standing in the doorway to the bathroom. You had something in your hand, and you were staring at it. I started to ask you a question, then I saw you were looking at my birth control pills. You were thinking about throwing them away or ruining them somehow, weren't you, Nathan?''

There was a long, heart-thudding moment of silence.

"I wouldn't have done it, Laurel."

"That's what I told myself. Until the fight at Subic Bay when you *demanded* that I throw them out."

"I wouldn't have done it!"

Laurel winced at the raw insistence in his declaration. She waited a moment, then asked calmly, "Are you sure, Nathan? Are you very, very sure that you wouldn't have decided the best thing you could do to *help* me get over my fears about starting a family would be to make me pregnant?"

"Lauri, no, I—"

"You think about it, Nathan. I've got to go now."

When Laurel hung up, Nathan slammed the receiver back on the hook and strode from the phone booth toward the car parked at the curb. The door bounced on its hinges under the force with which he yanked it open. The entire car shook when he slammed the door closed behind him. Then he sat at the wheel motionless—except for the muscle working in his jaw—and through the red-purple haze of anger that clouded his vision, he tried to think.

When had things gotten so out of hand? At what point had Laurel become so suspicious that she had guessed at the most reprehensible fantasies in which his guilty conscience had ever indulged? And even if she had guessed, how could she ever *dream* he would actually do something so detestable—not to mention professionally suicidal—as to tamper with her birth control? You didn't do something like that to somebody you loved!

But Laurel believed he would have done it to her. She didn't trust him not to manipulate her life as he saw fit. At this point, it did not even seem that agreeing to quit the Navy would undo the damage. But God Almighty, what *could* he do that he hadn't already done to win her back?

You jackass, the voice of his conscience sneered in pure disgust. *That's what she's trying to tell you. You've done too much. You've tried too hard. And you've lost her.*

Every nerve and muscle in his body tensed in rejection of the idea. There would be a way. There *must* be a way to get Laurel back. She loved him. She could not actually want to go through life without him, any more than he wanted to go through life without her.

Suddenly Nathan was overcome with a terrible, shaking feeling of dread. He had never felt so lonely or so shockingly alone. Never! Without thinking twice, he threw the car into gear and headed toward the one refuge he thought he might have left.

"Well, if you aren't a sorry sight."

Nathan's gaze dropped sheepishly to his feet, which were planted squarely on Louise Halliday's porch, then rose once more to face the old woman's appraisal. Her slight form was wrapped in a ridiculously large pink flannel bathrobe and a pair of purple scuffs that peeped out from under it. Her hair was disheveled, and it could not have been more obvious that he had awakened her. Still, she looked better than he did, and they both knew it.

"Did you go to bed last night, boy?" she asked with a pointed glance at his rumpled shirt and his unshaven face.

Slowly, Nathan shook his head.

"Got woman trouble?"

He nodded.

Louise had the temerity to chuckle. "I wondered how long it would take for you two to start hollering at each other."

"The hollering's over," Nathan said. "She won't talk to me. She's leaving tomorrow, and I can't think of a way to stop her."

"Leaving!" Louise exclaimed. Then a frown appeared on her brow. Obviously this wasn't part of the plan. "Well, come in, Nathan. I can't have you standing on my porch, looking like something the cat dragged in."

Louise fed him coffee, strong and black, and a plate of pancakes soaked in maple syrup. And only when his plate was empty did she seat herself to his right, her cup of tea steeping on the table in front of her.

"So, tell me," she ordered. "What have you done to Laurel this time to make her run away?"

Nathan flinched. He started to answer, then hesitated. Finally, his broad shoulders sagged. "I'm not sure I even know. I thought it was because she wanted a picket fence, and I refused to give her one. Now I don't think she'd take one from me if I had it gift wrapped. She says I act like I know better than she does what her needs are and what her choices ought to be. She doesn't trust me."

"Oh, pooh." Louise dismissed the conclusion. "It's not you she doesn't trust. It's herself. You've got her scared to death something awful's going to happen if she really lets herself love you."

"That's ridiculous," Nathan grumbled. "She never *used* to be afraid of loving me."

The old woman's brow arched. "That was before you kissed her and asked her to follow you anywhere—and she found out she'd be going places she didn't want to go.''

"But we *loved* each other, Aunt Louise!" Years of repeating the litany brought the words by reflex to Nathan's lips. "Nothing in the world should have been more important than that! My being in the Navy didn't have to make any difference to our plans for a home and a family. No matter where we were or what we were doing, our loving each other should have been enough!''

Louise grunted softly. "Well, Pollyanna, when you decide to cut your pigtails and face the *awwwful* truth that things might be a little more complicated than that, you let me know.''

Nathan stared at her for a moment in utter bewilderment. Then, as comprehension dawned, his brows drew together in a dark scowl.

"Don't look at me like that, boy. I'm not the one sitting here feeling like he just found out there's no pot of gold at the end of the rainbow." She shook her head. "And I'm not the one to tell you to stop looking for it, either. In your line of work, I imagine an extra dose of faith comes in handy. But hadn't you better admit you're in love with a woman who doesn't give a hoot and a holler about any pot of gold—except the one she found the day she met you?''

Nathan snorted. "If she feels that way about me, she's sure got a funny way of showing it. She may have followed me into the Navy, but she managed to make it clear she wasn't happy about it.''

"Kind of sticks in your craw, doesn't it?''

His frown was still in place as he cast her a questioning look.

Louise was quick to explain. "Your sweet little wide-eyed Lauri, who'd always thought the sun rose and set on you, wasn't smiling at you anymore. And you didn't like it one bit."

Nathan shifted uncomfortably in his chair, wondering why he had come here. He should have known Aunt Louise would take Laurel's side in this argument.

"Why didn't you tell her, Nathan?"

The question barely registered. "Huh?"

"Why didn't you tell Laurel the reason—the real reason—you wound up having to ask the Navy to send you to medical school?"

In a snap, his eyes were glued to the ageless, dark-skinned face. "You know about that?" he whispered.

Louise's chin lifted. "'Course I know. How much do you think went on at the Landing that I didn't hear about sooner or later? I could tell you things— Well, never mind. Mr. Jack was bellowing loud enough that day to be heard clear across the river."

Her black eyes softened with genuine sympathy. "They were awful things he said to you, Nathan. It was bad enough insulting Laurel, when the fact is, he liked her more than he liked most people. Oh, in the beginning, it's true, he let her come visit against his better judgment—because you wanted her and he loved you and was near frantic for ways to help you get over losing your parents. But that changed. I don't think he really understood it himself, how he could have come to like somebody whose blood wasn't as blue as his. And maybe he wished she'd had a string of ancestors as long as yours, but he didn't really hold it against her that she didn't. The day of your wedding, he was as happy as I'd ever seen him."

Overwhelmed with relief that he wasn't carrying the burden alone anymore, Nathan sighed. "I guess I eventually figured that much out. And when he and I talked before he died, he told me he hoped Laurel and

I would work out our troubles. I knew then it hadn't even occurred to him he'd ever insulted her. But what he said about my father!'' Nathan's jaw tightened. ''You can't excuse that. He knew exactly what he was saying.''

Louise shook her head. ''You still don't understand, do you, boy? I suppose that's not surprising, since you never really knew the whole story. But I was there when your uncle—he was twenty at the time—had to take over everything after his father died, including raising his younger brother. He worshiped Curtis, just the way he did you. And it nearly killed him when Curtis left home to go into the Navy. Without a woman of his own, no family left, he got to be a bitter old man long before his time. Still, he loved his brother, and I thought he'd lose his mind when he found out Curtis had been killed. I swear, the only thing that saved him was getting you. He'd have done anything for you, and you know it. You were his second chance. But it made him scared to think you'd leave him, too, someday, and I guess he thought he'd tie you to his way of thinking with all that talk about your father's *mistake*. All he ever wanted, Nathan, was your loyalty. He just went about it in the wrong ways.''

''And instead of winning me over, he ended up driving me away,'' Nathan finished, knowing Aunt Louise was telling him the truth. It saddened him terribly to realize how little he'd understood his uncle, but feeling sad about the truth was infinitely better than being perpetually angry over something that had never made any sense.

''His foolishness cost him, all right,'' Louise agreed. ''After that fight you two had, with him insulting both your father *and* the woman you loved, you did exactly what I could have told him you'd do.''

Sadly, Louise shook her head, and her look was kind as she concluded, ''I'll never blame you for what you

did, Nathan. It was reckless and spiteful, maybe, but
your heart was in the right place. I've always been
grateful you at least hung on to the notion of pursuing
your medical career. It could have been worse. You
could have hauled off and enlisted and given up your
dreams altogether. Then you'd really have something to
be miserable about."

Nathan's eyes closed on a long, shuddering breath.

"So, now, tell me why you didn't tell Laurel the
truth?"

"Why do you think?" Nathan returned bitterly.
"How could I tell her the man who was largely responsible for the only pleasant memories she had of childhood thought she was a vacuous, status-hungry social
climber?"

"You think it hurt her any less to believe you put her
after your own career? You think she never wondered
how you could have gone into the Navy if you'd really
loved her?"

"But I did love her! I do love her! More than anything in the world!"

"Then why won't you give her the picket fence she
thinks she's got to have?"

"Dammit!" Nathan's fist hit the table. "Doesn't
anybody understand? This is my life's work we're talking about! I've driven myself practically into the ground
for it! I *can't* just throw it away!"

An odd expression crossed Louise's face. "Why not?
You afraid of being out of a job? Can't believe a bright
boy like you'd have a hard time finding a place for
himself somewhere or other."

When the only response she got was an exasperated
sigh, her mouth thinned into a line of disgust. "Nathan St. John Coltrane, don't you think it's about time
to grow up? In every other way you're a man. But when
it comes to Laurel, you act like you're still a sweaty-
palmed young buck who spends all his time working out

ways to get his girl to let him do things to her he knows he shouldn't be doing. Why don't you take some of that experience and know-how you've got so much of for other things and put it to use? Now, out with it. Why won't you give Laurel her picket fence? It's the only thing she's ever asked of you, and I'll grant you it's a lot. But it doesn't seem like too much for the woman you say you love more than anything in the world."

When Nathan's reply was not immediately forth-coming, Louise answered the question for him. "You're still waiting for your Lauri to smile at you, aren't you? You want her to make up for all those years she didn't smile. You're trying to get her to tell you it doesn't matter that you took her picket fence away from her, and that she loves you anyway. You're not asking for forgiveness. You want *approval*!"

Nathan's fingers traced the checkered pattern on the blue-and-white tablecloth on which his gaze was fixed. It was a long while before he muttered, "Maybe I do. Maybe I want her to recognize that it was hard for me, too. I didn't want to go off on Reserve duty or ship out on an aircraft carrier for three months at a stretch. And I sure as hell didn't want to get two different overseas assignments in a row! But I did what was expected—even though I knew everything I did made her think *less* of me."

His mouth hardened. "Maybe once, I'd have liked her to go to one of those blasted parties I had to attend and try to make friends. Or say goodbye when I had to leave on special duty and not look like she was afraid she'd never see me again. Maybe once—" He broke off for a moment, and when he continued, his voice was hoarse. "Maybe once, I'd like to hear her tell me she thinks of me as something other than a . . . a damned vagabond."

Louise's hand appeared in Nathan's line of vision as the old woman reached over to pat the back of his hand.

She left her gnarled fingers resting on top of his longer, straighter ones as she spoke quietly. "She hurt your pride, Nathan. She didn't mean to—didn't even know she was doing it—but she did. Just like your Uncle Jack did. But are you going to keep on making the same mistakes you made when you were twenty-one? Are you going to make her pay—and wind up paying along with her—for the rest of your life?"

At the sudden constriction in his chest, Nathan clenched his teeth and swallowed convulsively, but he could not prevent the unfamiliar stinging sensation in his eyes from making the blue-and-white checks of the cloth blur.

Louise's voice was gentle. "I know there's things you're not saying, Nathan, reasons for the way you feel that you aren't ready to talk about—maybe aren't even ready to admit to yourself. But I tell you it's time. It's time to let go of the past and get on with the future. Laurel's a woman now. She's been trying for a long time to love you like a woman loves her man. Why won't you give her the chance?" Her knobby fingers tightened on his. "I've got a feeling you wouldn't be sorry."

Nathan's eyes were closed. All he could think of was the horrible, tortured look on Laurel's face after he had kissed her on the dock the night before. His throat hurt, and it was all he could do to whisper. "I think it's too late, Aunt Louise. I went too far this time. She won't want to see me again."

Louise studied him a moment, then nodded, once. "Well, I guess you'll have to figure out a way to change her mind, won't you? That shouldn't be too hard, with all the practice you've had. But this time, Nathan, I really think you'd better get it right."

Chapter Thirteen

Laurel fully expected to find Nathan waiting for her at Clarkson's Lodgings when she arrived there at six-thirty. But his car was not parked out front, nor was he in the parlor. She didn't know whether to be relieved or disappointed, but she felt a little bit of each when she took the sealed envelope Mrs. Clarkson handed her and noted her name written on the outside in a familiar, extravagant scrawl. She tore the envelope open and read,

> Lauri,
> Aunt Louise says my name should have been Pollyanna, but I still think we can work this out. Don't leave tomorrow. Please. I'll call you later.
> Love, Nathan

The phone was ringing when she opened the door to

her room. She felt her stomach muscles tense as she picked it up.

"The answer is no," she said, not giving him a chance to argue or herself a chance to waver. "I'm leaving tomorrow, and that's final."

There was a brief moment of silence before a male voice replied, "I won't try to contradict you, but I think you should reconsider."

Laurel's breath rushed out. "Oh, it's you."

"Hmm," her father confirmed. "I heard you come in. I take it you thought it was Nathan calling?"

"Yes."

"Your mind's made up?"

"I'm afraid so. Listen, would it be all right if I didn't come to dinner with you? I don't think I'd be very good company. I'm pretty wiped out."

"Of course, it would be all right," James replied. "We'll talk at breakfast. And I'm already looking forward to the week in July we've planned."

"Don't forget Christmas at Lilly's," Laurel reminded him with an affectionate smile.

"I'm counting on it. But about this evening. Are you sure you'll be okay? Do you want me to—"

"Don't worry about me," she interrupted before he offered to stay with her. "I'm going to pack. Then I'm going to bed early."

"All right, honey. I'll see you in the morning."

Laurel replaced the receiver, but the phone rang again before she had taken her hand off it. This time, it was Nathan.

"How was your day?" he asked in almost conversational tones.

"I survived it," she answered warily.

"Were your students disappointed to see the conference end?"

"Nathan, I can't talk to you like this."

"Laurel, I've *got* to talk to you like this!"

She sank down on the bed and, for a moment, considered leaving Annapolis that night. But then, that truly would have been running away.

"Please," he said. "Don't go tomorrow. Stay an extra day."

"No," she whispered. "Nathan, I can't take any more. I can't keep hurting like this. And I can't stand to watch you hurt, either. We have to—to end it. Now."

"But I want to end the *hurting*. Neither of us was hurting two nights ago, and I think it can be that way all the time. Sweetheart, please, listen to me—"

"No!" Laurel cried suddenly. "I'm *not* listening! I'm scared to listen! I'm scared I'll let you talk me into believing something I didn't think for myself. I'm scared I love you too much to say no when I should. I'm leaving in the morning, and *please* don't try to call me again!"

Laurel almost forced the receiver back onto the hook, but she had not risen from the bed when it rang again. She let it ring while she paced the floor, stopping every two or three turns to stare at it. When she couldn't stand it anymore, she snatched it up, begging this time, "Nathan, please! Don't do this—"

"I love you!" he shouted. "No other man is ever going to love you the way I do! Laurel, for God's sake—"

"Oh, Nathan," she moaned, "I love you, too, but we've run out of chances to love each other and have it mean anything except heartache. And I've got to say goodbye!"

Laurel pressed the disconnect button; then, before she could change her mind, she released it and called downstairs to say she did not want to receive any more calls that evening. Then, planning to be up and gone before the sun had risen, she wrote a note to her father, telling him she'd had to leave early and would call him to explain when she got home—though she rather imagined he would understand.

When she had put the note on her father's bedside table, she returned to her own room and began throwing things into her suitcase and garment bag, packing everything except her toiletries, the clothes she needed for the next day and her nightgown. Then she stripped off the clothes she was wearing, bundled them in, too, and proceeded to drown her sorrows in a bubble bath.

Laurel took the longest, hottest bath she could stand, willing herself to enjoy it. She was not going to cry another single tear. She absolutely wasn't. She had already cried more in one week than she had in her entire life, and she was beginning to see that one tear simply led to another and that there were some things about which one could cry forever, her fruitless love for Nathan being one of them.

For nearly an hour she soaked her tired body, emerging only when her skin was a glowing pink and her fingers and toes looked like shriveled white grapes. After drying off and rubbing her hair into a damp mop of curls, she massaged huge dollops of an outrageously expensive body cream into every square inch of skin she could reach. Her heart was not really in it, but she thought some pampering was in order. Besides, she hoped it would relax her enough to fall asleep. When she realized she had been standing in front of the mirror biting a fingernail instead of brushing her teeth, she knew it hadn't worked.

With a tiny, disgusted sound, she grabbed her toothbrush and applied it with a vengeance. Then, looking for her hair dryer, she frowned when she realized it was not on the sink. Thinking she must have packed it, she yanked open the bathroom door to fetch it.

The blanket descended over her head when she had taken one step into the bedroom—exactly half a second before she started to scream. But the scream was knocked out of her as she was tossed in the air and came down hard against something thoroughly unyielding. Before she could draw another breath, an urgent voice said, "Laurel, it's me."

"*Hhhel*— Who? *Nathan!*"

"It's okay. Don't scream."

"*Don't scream!* What are you *doing*?"

"Hey, cut that out!" He caught her foot with his hand as it connected with something that could have been his jaw.

"*Me?* You want *me* to cut it out? Why you jer— Ouch! Nathan, you bit me!"

"Well, quit kicking me! Now, I'm sorry if I scared you a little—"

"A little? Are you *crazy*?"

"Maybe," was his growled reply. He was wrapping another blanket around her bare legs and feet, rendering her completely immobile.

"Nathan, tell me this is a joke."

"Two hours ago, did I sound like I was joking?"

"Then why in blazes am I hanging here, suffocating? *Let me*— Hey. Hey wait! Where are you going? You're not taking me—Nathan, I haven't got anything on!"

"Yes, you have."

Laurel squealed when he actually had the gall to pat her bottom, which was poised somewhat indelicately over his shoulder.

"You're very well covered," he noted. "If you stay quiet and don't wiggle, nobody will ever know."

"Nathan Coltrane, you take me back to my room right now or I'll scream this place down! Do you hear me?"

Nathan's reply was succinct. "Shut up, Laurel. If you don't, I'll drop you. And I'll take the blankets with me."

"You wouldn't dare!"

"Would you like to bet?"

No. She definitely did not want to bet.

At that moment, he began descending a flight of stairs, and Laurel gritted her teeth against the bone-jarring bounces. Lord, he was made of rock!

"If anyone sees us and asks," Nathan told her in a husky whisper, "you're a sloshed midshipman I'm escorting back to his quarters. I'm in uniform, so believe me, I look a whole lot more credible than you do right now."

"You don't actually expect me to coop—"

"I swear, Laurel, I'll drop you if you so much as whimper."

She believed him. Dear God, she actually believed he'd do it. She was in love with a madman.

The madman carted her down the stairs. After that, Laurel had no idea where they were. She knew when they hit the sidewalk, though, because she could feel a draft of cool night air coming from an open space in the blankets. She chose not to think about where the open space might be. The blankets were scratchy wool. Her nose itched, and her right arm was going numb. It seemed like forever that she was jostled along like a sack of potatoes, and with every bump, her anger grew apace with her discomfort.

How *dare* he do this to her! How *dare* he use physical force to get his way! Talk about male chauvinists! Talk about spoiled-rotten *brats*! Just wait until he let her go. He wanted to talk? Well, she'd talk, all right! None of this 'I love you' stuff and poignant goodbyes. Oh, no! She had done the Sarah Bernhardt routine. This time it was going to be Kate Hepburn, spitting and caterwauling the whole way. A little impolite name-calling would do for starters. Ooooo! Was he in for it! Just as soon as she got rid of the headache all this upside-down bouncing was giving her.

It seemed as if they had been moving forever when Laurel felt Nathan slow his stride, hesitate, and then take a long step forward and down. Beneath the blanket, her sense of hearing was fully functional. She heard the sloshing of water against a hull and the sound of a wooden deck beneath Nathan's hard-soled shoes. In a moment of pure panic, she could not keep quiet any longer.

"A boat? Nathan! We're on a boat!"

"That's right."

Laurel felt him bend low and start down through a companionway. "No! Nathan, you can't do this! I'll never speak to you again if you do!"

His footsteps thudded on carpeted steps. "Seems like I've already heard that once or twice today, so I figure I don't have much to lose, do I?"

From his point of view, she thought, he probably didn't. Dammit.

It was a big boat, she guessed, given the amount of walking and ducking he did before they finally stopped. An instant later, the blanket wrapped around her feet was whipped off, and he slid her forward, down the length of him until her toes touched carpet. Fortunately, since her arms remained imprisoned, he did not let her go or she would have fallen.

"Oh!" Laurel whimpered, swaying unsteadily on legs that were half numb. "Nathan, I'm so mad at you."

"I know," came his quiet response as he held her up with one arm and pulled the second blanket off her head.

Her gaze flashed to his in the semidarkness, but he would not look at her directly. Nor did his eyes take advantage of her nudity as he wrapped one of the blankets around her shoulders and guided her toward a bench.

In a quick glance, Laurel took note of the large double berth and the shape of the room and concluded that they were in the stern of a large cruiser. "Where are you taking me?" she wanted to know, resisting every step of the way.

"I wouldn't try to stand up for a few minutes if I were you," he replied, finally picking her up and plunking her down on the bed.

His advice went unappreciated as Laurel surged—or, rather, wobbled—to her feet to follow him when he turned to leave. "How long do you expect this to go on?" she asked, grabbing at the edge of the bed for support. "You can't keep me here indefinitely."

His reply was cryptic. "I'm going to get us under way. There's a pair of jeans and a sweater stashed under the berth."

"Well, they can rot!"

Nathan stopped with his hand on the door to look back and give her huddled form a pointed once over. "Suit yourself. But if you aren't dressed when I come back, I'm stripping, too." And having thus informed her, he left, shutting the door behind him.

"Why, you arrogant, pigheaded— Nathan, you come back here!"

Laurel did her best to race after him, but the effort stopped at the door—which was locked from the outside. Rattling the knob produced no results, nor did

beating against the door itself. Nor did the long string
of unladylike oaths and demands she hollered through
the crack between the door and the frame. When Laurel heard the cruiser's powerful inboard engines come
to life, she knew she had lost any hope of escape.

Flinging herself away from the door, she stood,
fuming, in the middle of the cabin, every inch of her
body jumping with raw nerves. Of all the unpredict-
able, impulsive things Nathan had ever done, this was
the worst. The very worst. Did he think she would find
it thrilling to be captured, naked, and spirited off to
sea?

That thought reminded her of his threat to match her
nakedness with his own if he returned and she wasn't
dressed. Was he planning a big seduction scene, wherein
he would kiss her senseless until she admitted how
helpless she was to resist him? Incensed that he could be
so blind and that she could be made to feel so power-
less—for the awful part was, it was true, he *could* kiss
her senseless—Laurel stamped a bare foot and permit-
ted herself one satisfying screech. Then, fearing that
seduction was, indeed, what Nathan had in mind, she
concluded she had better look for the clothes he had
promised. And the more of them, the better.

Six portholes—two large ones behind the berth and
two each on the starboard and port sides—allowed
enough moonlight to filter into the cabin for Laurel to
find her way to a wall-mounted lamp. She turned it on,
then sank down upon the carpet to begin pulling open
the drawers tucked beneath the bed. The sweater and
jeans—and nothing else—were in the last drawer, and
it became immediately obvious that the clothes were
Nathan's. When she threw off her blanket and pulled on
the jeans, they fit the way his used to fit her—a foot too
big in the waist, almost a foot too long in the legs, and

indecently snug across the backside. The bulky black sweater engulfed her to mid-thigh, but by this time, with her hair still damp, she was grudgingly appreciative of its warmth. She rolled up the jeans, ran her fingers through her hair and squared her shoulders in preparation for battle. By God, this was going to be one time she let Nathan know how furious she really was!

She had a long wait. And while the cruiser moved relentlessly through the dark waters, she paced the floor of the cabin and let her anger stew. She absolutely was not going to think about how panicked Nathan must be to do something like this. She absolutely was not going to feel guilty for driving him to such lengths. And under no circumstances would she let her resolve to end their torturous relationship waver.

She had heard every love word he knew how to speak. She had felt all the kisses he was capable of giving. She'd had the best and the worst of him, and there was nothing he could say or do to change her mind. Nevertheless, when Laurel heard the engines cut and felt the boat's speed drop, it was fear, not anger, that made her tremble as she peered out one of the starboard portholes to see if she could tell where they were anchoring.

Moonlight painted the black, liquid canvas beyond the porthole with splotches of silver, and as the boat swung around on its anchor line, a long stretch of sandy beach appeared. There were no houses, nothing that might identify the shoreline—nothing but sand and marsh grass and a few scrub pines. But then, did it really matter where they were? There had been enough lunacy for one night. She wasn't so frantic to get away that she would jump overboard in the dark and swim ashore... was she?

She was pondering the question when the door opened.

With one knee planted on the bench beneath the porthole, Laurel pivoted, and her gaze locked with Nathan's. For a long moment they assessed each other. His eyes skimmed quickly over her clothed form. Her spine stiffened, even as she took note of how truly awful he looked. In the dim light she saw the haggard, drawn expression on his handsome face, the lines fanning out from his eyes and down from his mouth that made him look every one of his thirty-six years and then some.

Realizing she was starting to feel sorry for him, she jumped off the bench and faced him, her hands planted on her hips.

"All right, Nathan. This has gone far enough. Just what do you think you're doing?"

Nathan took one step into the cabin and stopped. "I thought it was obvious," he returned tiredly. "I'm preventing you from leaving tomorrow."

"Oh, well! I'm certainly impressed!" She made a sweeping gesture that took in the well-appointed cabin. "Is this supposed to convince me I was wrong, that you wouldn't think of manipulating my life to suit your purpose? If that's the case, I'll guarantee you, it's not working."

Crossing the room, Nathan folded his long frame onto the bench that ran along the cabin's starboard side and leaned forward to rest his elbows on his knees. As he spoke, he rubbed his eyes with the fingers of one hand. "I'm not trying to convince you of anything, Laurel. I only want to talk."

Refusing to be moved by either the sight of him or the quiet tone of his voice, Laurel drew herself up straighter. "What about my father? Don't you think he's going to wonder where I went? Don't you think *somebody*'s going to wonder why I left with my things spread all over the room?"

Nathan reached up to unfasten the top buttons of his white shirt. Then he removed his hat and tossed it onto the bench beside him. "I left a note for your father. I told him you'd be with me and asked him to pack your things and have the guest house hold them until you claimed them."

"How did you get into my room?"

"The door was open."

She started to say she didn't believe him, then bit back the retort when she remembered the phone had been ringing when she had entered; she must have forgotten to go back and lock the door.

"I was prepared to bribe the maid to let me into your father's room," Nathan continued. "I figured there would be a connecting door. But it wouldn't have mattered. I was going to get in one way or another."

"My, my, such determination!" Folding her arms, Laurel strolled over to stare out the port-side window.

"I was desperate, Laurel. Which is what I guess I've been for a very long time."

She twisted around to stare at him.

He went on, leaning his head back against the wall and letting his eyes close. "So, you can put this evening's adventure on your list of times I've 'done you wrong,' along with the house in San Diego and Mrs. Sato and the rest. And you might as well add the birth control pills to the list, too. If you hadn't left me and things had kept going the way they were, I'm not at all sure anymore that, eventually, I wouldn't have completely lost it and found a way to get around them. God knows, I thought about it."

Shocked beyond belief, Laurel actually forgot she was angry. Turning to face him, she said the first thing that came to mind. "But why? What could you have been feeling so desperate about all these years—almost from the beginning?"

His eyes opened to meet hers across the fifteen feet that separated them. "I've been terrified out of my mind that I was going to lose your love. The last three years have only been a confirmation that my worst fear had been realized."

Slowly, incredulously, Laurel shook her head. "But that's— Nathan, there've been times I was angry with you, but there's never been a single moment when you were in danger of my not loving you."

"Yes," he replied quietly. "I know. But I didn't know before, when I was doing all those things, trying to make sure you never stopped loving me. Trying to make sure the fact that I was wearing this—" his hand stretched across the bench to pick up his hat "—didn't make you hate me."

She started to speak, but he cut her off.

"Lauri, do you remember the letter you sent me when my parents were killed?"

Yes, she remembered it, but what on earth did it have to do with any of this?

"I suppose so," she replied absently. "But what—"

"Do you remember what it said?"

"That I was sorry to hear about your parents. But, Nathan—"

"Actually, it said a lot more than that. Let's see. How did it go?"

His eyes closed again, and Laurel frowned in perplexity as he began to recite.

"Dear Nathan. Daddy told me about your parents. I wanted to call you, but he said I should write first. Oh, Nathan, I think it's really terrible and unfair what happened, and I'm so sorry. I don't know what else to say. I wish more than anything that I was with you, because I know how scary it is when it feels like you're all alone. I never told you this before, but I'm going to tell you now. If you want, you can pretend I didn't. But it'll be true, anyway. I love you. And I promise, I always will.

Your forever and ever friend, Laurel.''

Nathan fell silent, and when his eyes opened to meet Laurel's, the astonishment he found in her gaze was reflected in her whispered words.

"You remember every word."

He nodded. "I ought to. I read them enough times, sitting on the dock with a fishing pole in one hand and your letter in the other. It got kind of ratty looking after a while. But I've still got it."

"You do?"

"Hmm. It's in a box in my bottom dresser drawer—along with every other letter you ever sent me. And my wedding ring."

Laurel's lower lip trembled, and she caught it between her teeth.

"I never told you, did I, how much that letter meant to me."

She shook her head. "It doesn't matter."

"Oh, but I think it does." Nathan leaned forward, resting his forearms on his thighs, his hat dangling in both hands between his knees as he turned it in slow circles. "That letter was the beginning of it, really. The beginning of my knowing that your love was vital to me. I'm not pretending I thought about it *consciously* at that age. I only knew that that piece of blue stationery meant there was somebody left in the world who knew me—really knew me—and who loved me, not because I was their nephew and heir, not because I was the son of a man they'd helped raise, not for any reason other than because I was *me*."

Nathan's shoulders rose and fell in a deep breath, his gaze fixed on the finger that was tracing the inner rim of his hat. "By the time you came to live in Annapolis, I think my subconscious had the rest of me convinced that nothing short of Judgment Day was going to keep me from showing you that your love was being well spent. It kept me pretty busy, too—living up to what I imagined your expectations of the perfect hero must be."

"Oh, no... Oh, Nathan." As understanding began to dawn, Laurel walked over to sink slowly onto the edge of the bed near him.

"'Oh, Nathan,' is right," he grunted softly, tossing his hat back onto the bench. "I got rather cocky about it, after a while, feeling that you were pretty well hooked on me. Especially after we started kissing. That was like magic. I can't begin to tell you how it made me feel— how it *still* makes me feel—when I kiss you and you look at me like the rest of the world could disappear and you wouldn't care."

"I wouldn't."

"I know. Which is why, when I kiss you and you *don't* look at me that way, it scares the hell out of me."

Nathan met Laurel's searching look steadily. "When that happens—like it did last night—I panic. And I do some terrible things when I'm panicked, Lauri. Things like moving us across town without asking if you want to go, when a coat of paint would solve the problem. Things like trying to make it look as though it's your fault when things go wrong, and getting angry when you won't admit it. Things like turning our marriage bed into the war zone, as you once called it, trying to make you give me back what I thought was mine."

"Oh, God, *no!*" Laurel's entire being rebelled. "Nathan, making love with you was never like that! I said those things when I was angry!"

Insistently, he shook his head. "I never forced you or hurt you, but I wasn't making love with you, either—not the way we made love two nights ago. I *was* making war, the battle prize being your complete devotion—the love that had become so important to me, I couldn't even imagine life without it."

Nathan dropped his gaze to his hands, which were clasped between his outstretched knees. Opening them, palms up and empty, he looked at them curiously. "From the time I accepted the Navy scholarship—which is the only thing I've ever done that I knew ahead of time would make you unhappy—I've been operating in crisis mode, trying to prevent the thing I feared most from happening: you withdrawing your love. But I lost. Or at least, I thought I had until this week. Until you told me you still loved me." His fingers curled in toward his palms. "Until you gave yourself to me the way you had on our wedding night. Then, all of a sudden, my world was right again. When you told me last night you were leaving and didn't want to see me anymore, I thought I'd lose my mind if I couldn't convince you to stay."

Clenching his hands into fists, he shook them once, vehemently. "But I *can't* convince you! And I can't go on trying to be the perfect man of your dreams. And I can't keep measuring myself by whether you approve or disapprove of what I do. My refusal to admit my mistakes—my fear of letting you see me as...as imperfect—has driven us farther apart than any mistake I ever could have admitted to. And there've been enough of them. I've cheated us both out of the chance to—" he shrugged "—to grow up, really, because I thought the

love you gave me when we were young was the only love
I would ever need or want, and I couldn't envision it
changing. Growing.''

Nathan lifted his head, and his eyes searched Laurel's. ''What I did to you tonight, Lauri, dragging you
here against your will, was a terrible thing. And I knew
it was wrong the entire time I was doing it. But I
couldn't let you leave. I couldn't let another day go by
without saying what should have been said years ago.''
He took a deep breath, and the words came, thick and
broken. ''Sweetheart, I'm sorry. I'm so damned sorry.''

''Nathan, I—'' Laurel choked back a sob, and in the
next instant she was kneeling in front of him, her hands
wrapped around his. The tears running down her cheeks
mirrored those glistening in his dark eyes. ''Oh, Nathan, I'm sorry, too! I'm sorry I hurt you when I left.
And I'm sorry for making you go to such extremes to
tell me this. But mostly I'm sorry you went through all
these years, thinking you had to work for something
that's always, *always* been yours! I *wish* I'd understood. I wish I hadn't been so wrapped up in my own
fears. Maybe if I hadn't hated the Navy so much, it
would have worked itself out.''

''Maybe's don't count,'' he whispered, his finger
tracing the path of a tear on her cheek. ''We'll never
know whether it would have worked itself out or not.
And both of us have wasted enough of our lives wondering what might have happened if I hadn't let Uncle
Jack goad me into the Navy.''

Laurel's eyes widened, and she started to speak, but
Nathan shook his head.

''I'm not going to tell you what he said. I've learned
some things that have helped make it clearer to me, but
it's still pretty raw. Someday we'll talk about it, and I'll
tell you everything. But right now all you need to know

is that it's true, he refused me the tuition. It's true that, after what he said, I wouldn't have taken another red cent from him for *any* reason. And it's also true that, even if there had been another way to get the money, I would have applied for the Navy scholarship."

Her question was barely audible. "It did have to do with your father, didn't it?"

Nathan studied her for a moment, then stated simply and with utter finality, "Yes."

Laurel didn't press him further.

"It doesn't matter anymore," Nathan went on, "how or why I got myself into the Navy. The fact is, my time's almost up. And here we are, loving each other more than ever. I'd have to be out of my mind to let the Navy keep me from having the one thing I want most in the world." His gaze dropped to look at her left hand, which rested in his right. "Lauri, I haven't accepted the contract yet. It's in my suitcase, at the cottage. I'll mail it back tomorrow, unsigned, if you say you'll marry me."

For one image-shattering moment, Laurel studied the man sitting before her. He had been her friend, her lover, her husband. Yet, she realized, this was the first time in their long life together that she was seeing him for what he truly was: a man. A mortal man who made mistakes, who cried, and who loved her with such power that it took her breath away. He sat before her now, with his weapons—every last one of them—lying scattered on the ground. And she knew that the time had come to lay down her own arms, for she would never need them again.

Her fingers trembled as they lightly traced the four gold stripes that rested on his brawny shoulder, and she spoke in a husky, quavering voice. "Have I ever told you how incredibly handsome you are in uniform?"

As though in slow motion, Nathan straightened until his eyes met hers. Just as slowly, he shook his head.

Her look was remorseful. "I was afraid of that. But it's true. And these bars look awfully good, too. Like they were made for you."

"I don't give a damn about the bars!" Nathan declared hoarsely as he grabbed her hand from his shoulder to capture it once more between his. "What good are they if they keep us apart?"

Laurel glanced down, inching forward on her knees until she was cradled as close to him as their hands clasped between them would allow. Then she lifted her gaze to his once more.

"If you let go of my hands, I'll show you how far apart your uniform is going to keep us."

She felt the tension coil in Nathan's body, felt the tautness of the muscles in his thighs as they hugged her ribs. His throat moved as he swallowed hard.

"You don't have to do this, Lauri," he managed raggedly. "Really. I'll quit."

Pulling her hands gently from his, Laurel framed his face between her palms. "My dear, precious love," she breathed. "Why on earth would I want you to quit? When I look at you like this, when I think about all the wonderful things you've done, it makes me so happy— so *proud* of you—all I can do is cry."

The beard-roughened skin beneath Laurel's hands moved as Nathan's entire face twisted helplessly in a swift gulp for air and a racking shudder. The next thing she knew, she was being crushed in an embrace that threatened her ability to breathe, but she barely noticed, and her own arms were locked around him no less tightly.

"Lauri ... Lauri ... Oh, dear God, I love you. I love you so much!" Nathan gasped out the words between kisses and the almost violent quaking of his whole, great body.

Laurel's vows of love were whispered as she surrendered to the frenzied progress of his mouth over her eyelids, her cheeks, her throat.

"Lauri, are you sure?" His fingers were tangled in her hair. "Are you really sure you want to give up your picket fence? I'd give anything to build you one."

"I know. I know you would," she answered, her lips tasting his as she spoke. "I've been an idiot. I don't need a picket fence. I only need you."

"And babies?" He pulled back a little, enough to look at her. "Will my staying in mean you won't want any?"

Laurel's eyes were cloudy with tenderness as they probed the depths of the dark gaze she adored. "Love, I threw my pills out three years ago."

His breath caught for a moment. "The other night—"

Slowly, she shook her head. "The other night was you and me. That's all."

It took Nathan less than a second to understand what she was telling him, and his stunned expression reflected every ounce of hope that lived within him. Laurel caught a glimpse of the look in the instant before his mouth claimed hers in a wild, sweet rush of joy and celebration.

Between kisses the words tumbled out.

"Why? Why didn't you tell me? I would've—"

"No. I wanted all of you. I wanted you to have all of me."

"Oh, Lauri, could it have—"

"Maybe."

"God, I want you now! Like that. Knowing."

So did she. And in slow degrees, they made their way toward the bed. At the foot of it, they stopped, both of them thinking how glad they were there were no memories to be found upon that unfamiliar resting place; there would be nothing to flavor the new beginning they were making.

"Nathan, I have to tell you something."

His lips paused at the tender spot beneath her ear.

"I never slept with—"

"Anyone else. Yes, I know."

"You do?"

"Hmm. You couldn't sleep with a man you didn't love."

"Oh."

"Lauri, I have to tell you something."

"Nathan, you don't have to say any—"

"I couldn't sleep with a woman I didn't love, either."

"Oh, Nathan . . . Oh, I do love you so."

It was a beginning filled with loving that flowed as easily as tears to mingle with the soft sounds of cloth being tossed to the floor. Panting, breathless moans of pleasure accompanied kisses scattered over flesh that hardened, softened, throbbed and grew moist. Caresses were soon bold, and heartbeats swiftly racing. There was no fear or uncertainty to temper passion, nothing in the way of their bodies coming together as love, rich and full and lasting, wrapped them in its nurturing arms.

The bed rose with the gentle rocking of the boat as they fell upon it, embracing, touching, whispering words that soothed and healed the hearts so badly broken.

"I don't know what I'd have done if you'd left."

"I don't know how I'd have gone on without you."

"I would've found you."

"I'd never have been able to say no again."

"Don't. Don't ever say no. Say, 'Kiss me, Nathan. Hold me, Nathan. Touch me.' God, yes, Lauri! Touch me. Please..."

Her mouth and her hands touched every glorious inch of him in a way that was both possessive and erotic. She knew his body as only a longtime lover could, but there was a confidence, a surety of heart that, at last, he was hers—really hers—and the knowledge rocked through her and into him.

He was thrilled. Enchanted. Aroused beyond speech. He was shaken to his soul when she glided her lissome body down over him, opened her thighs, and in one graceful motion took his hard, aching flesh into the softness and heat of her woman's depths.

"I promise, Nathan," she whispered as gray eyes held brown. "Nothing between us but what we make together."

"Lauri..." he tried to say.

And then she began to move.

He swore, he pleaded, he cried out with the pure ecstasy of it. With wondering hands and a fervent mouth he caressed her. With cherishing arms he cradled her against him. And when their flesh was slick with sweat and the tension inside them arched to the point of breaking, he rolled her beneath him. And there, he loved her with a majesty that brought every color in the rainbow pouring down upon them, bound them together in a wave of faultless motion, and left them shattered by the awesome knowledge that, this time, their promises had been made to last. Forever.

Chapter Fourteen

Owing to small matters such as licenses and three-day waiting periods, Laurel and Nathan were married the following Thursday by a justice of the peace. Louise Halliday was there, and so was James Randall. The former was smug; the latter, immeasurably relieved. Both were delighted. The only one to express a complaint was Lilly, who, when informed Laurel would not be coming to visit because she would be on her honeymoon, first burst into ecstatic squeals, then cried because she could not be there to help celebrate the happy occasion.

James, with the kind assistance of Mrs. Honey Clarkson, provided the beaming wedding party with an elegant dinner in Clarkson's Lodgings, after which Nathan and Laurel retired to St. John and Elizabeth's cottage, prepared to make the most of the remaining two weeks of Nathan's leave. Their second wedding night—which bore a remarkable resemblance to the first, with the notable distinction that neither of them could claim to be either nervous or virginal—came to its natural conclusion in the old bed upon which they had first discovered conjugal pleasures. Sated, tired and happy, they prepared for sleep, satisfied that the vows they had spoken that day had been properly consummated.

It was very late, and they had been quiet for some time, when Laurel raised her head a little from the pillow and spoke softly.

"Nathan? Why aren't you asleep? You've been tossing and turning for the last hour."

With a sigh, Nathan rolled to his back and turned his head to meet Laurel's gaze. There was a full moon, and its light poured in through the windows, illuminating her face and making it glow like the finest porcelain.

"I'm sorry," he replied in a quiet rumble. "Have I been keeping you awake?"

She smiled. "When a man as big as you is restless in bed, it's not a matter of falling asleep so much as not falling out."

His hand reached out to stroke her cheek. "I guess I'll have to get used to sharing a bed again, won't I?"

Laurel shifted the covers to slide over close to him. Dropping several fleeting kisses across his shoulder, she asked, "What's wrong? Haven't I tired you out sufficiently?"

He chuckled softly, his fingers threading through the silky hair at the nape of her neck. "Sweetheart, if the last few days and nights with you haven't tired me out, I'm not sure what would."

"Well," she drawled, trailing a finger down the flat plane of his belly as she nibbled at his jaw, "maybe I'm not doing it right."

"You're doing it exactly right," he growled, reaching for her. "So, come here and do it again."

A while later, a much more relaxed Nathan lay holding his wife in the circle of his arms as they drifted on the borders of sleep. Yet again he was brought to wakefulness.

"Lauri?"

"Hmm?"

"When will you know if you're pregnant?"

There was a second's pause. Then she laughed softly. "What sort of question is that coming from a doctor?"

"I'm not your doctor. I'm your husband."

"Let's say in a couple of weeks, I'd start to get suspicious."

"So you probably won't know until after I've left."

Laurel yawned. "I promise, if I've got anything like that to tell you, I'll call instantly."

"I don't know what the phone lines are like at Deep Freeze." He frowned. "I hope we'll be able to get through to each other."

Laurel whimpered a little, snuggling back against him. "Believe me, if I'm pregnant, I'll find a way to let you know. Please, stop worrying and go to sleep."

But Nathan *was* worried. They had spent most of the last few days preparing to rearrange their lives—or, rather, Laurel's life—so they could be together in Jacksonville. When they had talked about parenthood at all, it had been with pleasurable anticipation. They hadn't really considered the more practical ramifications of such an event. But lying there in the darkness, Nathan began to consider them.

What if Laurel had a difficult first trimester, when he wasn't there to help? What if she were ill and exhausted the whole time she was having to sell her condo in D.C., settle affairs at her office and move to Florida? She was healthy, and her age would not quite make her pregnancy high risk, but he knew the statistics on miscarriage and other complications in women over the age of thirty having their first babies. The odds, which in the past he had only thought of from a professional standpoint, looked remarkably different when viewed personally. And he did not like them one bit.

There were other things that bothered him, too. Given the nature of his work, it was not beyond the realm of possibility that the Navy would send him off on another special assignment some time in the next year. Besides the fact that he didn't want Laurel to face the ordeals of either pregnancy or childbirth alone, he had waited all his adult life for this. And he wanted to be there, dammit!

"I don't know," he said, thinking aloud. "Maybe we should have waited until I got to Jacksonville before we started trying to make you pregnant."

Clearly, Laurel was more interested in sleep than conversation, for she murmured almost inaudibly, "Don't want to wait. Besides, too late now. What's done's done."

Nathan's hand moved from Laurel's breast down over the flawless, ivory skin of her belly as he considered the very real possibility that, when he got on the plane the following Friday morning, he would be leaving her pregnant. Yes, he thought, what was done certainly was irrevocable. But, on the other hand, what *wasn't* done . . . well, that was an altogether different story.

Shifting the bag of groceries from one hip to the other, Laurel walked down the path toward the cottage, mentally going over the special dinner she had planned for Nathan's last night home. When she came to the edge of the cottage clearing, the sight that greeted her made her stop short. With one knee planted on the ground, Nathan was kneeling in front of the window of the great room. Approaching slowly, she set down her bag of groceries in front of the door.

"Nathan, what are you doing?"

He flashed her a quick smile. "Come look." When she had moved within range of his long arms, he grabbed her hand and tugged her down beside him, the fingers of his other hand touching the lower right pane of the old window as he urged, "Tell me if this looks right to you."

For a moment, Laurel could only study his oddly flushed face. There was a look of excitement so intense in his dark eyes that his whole being was alight with the almost ethereal quality of it. The hand that gripped hers was trembling with the same excitement. Finally, when she thought he might burst if she waited another second to comply with his request, she allowed her gaze to be drawn toward the window.

There were St. John's and Elizabeth's names etched into the glass, along with the date, 1661. But Laurel's breath caught when she saw what new claim had been laid upon that hallowed spot. Below the mark his forebears had made, Nathan had etched his own name, hers and the year.

Laurel's heart was melting as her eyes met Nathan's. "You're incurably romantic, and I love you for it." Leaning forward, she placed a soft kiss on his smiling lips, whispering, "It looks perfect."

He returned her kiss, then drew back, saying, "There's more." Pulling her to her feet with him, he reached into the back pocket of his jeans and withdrew a thick packet of papers, which he handed to her.

Laurel turned the envelope over, noting that it bore the name of his lawyer's firm on the front. Warily she began, "If this is your will or something you think I've got to have before you go off—"

"Open it."

Laurel's fingers shook as she broke the seal on the packet and unfolded the typewritten pages. A single word—*Deed*—caught and held her attention. Her eyes barely skimmed the rest of the page, only enough to realize what he had done, which was nothing less than giving her the cottage and a sizable plot of ground surrounding it.

"Oh, Nathan," Laurel whispered, raising tear-filled eyes to his. "This is a lovely gift, and you must know how I feel about it."

"The deed's to add to the collection in your box," he said, his tone gently teasing. "I didn't want you to have to wait too long to add your name to the ancestral roster. And I also don't want you to have to wait to—"

"But, Nathan," she began hastily. "I told you. You don't need to worry about me. It's really okay—"

"I'm not worried anymore. About *either* of us."

"I'm going to be fine, and—"

"My only concern is where to tell the contractor I hired to put your picket fence."

It took a moment for Laurel to catch up. When she did, her look became thoroughly bewildered and a little dismayed.

Nathan's look was positively ingenuous. With a sweep of his hand that encompassed the property he had given her, he said, "Well, it's a real problem, you see. I didn't know whether you wanted the whole parcel fenced or only the front yard."

Laurel knew then that she was being reeled in on a long line. But where did the line lead...? "Nathan

Sinjin Coltrane, you'd better have a darned good reason for teasing me about my picket fence."

He ignored the threatening note in her voice. With his arms folded across his broad chest and his feet planted wide on Coltrane soil, he frowned thoughtfully. "I figure we'll have to do some remodeling at the big house. I never liked the idea of having the nursery on the third floor. It'll have to be moved to the second. And the conservatory will make a great playroom. We won't touch your cottage, though. It'll be our place to get away."

"Nathan, exactly what are you saying?"

"Shall we ask Aunt Louise to come live with us?"

He turned to face her, and there was a long moment of deep-woods silence as their gazes locked—hers questioning, his answering.

With her heart pounding, Laurel whispered, "Oh, love, are you sure? You've worked so hard, and what you're doing is so important."

"Of course, we'll have to wait until January."

"But the ship—"

"It'll float. I swear."

"And a job—"

"Think I'll have a hard time finding one?"

"I think you should...think about this very... carefully."

Somehow, she was in his arms, and he was dropping luscious kisses on her lips as she tried to speak.

"Nathan, don't do anything...hasty. Think about it while you're at...Deep Freeze."

"I have thought about it."

"We'll talk...when you get back."

"Lauri, it's too late."

Her breath caught as their eyes met at a distance of mere inches, and there wasn't a drop of teasing left in his tender gaze or in the extraordinary words she heard him whisper.

"Sweetheart, I sent the contract back unsigned."

* * * * *

Silhouette Special Edition

COMING NEXT MONTH

#463 DANCE TO THE PIPER—Nora Roberts
When cheery Maddy O'Hurley (triplet number two of THE O'HURLEYS!)
scattered sunshine and color at cynic Reed Valentine, both were dizzied by the
kaleidoscope of emotions that began to swirl around them.

#464 AMARILLO BY MORNING—Bay Matthews
Chasing shiny city dreams, Amarillo Corbett tried to forget gritty Russ
Wheeler. But rodeo Russ kept bucking Amy's objections, refused to be thrown,
and vowed to hold on—forever.

#465 SILENCE THE SHADOWS—Christine Flynn
Pregnant, widowed and nearly bankrupt, Megan Reese had problems. Financial
wizard David Elliott offered assistance, but could he rightfully offer his heart to
his late best friend's wife?

#466 BORROWED TIME—Janice Kaiser
On the eve of Stephanie Burnham's wedding, tragedy struck, and the medical
profession abandoned hope for her fiancée. She found solace in compassionate
neurosurgeon Peter Canfield—until compassion evolved into something
more....

#467 HURRICANE FORCE—Lisa Jackson
Amid a hurricane and a storm of accusations, Cord Donahue had sailed away.
Heartbroken, Alison banning believed him dead. But now prodigal Cord was
back, accusing *her* of *his* crimes...and demanding sweet vengeance.

#468 WHERE ANGELS FEAR—Ginna Gray
When her twin tied the knot, Elise knew marriage was in *her* cards, too. But
could she accept intimidating Sam Lawford's chilly proposal? Find out in this
companion edition to *Fools Rush In* (#416).

AVAILABLE THIS MONTH:

#457 BEGUILING WAYS
Lynda Trent

#458 SUMMER SHADOWS
Pat Warren

#459 A DIFFERENT DRUMMER
Maggi Charles

#460 MOON AND SUN
Allyson Ryan

#461 INTENSIVE CARE
Carole Halston

#462 PROMISES
Mary Alice Kirk

ATTRACTIVE, SPACE SAVING BOOK RACK

Display your most prized novels on this handsome and sturdy book rack. The hand-rubbed walnut finish will blend into your library decor with quiet elegance, providing a practical organizer for your favorite hard-or soft-covered books.

Only $9.95

Approximately 16" x 8" when assembled

Assembles in seconds!

To order, rush your name, address and zip code, along with a check or money order for $10.70* ($9.95 plus 75¢ postage and handling) payable to *Silhouette Books.*

Silhouette Books
Book Rack Offer
901 Fuhrmann Blvd.
P.O. Box 1396
Buffalo, NY 14269-1396

Offer not available in Canada.

BKR-2A

*New York and Iowa residents add appropriate sales tax.

Silhouette Special Edition

THE O'HURLEYS! MADDY'S STORY

from
Nora Roberts

Dance To The Piper

Available July 1988

The second in an exciting new series about the lives and
loves of triplet sisters—

If *The Last Honest Woman* (SE #451) captured your
heart in May, you're sure to want to read about Maddy
and Chantel, Abby's two sisters.

In *Dance to the Piper* (SE #463), it takes some very
fancy footwork to get reserved recording mogul Reed
Valentine dancing to effervescent Maddy's tune....

Then, in *Skin Deep* (SE #475), find out what kind of
heat it takes to melt the glamorous Chantel's icy heart.
Available in September.

THE O'HURLEYS!

**Join the excitement of
Silhouette Special Editions.**

SSE 463-1